JOSH & SEN

SAVE THE MULTIVERSE

BOOK 1

THE PATH
OF ONE

D. P. Behling, JD, MD

Josh & Sen Save the Multiverse Book 1: The Path of One

Copyright ©2023 David P. Behling, JD MD

Published by Physicians Press

Paperback ISBN: 979-8-9886535-0-9
eISBN: 979-8-9886535-1-6

Cover Illustration: Danielle Zirkelbach
Cover and Interior Design: GKS Creative
Editor: Monti Shalosky
Project Management: The Cadence Group

This book is for Nina, my beautiful nine-year-old
daughter who defeats dyslexia every day.
I'm so proud of you, my love!
— *Dad*

TABLE OF CONTENTS

CHAPTER 1

★

Sen Is in Hell!

SENYAK MARZTANAK was the second-seeded heir of Tenyak Marztanak, the Steward Hegemon of the entire Polar Neutral Iteration. Great things were expected of Senyak... but he was failing. Not just slightly failing... full-on, lose-his-place-in-the-hierarchy and find-a-new-iteration-of-origin failing.

Senyak and Damni had taken on their first joint Masters' mission to stop an individual chaos actor who was harvesting mortal soul Essence from victims of genocides that the chaos actor, himself, was facilitating.

The Masters were a loosely associated group of Immortals whose goal was to prevent the probable extinction of all sapient-mortal life from the multiverse. Damni, Senyak's Ka bond, believed in their goal. So Senyak did out of necessity. Such was Ka bond, and Damni was a worthy Ka bond.

Senyak had initially thought their joint mission would only take him away from his responsibilities in the Marztanak Hegemoncy for one, maybe two Ka nexus revolutions, a mere twenty-five to fifty local solar rotations. An unnoticeable time for Immortals like them.

Upon arrival through the aspect doorway, Senyak's plan was to wrap up the mission quickly by trouncing the adharmic, genocidal cur in a duel for the iteration. He would beat him into a state of Ka exhaustion, which required him to return to his iteration of origin to replace his lost cultivation, then Senyak could return to the Immortal Core iterations before he was missed. No muss... no fuss! Defeating the chaos actor would not be difficult for Senyak, given his Immortal focus as a combat specialist. The plan played to Senyak's strengths... what could go wrong?

------------------------------------★------------------------------------

Sen and Damni had tracked the chaos actor's location via his immortal Ka signature, using their Ethos Combis. Combis were Immortal Ka constructs, obtained at the time of transcendence to immortality, which linked Immortals with all matter, energy, context, and meaning in any iteration they presently existed in. Combis provided information on probabilities of events, locations of all items, material or immaterial, and knowledge of all outcomes from performed or anticipated actions.

After Senyak had confronted the chaos actor and introduced himself as the second seeded heir of the Marztanak Hegemoncy and pronounced his formal challenge, the chaos actor presenting in a tall and dark-featured physical avatar, had agreed immediately to the duel. His only request had been, "A short time, just two Ka nexus rotations to prepare and make our duel honorable."

As the chaos actor was not a combat specialist, Sen had readily agreed. After all, there could be no glory in crushing a weaker, unprepared opponent.

Sen and Damni had used the fifty solar rotations <*Years... Yes, Damni...years*> as much-needed time alone away from the Hegemoncy. And they had, in fact, truly needed it! Their union had only grown stronger in the time... His and Damni's cultivations had both increased through deeper entwining brought about with the greater understanding of each other's motivations and goals. This was after all, the very nature of Ka bond, strength through union.

During this time, Damni, who had ascended to immortality by rising through mortal cultivation in a physical-matter iteration, had shown Sen many things concerning physical communion with his Ka bond while in the present material-matter iteration ... Senyak, who hadn't been born and didn't have her experience as he had been actualized as an Immortal through the wills of his progenitors, had not known such *joining* was possible ... Whether they were at the dense core of a singularity, inside the swirling tempest of local gas giants, even between the galaxies and essentially free of all forces ... the variations were all unquestionably worthy! They would have to take the time to come back to this backwater and further explore this aspect of their bond!

It was only when the time marked for the duel with the chaos actor arrived that Senyak's plan fell to pieces, plummeting Sen into the dark plight he was now suffering in!

The chaos actor hadn't shown up for the duel. He had even diffused his Ka signature to untraceable levels with some mortal-level, Techno-Lord Ka-severing device. They could no longer track him.

Senyak remembered thinking ... *It is the height of insanity that mortal-grade technology can obfuscate my Immortal Ethos Combi?*

But at that point, Sen's troubles had only just begun. It was now 500 solar rotations later, <*Years ... yes, Damni ... years.*> Senyak had repeatedly failed to stop the actor. At every turn, Senyak had been continuously outwitted and outmaneuvered.

Furthermore, it was becoming clear that the chaos actor was nearing the end of his adharmic essence collection. Combi estimates were that the actor had filled approximately 92 percent of his soul Essence gathering array.

In true Karmic balance, Sen was also nearing the end of his abilities. Realizing this, he finally turned to Damni for help—who until then had been quietly letting him lead their floundering mission. She was quietly biding her time because there could be no question that stopping the chaos actor was due to Sen's success. Anything else could lead to a legitimate challenge of his standing as a second-seeded heir. At this point, they both knew he needed help, and right now. So, it couldn't have been a surprise when he asked for assistance. Like the best of Ka bonds, she was ready for him.

"It's about time, honey," she said in a kind tone while rubbing his shoulders.

Sen returned her caring gaze as she looked down into his eyes from her ovoid face. The form she had chosen in this physical iteration had pale-blue skin with an elongated head that gently swayed on a thin, elegant telescoping neck, continuously waving as if gently pulled in an oscillating underwater current.

"Yes, I have a high probability-suspicion on where the chaos actor will have to move to finish his plans. Currently, he is at ninety-two percent complete per Combi evaluation. I also trended the occurrence and total life count of the ongoing genocide events over the last seventy-five years.

"It seems that our interventions have slowed the chaos actor. As this time stream plays out, there is a significant downturn in incidence and overall lives lost to genocide. In fact, there will be a complete cessation of genocidal events in this iteration by the year 2035. A downturn due to globalization of commerce, media technology, and decreases in the at-risk population of victims. I believe this is because we haven't been giving him enough time to destabilize these native trends before he has to run from us, so they are increasing. He is now dealing with diminishing returns on his investments here.

"If these current trends remain unchanged, the chaos actor will have to leave with an incomplete array. This will cost him *a lot* of essence when he moves to harvest it. Likely more than half of what he has gathered. Either that, or he will again have to enhance the probability of genocide events.

"Along these lines, the decrease in the at-risk victims of genocide can be credited to a single human woman for her actions in starting an organization to fund education, medical access, and feeding services to these victims of poverty. She is a true *origin motivator*! It is her rise that is responsible for the largest effect on the chaos actor's plans for a full genocide array. If he wants to reach his goal, he will have to eliminate her."

Sen's eyes bulged out as he swallowed with a dry throat. They had him! At least where he would need to be! Not only that but knowing where the chaos actor would have to focus his presence would prevent his Ka diffuser from blocking their Combis from detecting him.

Sen tasked his Combi, and it chimed immediately. The chaos actor was already on the move and striking. He had already expunged the origin motivator Damni had just told him about in four of the local cuboid's twenty-seven total iterations. The principal of iterational overflow was very clear that only a simple majority of the cuboid's origin motivators needed to survive the chaos actor's onslaught to save the native fate of the local iterational cluster and shut down genocide here. That meant Sen had to save at least fourteen of the twenty-seven origin motivators in this cuboid. But Sen was now down to only twenty-three remaining. Put another way ... if he failed ten more times, all was lost!

They had to move fast! Sen jumped up and flew to the pilot's chair.

"Sweetie ... where are you going?"

"Huh ... I'm ... we're going to stop the chaos actor ... Aren't we?"

"He's not directly interfering with the time stream. You know the Principal Master's Penta Protocol as well as I do. We can only interfere to the degree that he does. If he doesn't appear in a physical avatar, neither can we. So far, the actor is only instigating Ka dominion to use onsite mortals to affect his desired outcomes. So ... until he moves directly ... here we stay, sweetums." Damni finished with a raised eyebrow, her arms crossed over her chest.

The infrequently seen but known recalcitrant posture of his Ka bond destroyed all of Sen's hopes with more finality than a fleet of

Star Negator warships. Hopeless, his head banged against the console in front of him.

The Principal Master's Penta Protocol was the Master's only immutable requirement. This was due to the Principal Master's great power. No sane Immortal would attempt to contravene him. But, more than this, the Penta Protocol was also generally considered the best course of action for overall mortal protection. Before its enactment, direct intervention by Immortals, even the Masters themselves, had caused so much damage to the involved iterations that complete collapse of all temporal probability models had occurred. Many mortal iterations had imploded to primordial singularities from such *Immortal help.*

Sen and Damni would have to defeat the chaos actor from right here ... by basically talking the mortals involved through it.

Sen's head banged the console again, harder this time ... He was ... *Fucked ... <Yes, Damni ... fucked ...>*

———————————✺———————————

The chaos actor had chosen to strike at the origin motivator in a closed space with no chance of escape. Six other mortals were present as potential Ka dominions for him to kill her with. As of yet, all probability models indicated that the chaos actor had not, and most likely would not, directly intervene. Obviously, desiring to avoid having to deal with Sen in combat.

The chaos actor had also correctly determined that Senyak wouldn't match his actions and chose direct Ka dominion. Sen really couldn't. Ka dominion, a very effective way to accomplish one's goals via mortal agency, caused expungement of the mortal's soul tether. It was an adharmic action. Performing adharmic activities would be an irreversible choice for Senyak. It would start him down the adharmic cultivation pathways and prevent him from maintaining his status as heir. In fact, it would likely get him banished from his family and their controlled iterations.

Sen gritted his teeth realizing he'd given all of this strategic information in his simple introduction when he had challenged the actor to a duel. Now the chaos actor was using what Sen had foolishly considered innocuous to beat Sen about the head and shoulders with. An excellent reminder that there were more weapons than those that were held in one's hands.

It was plain the actor knew more about Sen and how to manipulate that information than the inverse. The actor's skills to leverage a favorable battleground with his manipulation could not be denied. Senyak's earliest combat instructors' teachings haunted him from some of his earliest memories.

"If you know the enemy and know yourself, you need not fear the result of a hundred battles. If you know yourself but not the enemy, for every victory gained, you will also suffer a defeat. If you know neither the enemy nor yourself, you will succumb in every battle. This is an Immortal Ka iterational truth we have dispersed to all sapients, even the mortals. Make it yours as well."

So far, Senyak had succumbed in every battle...

To change this, Sen needed knowledge. He put his Combi to work. It chimed and informed him of all the weapons in the boxed lifter. *<Elevator, dear ... elevator.>* There was not much. A large pair of hand shears in the bag of an elderly lady. Several flat yet hard communication devices *<Cellphones, dear>* could be used to bludgeon like rocks. A few metal-shod writing implements. Two leather belts. And, lastly, a metal and plastic four-legged stand that an elder used for support. *<Walker, dear ... walker.>* It was of minimal use, given the space limitations.

The elevator's occupants were even less helpful.

—The target. The origin motivator stood in the right back corner, talking on her communication device *<Cell phone ... yes, Damni ... cell phone.>* For this battle, she was a nonissue. Karma entwined Senyak, the chaos actor, and the origin motivator. The chaos actor could not just take her via Ka dominion and have her jump off a roof or slit her own wrists. If he did, Karma's balance would replace her with an unidentified origin motivator to perform the probability activity she would have completed if not for the violation of Karma. This would put the actor back to square one.

—Two males. Both with no combat training. One was an elder, seventy-five local sun rotations, weighing less than fifty kilograms and walking with a four-footed ... *walker* ... standing at the left back wall. He had one of the steel-shod pens in his vest. The second was middle-aged and heavyset weighing 120 kilograms. He stood in the back middle next to the origin motivator.

—Four women of varying ages. From nineteen to sixty-eight years old and weighing between fifty-five to ninety-four kilograms. The most senior lady at sixty-eight ... *years* ... had the large hand shears in her bag, standing in the front center and weighing sixty-five kilos.

The last finding was—

—Anomalous reading. 0.04 percent chance of occurrence per iteration.

Sen reviewed the Combi's information. There was no knowing what the fourth line actually meant. He asked Damni to follow up on it while he attempted to devise a strategy before the chaos actor moved on to another iteration.

Not a lot to work with were Sen's first and second thoughts. Unless he came up with something he wasn't currently seeing, the chaos actor would wade through these humans, reach down the origin motivator's throat, and tear her heart out.

His Combi chimed. It had identified the next iteration the actor was targeting.

Sen chose the origin motivator as the mortal he would reach out and communicate mentally with. Upon later reflection, he realized that this had likely been a poor choice.

"I don't know, baby … I guess we can get together after class today … *But what will you do for me to make it worth it?*"

"*Hello,* hello! *Origin motivator in the yellow dress. Your life is in danger. You must act defensively immediately!*"

"*You perv!* This is a private conversation! Get off this line!"

"*What? Line? You don't understand! Your life is in danger! You need to rally support to fight off the independent chaos act—*"

"*Your* life is in danger, you sleaze! When my boyfriend finds out where you live! Jack! Can you hear this guy? Kick his *ass*, *Jaaaaahhhhhhaaa-ahhhacck-glacc …*"

Two wet *thunks* and a sudden *snap* ended the conversation as the fat man next to the origin motivator gouged out her eyes and broke her neck with three quick movements.

Quietly, Damni suggested, "Maybe physically accelerating the next target's responses will give you some more time to talk with them …"

Sen attempted to recruit the fat man to defend the girl in the subsequent two iterations. Damni had been right about the physical acceleration. It changed the outcome, but not positively. Resulting instead in not only the origin motivator's expungement, but several other of the … elevator's … occupants dying as well. The girl had her skull shattered against the metal back wall of the elevator. The large hand shears were left deep in the carotid artery of the fat man as he tried to hold the elderly woman back as she cut through the elevator's occupants toward her target. The older lady had smashed the origin motivator's skull after disabling her with rapid strikes to the trachea. Prevented from choosing the fat man due to Senyak's mental linking with his psyche during their brief and useless conversation, the chaos actor had chosen the elderly lady with the shears. More importantly, now the chaos actor knew Senyak was on to him. This significantly worsened things.

Seven iterations left to stop him.

Two more times, Sen attempted to recruit the fat man and instruct him in basic striking and self-defense. This achieved only negligible results. The few seconds he had before the chaos actor moved were just not enough.

At this point, the iterational pattern of the chaos actor was clear. He was simply going down the metaphysical lines from left to right, superior to inferior within the local iterational cuboid's postulated structure. Even after the actor had learned Senyak was interfering, he had only laughed and mocked Senyak, continuing to slaughter all of the mortals in the elevator only because he knew Senyak was watching.

"C'mon Senyak, great and mighty second heir of the noble Marztanak Hegemoncy! Wouldn't it be truly dharmic ... not to mention much more honorable ... to accept your ineptitude and failure, rather than refusing to see that you have lost? All you are doing is increasing these mortals' suffering ... No? Here, let me show you exactly what I mean!"

The chaos actor then proceeded to mutilate every elevator occupant, leaving them conscious as they bled out. The fat man Senyak had linked to begged him to do something ... anything ... before succumbing to unconsciousness and a meaningless death.

Five iterations left.

Sen then tried to interact with the old lady. This only resulted in the fat man taking the shears away from her, killing everyone in the elevator, then himself.

"Surely you see that these mortals are just resources for us to use. This is not murder, Senyak. I'm just reaping wheat to make bread, for Ka's sake!"

Four iterations left.

Damni reached over tentatively with a hand and placed it on his forearm. "Sen, there is something you need to see concerning the anomaly I have been looking into. If the chaos actor continues in his current pattern, in four iterations, there are eight people in the elevator. This anomalous male is apparently a survivor of a violent attack that left him dead at a very early age in ninety-nine point ninety-six percent of all iterations. He's also carrying a *case of briefs*, which I believe will significantly change the probability outcomes compared to how things have occurred so far."

Mocking comments/bloodshed/slaughter...

Mocking comments/bloodshed/slaughter/laughter...

Mocking comments/bloodshed/slaughter/laughter/two rude comments about Senyak's avatar's genitalia...

One iteration left to stop him...

CHAPTER 2

✦

Go to Hell, Josh!

"GOD DAMMIT, Miranda!" *I could strangle you with your own hair!*

Startled birds squawked and took to the air from the overhead trees when Josh screamed out his frustrations. Several coeds had also turned in his direction at the sudden outburst in the normally quiet space of the botanical garden.

Overhead, the twelve o'clock bells started to slowly toll from the nearby Franciscan Mission. They pealed over the southern tip of Jacksonville and the botanical garden outside of FSU's satellite campus. The same botanical garden Joshua Elias Tanner, a forty-four-year-old part-time law professor was currently having his emotional meltdown in.

The neat sheaf of stamped and filed divorce papers crumpled into an interesting piece of abstract art that was remarkably similar to the balled fist currently holding them. In Josh's left hand he held the pink Post-It that had sat on top of his divorce's cover page . . .

Go to hell Josh! it read in Miranda's prim and proper southern-lady cursive.

Upon seeing the papers, he had jumped from his bench in the garden's quiet cove and reflexively moved to a fighting stance. A throwback to his younger days of constant threat. His heart was racing, and his breath came in deep gasps like he was on the fifth mile of a three-mile run. But his bared and clenched teeth said without question he was ready to throw down with all comers!

Come back to reality, Josh . . . His thinking brain reasserted itself. *Nothing is going to get done about it here in the park.*

Josh looked at the papers. Looked at the Post-It. He looked around the lush greens of the botanical garden and the stand of red bamboo behind the bench he had been sitting at . . . Finally, he took a cleansing breath and started to let his frustrations go.

Two breaths later, Josh flopped back down on his bench and let the returning birdsong wash over him while he rubbed his eyes and attempted to gain some focus. This was his spot after all. When he couldn't do so elsewhere, Josh usually found center space here in the quiet of the gardens.

Right now, he was in the time gap between his summer schedule's generic torts and advanced personal injury classes. Fortunately, he still had a few minutes to pull himself together and he straightened his Wayfarer shades that sat askew on the tip of his nose from his meaningless physical response to Miranda's emotional onslaught. Josh straightened them while the unknowing FSU students moved down the cobblestone paths to and fro around him.

Cool it, Josh! Almost announcing your wife's murder in front of dozens of future lawyers, justifiable as it may be, is not a good way to run a railroad!

Emotions on edge, he snorted at his own sad joke. But his brain was right, he needed to rein it in. None of what he had been doing was for him or Miranda anyway. Not the stepping back from his busy practice, not the sabbatical teaching law, not the countless hours of couples and family counseling they had gone through . . . It was all for his one true purpose. The only thing in this world that made any sense to him.

Sophie.

And as long as his four-year-old daughter Sophie was still willing to smile and hug his face when he blew raspberries on her neck . . . There was going to be hope.

I am not going to end up one of those weekends and every other holiday dads!

That was not good for Sophie. So, it was not in the program.

Josh intended on seeing Sophie and her morning wake-up smile that outshone the sun after an all-night thunderstorm every day!

You know you won't be able to stand putting her through the pathetic single-dad attempts at Thanksgiving, Christmas, or birthdays. She deserves so much more than what you had, Josh!

And it was true. For Sophie, all options were on the table. Whatever the personal and emotional prices Josh had to pay, they would be inconsequential for keeping Sophie happy and in a solid home.

The minutes ticked and the sun slid across the sky. Josh also slipped over to the right side of the bench to avoid the sun's rays as it peeked through the shading branches of the overhead cypress trees. Born and raised in the northern reaches of Chicago's south side. Josh was a foreigner to Florida's scorching summer heat. He needed to avoid it or end up sweating through his shirt and meeting his third years with dripping armpits. Josh might be a *northern barbarian* as he had heard whispered on more than one occasion at Miranda's parents' plantation house . . . But even he knew pit stains were not a good way to instill confidence in his students on the first day of the summer session.

Once adequately shaded, Josh loosened his tie, and his thoughts switched back to Sophie. Her small hand planted on his cheek. Her forehead resting on his. Giant, wide blue eyes to say goodbye after their past weekend together.

With full voice and no shame, she had said, "Don't worry, Daddy . . . I know you love me! It doesn't matter what Mommy says when she's mad and talking with Aunty and Grandma . . ."

"*Damn...*" Josh groaned rubbing his temples at the psychic pain Sophie's emotional fallout exposure caused him.

Miranda's carelessness at letting Sophie hear these types of things grated him like a face plant on a 100-degree asphalt road.

He rolled his eyes under his brows. Then Josh proved that his brain was fully reengaged and changed his perspective. The way only a soulless lawyer could, as a crooked smile crept upon his lips, and he thought it through.

Sophie's assessment of the situation and her delivery had been topnotch! She really did seem to have a decent handle on the ins and outs of her parents' dysfunction. Much better than either he or Miranda.

Josh chuckled darkly, muttering, "Maybe Sophie should be the one to give us counseling... Would have to be better than that three-hundred-and-fifty-dollar-an-hour shyster..."

He dismissed the ridiculous but happy thought. Then stood from the bench with fresh determination in his steps after the single bell at 12:30 had chimed. Sophie deserved better. He would give it to her. His working-class *northern brutality* would find a way to fix this for her. He didn't have any answers on how he would do it right now. But he did have what had carried him every day of his life so far. The willingness to do what it took to fix the problems that seemed insurmountable. And somehow, Josh would. That much was certain!

Josh walked down the winding path that led out of the park with much more purpose than when he had arrived. He crossed over the manicured Saint Augustine grass and exited under the shady lady, sycamore, and cypress trees, heading to the fifty-story building that housed the FSU satellite campus where it occupied the seven floors between forty and forty-six. On his way, Josh joined dozens of summer students who walked and laughed with each other, who much like Josh were oblivious to the grander events occurring amongst them.

The increasing heat from the sun beat down, and Josh moved with quick strides to save his shirt from the summer ardor. He led the pack of students and faculty on the sidewalk's edge as he sprinted across the street with the light change. Gratefully, Josh entered the skyrise's air-conditioned lobby. A quick check of his pits for sweat stains revealed a passable situation as he swept past the security desk. The overweight but friendly guard, his nose buried in one of his duty logs, absently returned Josh's wave.

Josh caught the elevator at the last second as its doors were closing. He slid into the last open spot near the front right-facing buttons and pushed the forty-sixth floor. Then he lowered his briefcase to keep it out of the way in the nearly full elevator.

Glancing around, Josh smiled warmly to Sadie on his right. She was the late sixty-something-year-old satellite school's head receptionist and had always been polite to him. Nodding to him with her silently administrative Monalisa smile, Sadie closed her eyes for the ride up to her floor.

Josh began organizing his thoughts on *Palsgraf v Long Island Railroad*, Chief Judge Ben Cardozo's seminal case, as the elevator started to rise—

—White light exploded across his vision. What felt like ice picks stabbing out of Josh's eyes from inside his skull immediately stunned all his thoughts. A young male voice spoke at a volume that seemed to blow off the top of his head!

"Techno-Lord piece of crap... Damni, you know this has taken a lot longer than we anticipated. Without question, my inferiors will challenge me as heir for my failure to stop the chaos actor so far. I couldn't even prevent him from facilitating the rise of all these mortal adharmic leaders... Stalin, Hitler, Pol Pot, Hussein... to help him filling his genocidal essence array—"

"Sen... honey! You are active."

"Wha-what!"

"You are now communicating with the anomaly, Joshua Elias Tanner."

"Oh... Oh! Hello, Human With The Case Of Briefs. Can you hear me? Joshua Elias Tanner, I am speaking to you!"

The young man's voice burst from inside Josh's head.

Incredible volume split through Josh's mind, leaving him dumb-founded in the agony of a cluster headache piled on top of a migraine and what felt like a claw hammer smashing the back of his skull in. Josh blinked slowly and braced himself against the front elevator wall with his right hand. Absently, he felt what must have been blood slowly drip-ping down from his left ear.

Then, gratefully, the female spoke again. Much more quietly and with a voice Josh would describe as kindly.

"Yes, Sen, it's working. You need to back up from the transmitter and adjust your psychic output ... Or you will most likely burst his cortex, sweetie."

A momentary pixilated mental image flashed through Josh's mind. It was composed of black dots on a white field, showing a thin hand with several too-many finger joints reaching to pat Sen's shoulder with approval, then staying there reassuringly.

Sen was, apparently, the male voice. His image also consisted of black pixilated dots on a white field. From what Josh could tell, Sen was a mostly bald young male with a long topknot that swung quickly with his energetic movements. In response to the female voice's hand, Sen turned forward, smiling. The move gave Josh a momentarily pixilated full view of a face with Asian features.

"Oh ... Oh! Right! Sorry!"

Pain again spiked in Josh's brain form Sen's output that was no less than the first time. With his eyes freely watering, Josh rubbed his temples with both hands, letting his briefcase slide to his feet. He also acciden-tally leaned against the elevator's buttons, causing several additional low-level floors to light up.

Sadie's eyes narrowed and were briefly filled with concern as she looked at Josh's crumpling form. Seeing he wasn't immediately going to fall over, she looked away and started muttering about law professors with too much time on their hands.

Another pixilated flash showed a strong hand, with the standard four fingers, one thumb, and three finger joints adjusting two knobs and a toggle.

Sen then spoke again. Still in a loud voice, but much less than the previous mind-splitting airhorn range from before.

"Okay, okay, okay! Listen! We only have a little time, mortal. I'm going to speed up your perception and reaction speeds while I explain things. Just so we don't run into the same problems of the previous iterations, where everyone died— Where we failed, I mean . . . You will feel a little lightheaded, and your heart rate will increase. Don't worry. We should *be done before your internal organs lose cohesion from the strain."*

Josh's vision swam as he felt what he could only describe as the center of his brain, *releasing*. He also experienced two sharp, but not quite painful, feelings from his flanks above the kidneys.

"There. Now, your metabolic and sex hormones, catecholamines, and the endocrine proteins from your pituitary, thyroid, testes, adrenal glands, and pancreas are all maximized. We have also increased your cells' endocrine receptors with an organic stasis field limited to within the space of your physical body. The stasis will prevent the reabsorption of these biologics for the next few minutes. You should notice you are moving and thinking faster. While everyone around you should be doing so much more slowly, to your perception."

And they were!

Josh turned his head to see the body movements of everyone in the carriage were much slower and more deliberate. The lights indicating the elevator's floor change were now taking much longer between switching as the car climbed. Even the scowling Sadie seemed to mutter in slow motion as her lips puckered and frowned in distaste. She even seemed to recoil belatedly to what must have looked like the very disjointed and rapid movement of Josh's head turning to her. He must look like a crack tweaker in a mosh pit.

Sen's voice continued. *"There is an origin motivator in that vertically ascending metal car with you. A chaos actor has targeted her for expungement. In twelve seconds, this chaos actor will purge the soul tether of the old lady next to you, forming a Ka dominion over her. He will then use her body as a vessel for his physical intervention. The chaos actor will most likely use the shears the old woman is carrying to attack you … Is that the correct terminology, Damni, old woman?"*

Another pixilated flash. Damni nodded affirmatively to Sen.

"Yes. The old woman to your left will use the desk shears to cut her way through you all to get to the origin motivator and expunge her from this iteration. The origin motivator's expungement will result in the death of trillions. Both from mortals in your iteration and the deaths that cascade in all twenty-six associated iterations in this cuboid cluster. Perhaps even extending further out three to four clusters deep. You need to stop her! Your portable shield is the reason we have chosen you … Your case of briefs … Is that the right word, Damni?"

A pixilated flash of Damni's confirming nod. Josh noted at least three pigtails were shaking as her head moved on a long, thin telescoping neck.

"Yes, your case of briefs … Which you have … um … dropped! *Your* case of briefs! *Please pick it up right now!"*

Despite the surrealism of the situation, for some reason, Josh did lean down and pick his briefcase up. Holding the thick worn leather brought him a sense of security as he hugged it to his chest while praying that the voices and visions in his head would go away …

Sadly, no such luck.

"Because of your case of briefs, our Ethos Combi predicts that you have a fourteen percent probability … errr … a much better chance *than anyone in this, or all the previous iterations' elevators, of stopping the chaos actor's first selection for his Ka dominion. This is true even though you are an outlier existence and only have a manifested physical presence in less than zero point zero four percent of all iterations at this point in your time stream.*

"Also, please note that the chaos actor, while not a combat specialist, is a very clever Immortal. His choice of Ka dominion will not be limited to their usual physical abilities. The dominion will be significantly accelerated

and benefit from the chaos actor's knowledge and understanding. To stop this old woman, you must dig deep and carry it ... err ... I mean, send it! Is that the right choice of term, Damni?"

Pixilated flash, Damni again nodding affirmatively.

"Yes, send it! Now listen. Are you ready? We have less than eight of your seconds in local physical time before the chaos actor forms his Ka dominion. From there, he will likely attempt to penetrate your jugular veins and carotid arteries with the ten-inch desk shears the old woman carries. If you have any questions or comments, now is your chance. If not, and you are ready, please acknowledge you are so ... I think we have done it this time, Damni!"

Josh tried to speak, only a tiny choking sound made it out of his constricted throat. Only one thought made it through his hormone-accelerated consciousness.

I've gone insane! My separation has finally cracked my mind, and I'm trapped in a cheap James Cameron-John Daly rip-off.

"Whoa! Whoa! No, Joshua Elias Tanner, you are not insane. You are, however, our last chance to stop this loss of mortal life throughout your local iterational cuboid. If the origin motivator is expunged in one more iteration before she can institute her probability changes ... The changes that prevent local iteration genetic cleansing I mentioned ... I mentioned those, didn't I, Damni ... Never mind!

"If the origin motivator gets expunged in that metal car, her origin intention will never reach the critical weight necessary for overflow to the adjacent iterations. This is true even if we succeed in all the remaining iterations. Humanity will suffer the loss of trillions from genocide!

"I have failed to stop this chaos actor for the last five hundred of your solar rotations ... Years ... Yes, years. This is my last chance ... You *are my last chance!"*

Joshua's eyes glazed over at the ridiculous explanation. He only understood the part about not being insane. As for the rest ... He could understand the words ... but they had no contextual meaning to him.

One thing Josh knew for sure ... He wasn't going to stop anyone with his briefcase. And that included Sadie! What did that even mean? Death of trillions? If he remembered his facts right, there were only about eight billion people on Earth!

Pixilated flash to Sen's scrunched-up face with tense shoulders.

"Damni, I think I've overexplained ... I'm going to fix it!"

"Listen to me, Joshua Elias Tanner! Unless you stop her, in four Earth seconds, the lady to your left will take her scissors out and start killing everyone in your elevator ... starting with you! She is a highly skilled and deadly martial arts expert. She will slaughter you all if you don't act now! When she takes out her scissors, smash her skull with your case of briefs! Got it?"

Pixilated flash.

Sen leaned in close to Damni and whispered, *"Do you think I've obliterated his mentation? My Combi predicts only a four percent chance of survival if he doesn't strike her down first ..."*

Josh slid over against the sidewall and away from Sadie, looking at her in horror. She turned slowly to him at the reduced speed of everyone else in the elevator. Her eyes widened in surprise for a brief moment—

—A feeling of electricity suddenly flooded the elevator car.

Sadie straightened rigidly, her whole body trembled as she oscillated back and forth from her heels to her toes. A few seconds passed and her shoulders relaxed. She then adopted a new body language and stance that spoke of coiled strength and violence. She also moved a lot faster than all the other members of the elevator car—including Josh!

Sadie slightly turned her head and looked to the right and the left while at the same time reaching into her bag. With purposeful deliberation, she removed a new pair of scissors she must have just gotten from the school supply room on her lunchbreak. Josh couldn't help but read the tag still on them, $11.99! WHAT A DEAL!

Sadie raised the shears in her hand, expertly adjusting her fingers on the ten-inch-long blades to just below the finger loops and forming a hammer grip. She pointed the tips of the shears at Josh with unmistakable hostility, a wicked smile showed way too many of her age-stained teeth.

"Oh, sweetheart! You are new here . . . You're first, then!"

Josh could barely see the scissors as she lunged at him.

CHAPTER 3

✦

Physics Can Be a Bitch

JOSH HAD been involved in striking and grappling as a younger man, like most kids from the inner city. But he had never faced anyone who moved as fast as Sadie moved right now.

The scissors came down one-two-three-four times from all directions at his face. Already holding his briefcase to his chest in both hands, it had been instinctual for him to duck under it. The tip of the shears punched through the leather, ultimately stopped by the books inside his case.

Sadie withdrew the blades even faster than she put them in, and they sharply screeched against the case's metal frame as they went in and out. She had also struck him two times in the groin with her right knee and two times in the solar plexus with her left hand as the scissors were coming down. The attack had been so fast Josh didn't even have time to feel the pain. Having experienced cheap blows before, Josh knew he would soon have wobbly legs followed with expanding pain and weakness in a few seconds.

In truth, the briefcase was a mixed blessing. While it protected Josh's face, the downside was that it blocked his vision and left him vulnerable to the next thing Sadie did. Her left foot hooked into the crook of his right knee, then she leaned back hard, pulling said knee out from under him. Because of Josh's greater size and strength, Sadie had needed to overextend her pull-back to destabilize him. This led to the unintended consequence of bowling over the rather heavyset woman in the left front corner of the elevator. The fat lady slammed her face into the side wall and rebounded to crash back into Sadie; interrupting her planned overhead-hammer blow and pushing her toward Josh.

At the same time, Josh, having lost the support of his right knee and in the process of lowering his briefcase to a more central position, made the conscious decision to let the case edge lead the way and push Sadie away as he fell.

Even the killing machine that Sadie was still had instinctual reactions to large objects falling on her. Such as a 200-pound man with a large steel-framed, leather briefcase. These reflexes pushed out with both hands to force Josh onto his back foot. From there she could follow up with more hammer blows to his head now that the case was midlevel.

With whatever next-level acceleration Sadie had received, she pushed hard before the case could make contact with her. Not only did she manage to force Josh away, but she lifted him off the ground throwing him into the steel sidewall of the elevator. His body caused a loud *thunk* that rang in the car and reverberated up and down the elevator shaft.

The chaos actor had expected Josh to be pushed off of his feet. That was expected. The surprise was that Sadie's right hand, via the two fingers instinctually hooked through the shear's finger-loops, along with her right arm, were pulled to full extension along with Josh's frame. Sadie's hand, arm, and the rest of her much smaller body followed Josh across the elevator. The laws of physics pulled the much smaller woman off the floor with Josh. Instantly realizing his mistake, the chaos actor reversed his grip to his previous hammer hold and brought the shears back for another series of attacks. But it was far too late for that to make a difference.

———————✳———————

Josh's bell was rung when his head slammed into the elevator's metal sidewall. But without question, he had heard the squeal of steel on steel when Sadie had flung him. He also felt her pull hard on the scissors, almost yanking the case out of his hands.

The scissors are stuck in the case's metal frame! His accelerated brain realized this . . . and that he had an opportunity. *If* he was so inclined.

It would be a lie to say there wasn't still a very small part of Josh's brain yelling at him to stop and think about what was going on. Along with what, in the name of all that was holy, was he doing in response to his sudden arrival in the *Twilight Zone*?

Look at the facts, this analytical side said to him.

—You are suddenly hearing multiple voices in your head.

—You are imagining that you are moving faster than everyone else around you.

Except for Sadie, that is. His brain conceded.

—And, only seconds after the first two points, you are about to slam your briefcase down on Sadie's head in a public elevator. A woman in her late sixties that you have known for the last six months. An old lady who was an all-in-all nice person until she started trying to perforate your face like Anthony Hopkins in a dress. Screech . . . Screech . . . Screech!

Without a doubt, there was something wrong with him. Several possibilities came to mind. He could have had a psychotic break. Someone could have slipped something into his coffee this morning . . . A very vivid nightmare was not impossible either. If this was really happening, there was a better than middling chance he would get locked up in an insane asylum on his way to the electric chair! Florida was one of the southern states that still enforced the death penalty for excessive crimes. *You could fry for this!*

But ... and this was a big but ...

Josh told that part of his brain to *shut the hell up!*

This chick has drawn steel on me more than five times and kneed me in the crotch at least twice.

On top of this, Josh was pissed! Not just regular pissed. *He was race-car-in-the-red, mushroom-cloud-laying-motherfucker pissed!* And not just at Sadie ... This whole alien-mind-screaming, *Psycho*-slashing, surreal event was an excellent place to put the blame for all the bullshit that had gone down in the last year of his life, i.e., his frustration with his wife Miranda and her family. Rage from being separated from Sophie when she was so small and unprotected from sick people like them came to the surface. Sadly for Sadie, it was fair to say Josh had some significant unresolved issues he had built up, and there didn't seem to be an encounter group in the immediate vicinity for an intercession. Lastly, Sadie was trying to kill him with a set of scissors the size of Freddy Krueger's claw glove!

Josh had never been accused of being a slow thinker, unable to react in a crisis situation. This quality had helped him as a child as it helped him here. Josh also absently noted the hormone-acceleration-blender his mind had become was also lending him a helping hand in making quick decisions.

Before Sadie could regain solid footing from her overextension, Josh switched his grip on the case with both hands and slammed it down on her head—once, twice, *three times a lady.* She might have been much faster than him, but she was not stronger. He was a lean 200 pounds at six foot two compared to Sadie's five foot four and dumpy in sensible heals. Physics was still not on her side. And one thing Josh had learned as a young man, physics was a true bitch when she wanted to be.

Sadie had also made a mistake refusing to let go of the scissors as he slammed the case down on her. The thin bones in her hand and arm shattered with every hit. On the third time down, ominous snapping sounds also came from her neck, followed quickly by her body dropping into a pile of broken bones and shallow breathing on the floor.

Josh's harsh breathing filled the elevator as he realized Sadie was down. He lowered the briefcase with the scissors still sticking out of the top left corner. Due to how fast he and Sadie had been moving, only now did the others in the elevator start to react to the mayhem before them. But their actions were still moving like a slow-motion scene in an old-school movie. Josh heard them speaking in low drawn-out sounds, but at this point, he was so amped up he couldn't concentrate enough to give the drawn-out words any meaning.

"You did it! I can't believe it!" Sen's voice rang out in Josh's head. Clearly, as surprised as Josh was that he hadn't been savagely murdered by the old lady. *"Err, I mean, good job, mortal! Err... Joshua!"*

A brief pause ended with Senyak speaking even faster and with more concern in his tone. *"Now, I need you to stop her from expunging! If she dies, the chaos actor will be able to abandon his Ka domination and escape to the other iterations, where you will not be there to save the people in the elevator. You are an anomalous existence, after all. Quick! She is going into cardiac arrest! Do you know how to reactivate her function?"*

As his vision dimmed, Josh shook his head *no* to Sen's anxious voice.

"No? Oh, ahhh... okay! We will send the information to your cortex so you can implement it!"

CPR? That's what he meant right?! Josh had no freaking idea how to do it. He had seen it on TV. But that was it. Suddenly, like strong hands squeezing, a heavy pressure felt as if it had crashed through his skull and crushed his brain from all sides. He couldn't breathe and his vision seemed to double for several seconds...

And then he did know CPR. ABC assessments, cardiac compressions, chest thumps, even the administration protocols of epinephrine, atropine, and lidocaine if he had had them. Josh got down on his knees and moved to resuscitate the elderly lady ... *Sadie* ... who now seemed so very small and frail. No matter what, Sadie surviving this was a good idea for him and that small part of his brain that he had so recently told to *shut up*.

Josh's hands moved as they expertly straightened out Sadie's airway. Her cervical spine was obviously broken, and her head lolled grotesquely as he aligned her head and upper body.

At some point, Sadie had evacuated her bowels and bladder, leaving a wet stain on the front of her thin skirt and the elevator filled with pungent odors. Josh made sure Sadie's tongue wasn't blocking her esophagus. His index finger on her wrist's pulse point told him she didn't have one. He then gave her fifteen chest compressions, sharp and strong. The pulse hadn't returned. He gave another fifteen compressions, then he did it again. Sadie's pulse finally, but weakly, returned. By now, the elevator doors had opened, and a crowd had gathered in front as the other occupants ran out screaming. Likely heading for security and, hopefully, to call an ambulance.

"Well done ... again, mortal ... Joshua! There is much I would tell you. However, the biologic-acceleration we have enacted in your body is about to wear off. When this happens, you will experience a severe decrease in function and likely lose all conscious mental capacity."

The lights were steadily growing dimmer. Josh's hands felt blunt, heavy, and numb.

"But do not worry! Death is a much lower probability than when you faced the chaos actor! Significantly down below fifteen percent by our best calculations."

The silhouettes of people surrounding him stretched out, and they seemed to move from standing on the ground to standing on the side-walls. Josh's fried nerves didn't even feel it when he collapsed onto his face over Sadie's body.

"We could continue your acceleration ... but you would likely suffer multiple burst blood vessels in your cerebral cortex and cardiac muscles.

This would significantly increase the probability of death far above the seventy-fifth percentile. Permanent disability would also be guaranteed."

Josh managed a dissatisfied, "*Mwraaaaa...*" Then all he knew was blackness.

CHAPTER 4

———————★———————

Ow . . . Again!

SENYAK JUMPED from his seat and turned to Damni, screaming in exaltation. "He did it! I did it! We did it! *Whooooooo*, I can't believe it!"

Damni was all smiles as Senyak fist-pumped the air.

"*Independent chaos actor, my posterior fleshy seating pads! I shoved my foot up your internal and external sphincters! Woooooooooooooooo!*"

"Very well done, honey! I'm so proud of you! But I think that wearing this human form is starting to increase your emotional responses. Why don't you dial back your emotion centers for the next few minutes? We still have some work to do." She gently tried to wave him back down to reality . . . and what little dignity he still had.

Senyak, currently standing on the ship's command chair spinning around, shaking his booty in the chaos actor's imagined face, suddenly got a serious expression and looked around to ensure that no one else was in the cockpit with them.

Standing up, he straightened his robes and topknot ponytail, coughing into his hand. "*Ahem*, perhaps you are right, Damni. There is still much to do." He stepped down from the chair and embraced her, gazing up into her eyes as her three braids waved above his face on the sides of her oval-shaped head. "I owe it all to you, my Ka bond. You lifted me up when I was at my lowest. You guided me when I was lost. I have no words, but I will show you over and over just how much you mean to me."

A dark shadow crossed her countenance and was gone so fast that Senyak thought he must have imagined it.

She then smiled in her warm, kind way. "I know you will, Senyak. You are my heart as well... You know... there are a few more things about material-matter Ka bond joining that I was saving for commemorating your victory... I could show you now..." Her telescoping neck arced down to him, her lips nuzzling his ear and humming.

Senyak experienced a break of emotional control again, with his physiologic responses taking hold. Starting with an accelerated heart rate and quickened breathing followed by anatomical alterations in other areas...

He had just convinced himself to begin responding in kind when his Ethos Combi chimed. *"Ka dominion's life force critical. Recommend immediate acquisition."*

Nothing was stopping them now. If the Ka dominion was dying, the chaos actor would present in this iteration with a physical avatar. Even by the Principal Master's Penta Protocol, they were clear to intervene directly.

Two sharp pops in the thin air of the cockpit occurred as Senyak and Damni translocated to the dying Ka dominion.

———————————★———————————

Hantal Brundox was a cautious Immortal. At least, he had always considered himself so. When he decided to fully follow adharma and harvest soul Essence from genocide victims in order to further his cultivation, it had only been the last resort. He had been stuck in a bottleneck at the Awakening Tier, the third of the seven Immortal tiers of cultivation, for over five million years. At that point, he had no choice but to walk the dark paths of adharma.

His loss of momentum at that time was only made more bitter because his earlier progression through the Common Logos and Revelation Tiers had advanced so rapidly. His clan had even considered him a prodigy for a time. His revelational Ka truth, the gateway for Immortal cultivation to the third tier had also been surprisingly easy for him to find. He hadn't had to undergo eons of seclusion and soul searching or perform the obligatory acts of deprivation to find his core-motivational concept. It had come almost the first time he had thought about it. "I stand alone."

And he always had. Doing so had worked out pretty well for him . . . up until he had hit his bottleneck.

At that point, Brundox's advancement on the dharmic path had slowed down dramatically. The Awakening Tier required cultivators to form bonds with other cultivators and their iterations as a whole . . . In retrospect, this was not something he should have expected to succeed at . . .

So Hantal began, for the first time that he could remember . . . to fail. Trying to reverse this, he had made several adharmic choices to eke any cultivational advancement and form the required bonds. His decisions had seemed to make sense at the time. He had exterminated a fascist regime covering multiple sectors of space. Then he had eliminated hunting societies that focused primarily on unique animals and rare species. But Hantal had learned too late that it wasn't his ultimate goal . . . but the steps taken to accomplish that goal which made the distinction between dharma and adharma. Furthermore, the complete elimination of any mortal spirit beings was adharmic . . . Hantal had known that . . . but it had all just felt so good while doing it! And taking the necessary time to reflect on every single one of his choice's end results . . . Really? Who could stand the bother?

Thus, Hantal ultimately diverted his cultivation down inimical roads. Upon hitting mid-tier, he was more and more sure he would have to convert fully to adharma to continue his advancement. Finally, after five million years of complete stagnation, it was indisputable, and he accepted his dark future ... and he had never regretted it. *Standing alone* was much better suited for the shunned and shadowed tracks of adharma.

Even so, Hantal had continued to be cautious and circumspect in his actions. He had chosen a very out-of-the-way, Essence-deprived backwater cuboid, providing reduced spiritual payout to increase his probability of not being detected. Being a full eight aspect doorways away from the main Immortal-occupied realms provided quite a buffer from almost all probability searches ... but, as his current situation showed, it obviously had not been far enough away from the Principal Master and his goon squad.

At first, however, his caution had paid off. For going on nearly one hundred thousand local solar cycles, he had continued undetected with free reign over the entire iterational cuboid. Immortals generally shied away from this place with a passion, it being so far off the beaten track.

Along with the removed location, he had taken the precaution to set up several redundancies of escape and a few quick solutions to antic- ipated problems if and when other Immortals attempted to intervene in his plans. In the unlikely event he was discovered by some agents affiliated with the Masters, Hantal had been adequately prepared for the usual snares they might use to further their ill-conceived goal of preventing mortal sapient extinction.

Hantal laughed in the emptiness of his Ka dominion's broken mind. What a farce the Masters were! Preventing the multiversal extinction of all sapient mortals? Really?!? Why, in the name of Ka would that need to be done? Mortals were just a cultivation resource for Immortal discretion. To be consumed in a *use-as-you-can* manner. After all, they were only *physical entities*, for Ka's sake! Couldn't they be cloned any time their numbers significantly decreased? Whole iterations could be seeded with the genetic material necessary for their growth if a given

Immortal preferred organic development over breeding in static farms. Mortals were nothing more than a resource *to use as Hantal saw fit.* And he should know. Unlike most Immortals, he had transcended through mortal cultivation to the Immortal Realms. There was nothing those pompous asses calling themselves the Masters knew about mortals that he didn't.

Hantal still wasn't sure how Senyak had accelerated his inept thinking and realized Hantal was facing diminishing returns ... but, somehow, Senyak had. Even still, it was apparent there was no way the artless cretin was going to use Ka dominion against Hantal. It would undoubtedly result in diverting his cultivation from dharmic to adharmic.

It really was too bad Senyak hadn't chosen the adharmic path ... an evil glint flashed through Sadie's otherwise unresponsive eyes. It would have been nice to drag Senyak into the dark with him. It was true that Hantal *stood alone* ... What misery didn't love company on the way down?

Immortal intervention aside, it was still a sharp slap in the face that Hantal had ultimately been stopped by a 0.04 percent anomaly in that last elevator car. He was really starting to think that someone above Immortal Transcendence was out to get him ...

Now laying immobile, uncertain why Senyak hadn't yet come and forced him into banishment through Ka exhaustion to protect his precious sapient mortals, Hantal decided it *was time to leave.* Even though harvesting an immature array would result in less than half of his collected resources ... it was time to take the money and run.

Reaching out with his Ka, Hantal called into play one of his contingencies. An array-tether. He had paid a sizable portion of his Awakening Tier cultivation for it before coming here. Using it would cost a full half of the growth he could anticipate from what he expected to collect. Alas, some were better than none. And, if Brundox stayed stuck in Sadie's fading soul any longer, getting none and losing even more looked more and more probable.

Using the tether to open the immature array and expose its densely concentrated soul Essence would definitely over-accelerate the weak cosmic fields tethering mortals' Essence to their bodies. Doing so in the presence of this mortal would absolutely kill her and all the mortals within one thousand meters. In fact, the mortals' souls would essentially cease to exist. Not even being able to send their tiny spirits to the mortal nexus for rebirth . . . and that was really too bad for them. *It frees me from this anchor and gets me my Essence, so it's definitely happening!*

Hantal activated the tether attached to the center of his core, warping the relatively fragile fields of time and space in the Essence-deprived material iteration they were in. Transparent sigmoid waves whipped up and down in expanding circles from the center of Sadie's chest and the immature Essence array materialized in front of her dying body. Luminous brilliance from the hardly restrained Essence of countless adharmic warped souls filled the back of the ambulance. The energy crackled with violet arcs of power as it surged out of the patient bay unrestrained.

Now that the array was present, Hantal activated its release to transfer the Essence into his core. Exposure to the intense power also had the desired incidental effects of instantaneously disassociating her physical body to less than subatomic particles *and* complete spiritual dissolution of her comparatively feeble mortal soul tether. In short, complete expungement. No physical or metaphysical traces remained that she had ever existed.

The same was true of the EMT next to her, the driver, and 4,094 occupants of cars and buildings in a 1000-meter circle of Hantal's core.

Finally freed from his Ka dominion, Hantal manifested in his physical avatar. *The brooding mystic.* A broad-chested, dark-haired man with a tall frame and full but closely trimmed beard. His physical form floated through the open doors of the now out-of-control ambulance and hovered over the street as Essence from the array still flowed directly into his core.

Hantal admired the devastation around him during the several seconds the array needed to transfer its violet torrent of Essence. The now driverless cars around him careened out of traffic as they flipped over each other, crashing into themselves and the surrounding buildings. Orange and yellow explosions erupted as fuel fires blossomed in all directions.

The transfer ended in a trickle and Hantal moved to convert back to pure Ka for his travel to the nearest aspect doorway and away from here—

However, before he could Intend the shift . . . he felt the last thing he had expected. The slightest trace of a specific mortal's Essence. Easy to miss if he hadn't been intently aware of his surroundings, but after being felt it was absolutely unmistakable to his avatar's perception.

The mortal in question was also traveling in the back of an ambulance. In fact, his vehicle had collided with the massive pile-up Hantal had just caused and was, even now, flipped on its side and sliding to a rest in the growing snarl of wrecks clogging the road.

"Senyak's anomaly!" Hantal hissed.

If anyone needed to pay for Hantal's losses, it was him!

Even so, for a moment, Hantal's cautious nature warred with his depraved motives. He really needed to leave before the heir arrived. It was, in fact, very sloppy of Senyak not to have taken care of Hantal immediately. Trapped as he had been . . .

Yet, as much as Hantal would prefer *not* to consider himself a *bitter bitch* about failed plans, in truth, he *really was one!* A murderous smile slowly spread over his features at the satisfaction he would have in torturing this mortal for Senyak's interference in his plans. Hantal would only be giving him the release of expungement when his senses had finally tired of the mortal's cries begging for it.

The actor streaked over to the flipped ambulance and pulled the backdoors off, flinging them over the nearby skyscrapers for effect. There was a dead EMT in the compartment, an unconscious driver belted in the front seat, and Joshua Elias Tanner, the divergent anomaly who had cost him so much. The anomaly was working over the dead EMT to no effect.

Still grinning wickedly, Hantal leered as Joshua flinched at the ambulance doors ripping from their hinges.

"Sweetheart! Do you remember me!?"

Josh froze in the middle of checking the EMT's missing pulse. Until then, Josh had wondered how he'd even known to check for the standard signs of life. Somehow, he just had the knowledge. Probably part of the CPR information smashed into his brain . . .

Looking up at the bearded, dark-haired man he had honestly never seen before, who also happened to be . . . *floating* . . . Josh had absolutely no trouble recognizing the smile and the dark glint in his eyes. This was the monster that had forced his way into Sadie. No mistake, one thousand percent.

"Ahhh . . . yeah, sure . . ." Josh started slowly rising to his feet in the wrecked med bay. "You're the reason my balls ache!" Josh said, standing with a quick pivot to his right in one move.

The broken top half of an IV pole in his closed fist smashed the monster in the left side of his face with what should have been crushing force. It was a good hit. A solid hit. The monster hadn't even tried to get out of the way. A crack like this would have taken out Sadie at the beginning of their fight, and she had been an absolute animal! Even against the half-inch, solid-steel pole, it was a telling blow as Josh's weapon of opportunity bent into a *U* around the monster's head. But, against this . . . *thing* . . . it did nothing but make Josh's hands and shoulders hurt from the impact.

The floating man *tsked*. "Foolish, foolish, foolish . . . I'm immortal. *You can't* hurt *me*, Joshua." The hovering man said, straining the pronoun, then cheerily adding, "But I can hurt *you* . . . *Let's give that a try!*"

The chaos actor's hands flashed into the back of the ambulance and facepalmed Josh. He then nonchalantly slammed Josh's head into the asphalt. For the second time in so many hours, Josh knew nothing but blackness.

An evil cast came over Hantal's face. "And I plan to continue doing just that..."

CHAPTER 5

————————⭑————————

Time to Pay the Piper

"NO, NO. *No! No! No!*" Senyak yelled to himself as he appeared at the last known location of the Ka dominion.

A large pile of wrecked automobiles littered the street and sidewalks, several having crashed into nearby buildings before coming to rest.

"Combi! Locate the chaos actor's Ka signature." Then, he spoke to Damni while casting a worried glance around the destruction. "I don't know how he got out of the Ka dominion. Perhaps it was this massive transport accident that caused her death?"

Damni looked around at the destruction. There was a complete absence of mortal victim remains to be found. No bodies, no blood, nothing alive or dead at the original location. This was no mortal accident.

"Automobiles, honey... automobiles... It is more likely the accident was caused after his release from the Ka dominion. As for how he got out? There are expensive ways he could have facilitated her death. But regardless... without a doubt, the chaos actor has activated the Essence array. Feel the wild Essence flooding this area!"

Sen nodded. Any massive release of Essence that left so much residual behind would have destroyed any mortal soul tethers in the area. Sen sighed. *What despicable things wouldn't this chaos actor do?*

Sen's Combi chimed, reporting something very difficult to believe. *"Immortal Ka signature seventy-five meters to your right."*

Senyak and Damni turned with incredulous looks on their faces. He was right there! Smashing a mortal's face into the ground next to a flipped transport. *Is that Joshua Elias Tanner?* Senyak didn't know why the chaos agent was still here or how he had apprehended Joshua. But he did know questions were for later. The chaos actor had finally made his first mistake. Senyak was going to capitalize on it. Signaling Damni to stay back, Sen moved in.

Physical combat was new to Senyak ... In fact, it was unknown to most Immortals, who generally considered it pointless. Ka couldn't be destroyed through physical means. There weren't many non-physical means to destroy it either, hence the term Immortal. But here, in a material realm, physical combat held validity. Because of this, Senyak had studied it for the last five hundred local solar cycles <*Years, Damni ... yes ... years*> for just this event. Rolling his shoulders and loosening his neck, Senyak activated his *acceleration strike*. His favored physical attack.

Channeling Ka from his Immortal core, Senyak increased his physical avatar's overall mass, almost instantaneously reaching a density equal to that of an atomic nucleus. The same density that the heart of a neutron star reached just before forming a singularity. Simultaneously, he launched himself forward by opening a focused micro-gate from the center of the local star.

"The sun ... yes, Damni ..." Senyak muttered with his eyes dead ahead on the chaos actor.

At once, the force of the sun's nuclear fusion, turning 600 million tons of hydrogen to helium per second, accelerated his body to just under the speed of light in less than two nanoseconds, providing Sen with the needed acceleration for his attack. Sen sighed to himself. This attack really was lacking in style. But confined as they were to this physical iteration, along with the limits of the Penta Protocol concerning collateral damage, it was the best he could do.

Surprisingly, Sen found that sometimes just plain hitting things was quite cathartic. In this instance, it also served the purpose of causing the chaos actor to spend significant amounts of his Ka. And when his Ka was depleted, his consolidated cultivation would have to be converted to maintain his physical manifestation in this iteration. When both were consumed, he would be unable to maintain a physical form. Thus, unable to impact this or any material realm until it was replaced. His only course would be to return to the Immortal realms and rebuild his cultivation over the next millions of local solar—<*years!*>

While it was technically accurate that battling Immortals could abandon their physical avatar for their Immortal Ka form, if the chaos actor did that, he would be at the mercy of Senyak in his. *If only he was that foolish!* Sen found himself salivating at the thought. Sadly, Sen was certain the actor was not interested in facing him, a fourth-tier combat specialist, in his Immortal form.

In the long nanoseconds it took Sen to close in, he couldn't keep a smile from growing on his lips. *Transcendence! This is going to feel good!*

Senyak's first strike was a vertical hand blade severing the arm holding Joshua Elias Tanner. In the same motion, Senyak kicked the actor with both legs as his leading hand slid along the ground like an outrigger to maintain his position.

The chaos actor had no chance to react as his avatar's just-filled-with-lethal-mortal-soul-Essence-core was shattered by Senyak's double-leg attack. Mortal Essence so dense it formed a violet-hued, semi-solid plasma, exploded in a nimbus around them, covering everything in a fifty-meter diameter. Including Joshua as he lay unconscious at the feet of the chaos actor.

Exploding Essence geysered out behind the actor in a firehose-thick stream, visible even to mortal eyes, as the chaos actor was hurtled down the street from the impact. Having finished his opening salvo, Senyak followed up with multiple dimensional displacements, striking and restriking the actor dozens of times to prevent him from regaining his footing.

Sen ultimately directed the sack of broken bones and physical distortions serving as his opponent's avatar into the mass of piled up—<*automobiles... yes, Damni.*> The burning autos' frames spun on their flat roofs and slid on their sides as Sen slammed the chaos actor repeatedly into them.

Finally, when the stolen Essence blasting out of the chaos actor's fractured core was down to a mere dribble, Sen let the avatar roll to a stop in a heap of jumbled limbs near the center of the street. The chaos actor's appendages were hopelessly bent in useless shapes and a large portion of his hair and face had been scraped off as it tore up the asphalt of the road he stood on. Senyak mused that being used like a baton ball would usually have such results on one's physical avatar.

All this damage had forced the actor to burn through his cultivation. But really, it served as an outlet for Sen's twenty Ka nexus rotations of frustration. The chaos actor's cultivation was still nowhere near depleted. Senyak would need to hurl him through the core of the local gas-giant planets to get him to complete Ka exhaustion. *First, things first though!* Sen needed a bit more payback for all the disrespect he had suffered at the chaos actor's hands.

Slowly, Sen walked over to the beaten avatar. There had never been a question of combat's outcome between them. Senyak had always just had to corner him.

Grabbing the actor by his collar, Senyak yanked him from the street.

Looking into what was left of the actor's eyes, he said, "Now it's time for proper introductions. As you know, I am Senyak Marztanak, second-seeded heir of the Marztanak Hegemoncy."

Senyak punctuated his last words by headbutting the chaos actor, caving in what was left of his nose, and slamming him once again to the ground with muffled grunts. "Now, let us have your name, please."

Hantal, unable to compete with Senyak in combat, had used the quality time over the last several minutes of being battered and rolled around the street to think his situation over. During this time, Hantal had made some essential realizations.

Realization number 1: From a combat standpoint. All Hantal could manage in the physical realm right now was to maintain his physical avatar's form. As it was, he was already on the edge of burning his cultivation to keep achieving that.

Realization number 2: Clearly, Senyak was a combat specialist. At least one tier above Hantal's current level of cultivation to boot. Hantal's cultivation area was self-realization and energy utilization. His focus allowed for alternative cultivation methods and finding Ka truths.

Realization number 3: Given the difference in their cultivation bases, and specific applications, Hantal's chances of winning were bleak in a straight-up fight. He had zero probability of victory in direct combat. All he could hope for was escape. However, given the right circumstances, perhaps Hantal could recoup some of his losses . . . if the opportunity presented itself.

Realization number 4: As it turned out, Hantal suspected that the right opportunity for escape and recoupment would definitely present itself . . . all due to his usual cautious planning.

Hantal's bloody lips formed a twisted smile as he put his plan into play.

"*Mmmfffffnnngggfffff...*" Senyak heard the chaos actor attempting to speak through torn lips, shattered teeth, and a shredded tongue.

Sen leaned in. "What was that? I didn't quite make it out!" Senyak spoke good-naturedly, quite enjoying himself as he shifted back for the satisfaction of another headbutt on the chaos actor's ruined face.

But the headbutt never landed. Instead, Sen stood rigid. Frozen in place. His hands wrapped around the actor's collar. A half smile that was no longer reflective of his mood mocked the irony of his predicament.

At some point, the chaos actor had stuck a metallic orb to the middle of Sen's forehead. Green and purple lights studded around its diameter blinked steadily in his upper peripheral vision.

This is not good!

Slowly at first, and then in an instant, Hantal broke from Senyak's paralyzed grip. Hantal stood up and straightened his limbs. His dark features returned to his reforming face with an invisible pulse of Ka burned from his Awakening Tier of cultivation. Standing straight, he loomed over Senyak's unmoving form in the center of the destroyed street.

"I said ..." Hantal highlighted his words with a wagging index finger pointed at Sen's face. "You are a fool and easily duped." He shifted his index finger to the orb stuck to Senyak's head. "This is a physical-matter immobilizer. It is something the Biologic Union worked on together with the Techno Lords ... and quite possibly some covert agents from the Masters themselves. Its main purpose is to stop Immortals from running amok in the physical realms. Just like *you* apparently have." Hantal finished by tapping Sen's forehead on the pronoun with a genuine smile on his once again darkly handsome face.

Glancing left and right, taking in the destruction all around them, Hantal shrugged. "It does seem that we tend to wreak havoc when we show up unsupervised . . . but I digress . . . This immobilizer cost me more than I want to admit. Use of it will definitely make this trip a complete loss. Especially as you have cracked my physical core and spilled my *very recently* acquired Essence *all over the* Ka forsaken *street!*"

Hantal leaned over and tensely smiled in Sen's face. "But don't worry about me! To compensate me for this loss, you will donate all the cultivated Essence in your physical core. Just as you were planning on depleting mine."

Chuckling to himself, Hantal reached into an astral space and pulled out a blade approximately sixty centimeters long as he continued talking. "I mean seriously, Senyak, if I had known it would be this easy to harvest cultivated Essence a full tier above mine, I would have shown up to our *duel* five hundred solar cycles ago. Forget about the adharmic genocide Essence. Thanks for being so predictable . . . again!" Hantal's face beamed with glee and malice.

Senyak's eyes quivered in his face as he struggled to move . . . to cycle his cultivated Essence . . . to accomplish anything! Anything, but fail as horribly as it seemed he was . . . *And so, so foolishly . . .*

"Struggle as much as you like. Inside a physical body, within a material realm, we are bound by all the same laws as these mortals." Hantal continued whimsically, "We typically have a great deal more power than they do, for sure . . . but you won't break through this with your cultivation channels interrupted. The wires have been cut from your batteries, boy! What is it that the local mortals say? *Why run from me? You'll just die tired!*

"But keep trying! It does my heart good to see you struggle so futilely." Hantal widened his eyes as he cackled madly.

Hantal stood there waiting as Sen's struggles inevitably lessened and stopped. The shame of failure hung about his still form like foul air.

"There you go! I knew you would see it my way!" Hantal spoke in a bright tone, tilting his head and sending a cheerful wink at Senyak. "The name is Hantal Brundox, by the way. And this . . ." Hantal slowly raised the blade through the small space between their faces in a menacing manner, but his friendly, upbeat tone did not change. "This is an anti-serene core blade. It can take the dharmic core from those insufferable white-hat-wearing busybodies who run around for the Prime Motivator."

"Yes! Even with their internal cultivation shielding in place." Nodding, Hantal answered Sen's imagined question.

Leaning a fraction closer to Sen, he smiled widely and hissed though unmoving lips, "I'm sure it will have *very little trouble* harvesting yours."

Hantal's smile was quickly replaced with his bared, clenching teeth. "Do you know how much you have cost me with your silly hobby of trying to save mortals?" Hantal's face hardened into a severe expression as he raked fingers through his hair. "I'm going to tell you something for free, Senyak. Maybe get through that thick skull of yours. I've been here for the last four thousand Ka nexus cycles, one hundred thousand local solar rotations of this planet. I first got here when these mortals were still traveling in incestuous family groups hunting beasts and gathering berries in the forests. Before even an agrarian society existed. I fostered those civilizations to boost their numbers and raised them like cattle for my own purposes. I know them like a mortal parent knows their own children. They have been, and always will be, a murderous, uncaring group of powerless monsters. They have never changed, and they will never change. Not one little bit. Why do you think it is so easy to get them to kill each other with such wanton abandon, hmmm? Believe me when I tell you, *they aren't worth it.* Nothing more than a distasteful, hopeless group of smelly, unenlightened sheep." He shook his head as he could see his words were wasted. "Anyway, if you don't get it now … you never will. For that, I should end your Ka on pure principle. And I would. But, sadly, all I can do is pack you up and ship you back to your Polar Neutral iteration of origin. Minus your current tier of cultivation and your physical core, of course. I'll be taking those with me. They will fetch a reasonable price on the grey markets and help me recoup my losses … so my time spent here will not have been a total waste.

"Never fear, though. I'm sure you and your family will have quite a few things to discuss when you finally make it back. Good luck, Junior! Oh . . . and I haven't forgotten about that mortal you involved in this. Joshua? Was that his name? He and I will be having extended conversations for the next several Ka nexus rotations."

Hantal took a moment of thoughtful repose and exhaled a cleansing breath. "Well, let's get to it!" He smiled maniacally and slowly raised the blade to Sen's physical core. The tip touched Senyak's abdomen and slowly slid into his skin and muscle . . .

--------------------✶--------------------

Burning pain and—fear?—erupted in Senyak's mind. After penetrating a centimeter in . . . the chaos actor suddenly stopped. The rest of his body was also unmoving.

A disembodied voice spoke deeply, "**Yes, we surely do have a lot to talk with him about.**"

A strong hand erupted from Hantal's chest, simultaneously holding his Immortal Ka core and his physical cultivation core. Something Senyak had thought was impossible to accomplish outside of an Immortal iteration, until this very moment at least.

"**You, on the other hand, have said quite enough. I find you detestable. Good riddance.**"

Desperation flooded Hantal's eyes for the briefest moment as he found his immortal center cut from his physical body and crushed in the disembodied hand. A small squeak made its way from his unmoving lips. Then the blackness of oblivion swallowed him. And so ended the path of the Immortal Hantal Brundox.

The lights on the orb stuck to Senyak's forehead stopped blinking, and it dropped to the street with a heavy clunk. Absently, he sensed Damni being released from some form of suspension and flashing to him through material space. Senyak held up a hand behind his back and motioned for her to stop where she was. He then stood straight and brushed off his clothes.

Swallowing past a lump in his throat, Sen's voice cracked as he spoke with a dry mouth. "Grandfather?"

CHAPTER 6

✶

Being Dumb Costs a Lot

"WE NEEDS be gone."

Senyak's grandfather waved a hand. Instantly, Senyak and Damni appeared before him on the bridge of a much larger and more well-appointed . . . *spaceship* . . . than Senyak had ever been on before. A large view screen took up the front of the room upon which large clusters of galaxies, stars, and nebula were displayed with amazing visual clarity. However, while they were still in a material matter iteration, Senyak had no idea where they were without his Combi. Or if they were even in the same iteration or cuboid that he had just spent the last twenty Ka nexus cycles with Damni.

Mortals and Immortals, all uniformed in his house colors of navy blue and silver, scurried about on two, three, and four legs, some waving tentacles, some hovering. Most were in a predominately bipedal form with blue-tinted skin, telescoping necks, and more articulated joints in their limbs than humans. This one species, the Jaralon, manned the bridge at its various stations. Reading sensors, checking logs, and reporting to one another. About what, Senyak had very little idea. But the fact they were the same race as Damni's chosen-physical avatar made alarm bells start ringing in Senyak's mind.

Looking up at his grandfather, Senyak still had a hard lump in his throat. It was larger now, if anything. He also noted a cold sweat forming between his shoulder blades. And he was sure of only one thing—if his grandfather was here, things were far worse for him than he had thought. Without a doubt, Senyak would be facing some form of discipline from his family for failing to deal with the chaos actor definitively. But never would he have believed that his grandfather would be directly involved in such a small matter. Senyak wasn't even the first-seeded heir. That honor fell to his elder brother, Denyak. The first child propagated by his parents.

All Sen's life, his significance had been negligible. He was only the spare heir after all. Reflective of this was the number of times he had been alone in his grandfather's presence—exactly zero. Zero in six thousand Ka nexus cycles. Not that Senyak didn't know of his grandfather's history and accomplishments. They were required knowledge for all seeded heirs. The deeds and methods of Zenyak Marztanak, *Bulwark of the Polar Neutral Iteration; the Axe Blade of the Hegemoncy, Immortal cultivator without equal. Honored. Respected, and above all things ... feared.* A fact Senyak was very aware of right now.

"Say what you must. Then I will speak."

"Grandfather, *errr* ... thank you ... I am in your debt!" Sen dropped to one knee and lowered his head in supplication.

Rolling grey eyes under furrowed dark brows, his grandfather lifted a finger, and Sen was raised to his feet. Zenyak's gaze, if anything, grew more penetrating. Another thing Sen hadn't thought was possible.

"Anything else?"

Sen internally panicked.

Say what?

I'm sorry?

I failed?

I'm not worthy of being a seeded heir?

I was led around by my nose for twenty-five Ka nexus cycles by a cultivator one tier lower than me, and if it wasn't for Damni, I would still be lost and stumbling while he absconded away with his ill-gotten gains?

Family creed strictly frowned upon showing weakness, particularly in front of an accuser. *Always show strength and control. In every situation.* Senyak had heard his father say this on uncountable occurrences.

But there was nothing even remotely positive to say about his performance. Nothing could even come close to exculpating him and his actions. Nothing to show his strength or help him maintain his control.

Sen's internal conflict raged and paralyzed his thoughts. He looked to his side where at least he could borrow some of Damni's unflagging positivity. He needed his Ka bond more than ever right now.

Damni...

She wasn't at his side... the place where she had been for the last one hundred Ka nexus cycles!

Looking up, he saw her positioned two steps behind his grandfather. Her gaze was downcast, and she was looking decidedly uncomfortable... she was also wearing a crew uniform in the Marztanak blue and silver.

"Damni?" Sen's voice squeaked while his apprehension screamed.

He reached out to her through their Ka bond. Not meeting his gaze, she pulled her Ka back and turned away from him. His mouth fell open, and he goggled after her. A feeling of complete loss came over him as his thoughts raced—

But... but he was hers... She was his... The very definition of Ka bond! Still, she turned from him.

Sen's eyes narrowed. Only now did he begin to sense the depth of the waters he was swimming in. Wheels were turning inside of wheels around him. As was all too usual recently, Senyak had no idea if the ground where he stood was solid. His shoulders drooped in resignation, and he waited for the bulwark to drop his axe.

"Okay. This has gone on long enough." Zenyak wearily huffed out. "Senyak, sit."

Two chairs appeared facing each other. Zenyak comfortably leaned back in his; Senyak sat on the edge of his with dejected acceptance hanging over him like a shroud.

"**Damni is my loyal agent, not your willing Ka bond. She has had you under my surveillance for the last five hundred Ka nexus cycles. Her report of your actions showed me your failure at every turn, requiring me to present an end this fiasco.**" Zenyak clenched his fist and yanked minutely. "**This is no longer needed.**"

And Damni's tethered presence was gone from Sen's Ka core. As if her imprint had never been there . . .

There were also none of the expected penalties for breaking their bond. Senyak had neither loss of Immortal Ka capacity nor cultivation tier. He would have lost both if he or Damni had broken the bond. No, it was as if the bond had never existed.

Remorse clouded Sen's thoughts and feelings. An emptiness lingered over him in a way he would not have expected to feel before this *mission*.

Stunned and silent, Sen sat and tried to accept his loss . . . it had been real for him . . . obviously, not her.

Zenyak continued, "**There are things of import you are not privy to and that exceed your ability to understand. These events reach beyond your father and even my ability to completely control. They affect the Immortal Transcendence to the limit of known aspect doorways.**"

Zenyak paused, allowing his words to sink in for all the good it did. Sen continued to sit in a subdued manner, not grasping the full extent of what Zenyak was telling him.

Zenyak sighed deeply and rolled his eyes. "**Moving to things within your grasp . . . every seeded Marztanak heir, including your older brother, Denyak, has failed my surveillance. His failure exceeded even yours, showing only a continued recalcitrance to alter his obtuse and concrete thinking. Because of the seriousness of what we are facing, I** have disqualified him from his seedency. As I have for the overwhelming majority of your siblings. Every problem is not a nail to which you are all hammers. Your failure as heirs is in large part due to the deficiency of your father in raising nothing but combat specialists. Ignoring the importance of walking a well-balanced path through existence. He has focused only on Immortal concerns, ignoring the totality of the underlying realms. Mortals, Biologics, Necro and Techno Lords, Undead Commandants, Mana Usage, Primordials, gods, demigods, demon spawn, and all lines of lower realm cultivation, to name but a minuscule part of what is missing.

"Knowledge from the lower realms should always be considered and utilized where appropriate. Such knowledge is a force multiplier when properly implemented and applied to Immortal Ka. When not . . . it is a devisor leading to complete collapse and defeat. A thorough understanding of mortal-level Essence and the mortal realms is an irreplaceable foundation for successful Ka cultivation and Ascendance.

"You have most aptly proven this with your extraordinary failings in dealing with Hantal Brundox. A very distasteful creature that I'm almost sorry I utilized. Yet, he clearly defeated you while being a step lower than your cultivation with nothing more than his knowledge of what was available in the mortal realms. That and his willingness to use them. I cannot stress enough how handily you were defeated at the hands of an immortal who, by all standards, was inferior to you . . . save for his knowledge of mortal concerns . . .

"Didn't Damni's report say that Brundox stopped you from halting the rise of a mortal-genocidal dictator . . . one Adolf Hitler . . . with, of all things, something as low-tech as a nuclear fission device and its resulting EMP. Disabling your transport's engines and leaving you like, and I quote, 'a dead duncro, bobbing in the sea.'"

Sen blushed in shame at his Ka—his former Ka—bond's unkind but accurate description . . . then did a double take, his mouth falling open again. "This was all a setup? The entire thing! *You controlled the chaos actor?*"

"Of course, he was under my control. Though he didn't know it. I have controlled all the events surrounding you since you and Damni formed your Ka bond ... such as it was." Zenyak had the good graces to move on quickly from the fact that he had dropped his own descendant into a fictional Ka bond.

"Know this, all of the Marztanak failures, up to and including your father's, are ... largely ... my fault.

"I failed to instill in your father how important it is to teach you all the underlying mortal precursors of Immortal Ka. I had the mistaken belief that what I was ... he would also become. A simple fact that the mortal concept of entropy would have reminded me of ... if I had considered it.

"I was wrong to let him focus purely on the Immortal realms. He did so because it was easier and less tedious. My shortcomings were in wanting my child to be happy to the point that I spoiled him.

"Know that what has happened to our family is not uncommon. When we focus on the Immortal and forget the foundations from where we come, we are always less. Much more vulnerable to the actions of those who can join both Immortal and mortal knowledge when acting. The only reason I dominated the Hegemoncy when I transcended was that I took it away from privileged Immortals who had similarly forgotten the trials and tribulations of their ancestors. Forgetting the very face of their fathers ..." Zenyak trailed off.

Sen looked up at that. His Grand Patriarch's admittance momentarily made him forget his own dejected feelings. Sen was further surprised to note a rare forlorn moment crossing Zenyak's features. As if his grandfather was reaching back to memories beyond him. Hoping for a chance at change, though he knew it was beyond even his vast powers to do so.

Sen took the small gap to interject the question spinning in his mind. "Grandfather, I understand I failed. To be honest, I have known this for a long time. What is to become of me?"

Zenyak looked up from his troubled revelry and focused a piercing gaze on Sen. **"You are all we have left, Senyak. I am going to have to use you to face what is coming. But I can't use you as you are. You will need a complete . . . what was the mortal term? Made over. Yes, you need a makeover.**

"You will start with zero tiers of cultivation and begin again. If you can restore yourself with the appropriate foundational support, you will inherit the entire Marztanak Hegemoncy as its sole heir. Then, with the proper foundation, my greatest hopes are that you will have the strength to rebuild what has fallen. If not . . . you will perish." Zenyak's serious and unwavering gaze left no doubt in Sen's mind that his grand-father was not exaggerating in any way.

"Your only other option is to be cast adrift from the Hegemoncy . . . our family . . . our iterations of origin. I won't lie to you. This has already been the fate of the majority of your seeded siblings. Most of their fail-ures were so great I simply cut them off from family resources and banished them. The very few that did qualify for an offer of rehabili-tation have refused it.

"Senyak, the choice is yours. If you prefer to continue an unsup-ported Immortal life, I will let you keep your Ka. You are already at the fourth tier. Who knows? Perhaps you could continue on your own through the last three tiers . . ." Zenyak stopped speaking, and silence fell over the front of the bridge.

The crew milling around during the start of the conversation had the common sense to keep back and quiet, the weight of what was being discussed far beyond them.

"Senyak, only seeded heir of the Marztanak Hegemoncy, what choose you? Do you wish to continue in the seedency? To try again? To grow with the proper foundation? Or will you be cast from the family to find your own way?"

Sen's mind whirled. Of all the things he had expected, this was never one. He had even asked his Combi to calculate its probability. But Zenyak had apparently cut him off from his Combi during their conversation. Senyak was well past the midpoint of his fourth tier. It had taken him one hundred thousand Ka nexus cycles and would take much more to get back here with the proper foundation his grandfather was talking about. He didn't even know how to start getting that information. Perhaps his Combi could help him when he could access it again. Sen's alternative of going on alone? That was terrifying as well, but not impossible. His Immortal foundation was solid, and he had already benefitted from his family resources thus far. Sen might be able to make his way if he could gain support from an independent combat specialist society or clan...

But, going off on his own...just wasn't him. If Senyak was anything, he was loyal to his family. He was grateful for the support that he had received from them. Searching deep, Sen realized he was willing to sacrifice his four tiers of cultivation for his *makeover* if necessary to help him regain his place among them.

His choice made, Sen bowed at the waist to his grandfather. "I will continue my seedency. I choose the makeover. I will not let you down. I will cultivate my Ka growth with the proper foundation to face what is coming." His mindset had never been more determined.

"Excellent choice, child. So it is decided. So it shall be."

Sen stood tall and straightened his clothing. "I'll return to the Polar Neutral Ka nexus immediately for retraining..." Sen's voice trailed off as Zenyak's head was shaking in the negative, a mischievous smile spreading across his face.

"No, child, you are mistaken. To be sure, you are starting over, but not as an Immortal. You are returning to a prime-material iteration to begin cultivating as a mortal. From there, you must rise to the Immortal realms and beyond. Just as I did ... Blessings to your cultivations, young one!"

Say what?!? Senyak saw the schadenfreude in his grandfather's twinkling eyes for the first time. Then, the entire world disappeared without giving him the time to rally his thoughts and call his grandfather the *deceitful and conniving old bastard* he was.

The next thing Sen heard was a groggy but recognizable voice.

"Wha ... What the hell is going on ... Who was that old guy?"

"Joshua?"

CHAPTER 7

Put It Away, Sen!

THEY HAD appeared in a dark alley next to a dumpster reeking of rot, death, and worse. It was lightly raining, and thunder could be heard rumbling softly in the night's distance. Several large dark plastic rubbish bags lined the wet wall next to the dumpster. Josh's slightly stirring body lay face up on them. Twenty-five meters down the alley, there was a traveled street. The light of passing headlights reflected from the wet asphalt as the cars drove by. Several overhead lamps were out, creating a flickering shadow scape as the wind caused loose lines to sway overhead.

Joshua Elias Tanner had indeed been returned to this iteration with Sen. Wherever they were, it was unlikely where they had started, given his grandfather's desire for Sen to be *made over*.

Upon first arriving, Sen had turned to Joshua and made clear eye contact. An initial look of horror had come over the mortal's face. Then he had proceeded to pass out. His loud snoring was the only sound save the wind and dripping rain. Sen was unsure why his grandfather had gone through the trouble of sending Josh along. However, Joshua was no immediate threat, so Sen disregarded him, letting the human continue to sleep on the plastic waste bags he had collapsed back onto.

"Combi, identify current space-time coordinates."

No response ...

Very disturbingly, there was also no sense of his Ethos Combi being bonded to his Ka core either.

In fact, there was also no sense of the overwhelming dominance of his Ka core ... the center of his Immortality that had presided in the center of his being from his initial dawning in response to his progenitors' wills fifteen thousand Ka nexus cycles ago. Senyak's Immortal axis, the immutable aspect that joined him with everything around him, spiritual, physical, metaphysical, current, past, future, material, immaterial. *Now nothing ...*

Still, he attempted to open his Ka core and restore his Immortal Essence. To rejoin his transcendent form. *No effect ...*

He repeated the process, again, again, again and again. His fists were like stones, jaw clenched, eyes closed, desperation increasing with every failed attempt. After what he considered *a few tries*, Sen stopped the futile effort. Perhaps 1,049 times over the previous fifteen minutes. Just to be sure ... *but who was counting!?*

Then, just to be absolutely sure ... as if Sen's Immortal transcendent form was a cagey animal he could sneak up to and suddenly pounce upon, he did it again another 150 or 200 times ... *Nothing ...*

The rain had stopped, and the stars wheeled overhead through the breaking clouds as Senyak realized he couldn't even really remember exactly what it felt like to have his Ka core. Being separated from it seemed to remove its very memory. Focusing his concentration, Sen could barely appreciate its fading loss, a thing just beyond his fingertips.

Then even this impression quickly faded. In minutes it was totally gone.

I'm mortal ...

Unable to think of anything else to do, Sen called out to his grandfather. Each time addressing his failings and promising to make the necessary changes. Each time it ended with him begging to be taken back and restored to his Immortality. Each time his pleas went unanswered. He had even once called out to Damni, who he was sure could hear him if she so chose. *There was no response then, either.*

Finally ... giving up ... Sen crouched over his feet and took stock of what he did have ... in what he could feel ...

Concerning his physical being, subjectively, he couldn't identify anything that seemed different from his transcendent form. He was still strong and capable in a combat sense. His thinking processes also seemed to be intact. His knowledge base didn't seem to be altered either. He could still remember his family, their iterations, the stages of immortal cultivation, etc.

On the spiritual level, however, there was one difference he appreciated. After sitting quietly for a few seconds, searching his body, Sen was confident that there was a minuscule, centrally located, mortal-spiritual source. A 1.5-centimeter spherical structure, gently glowing in his strange mortal ... aural *sight* ... <Is that the word, Damni?>

No response ...

A bitter smile carved onto his face as he caught himself slipping back into his old habit. That was going to have to end.

Yes, aural sight was right. Sen's mortal Essence core, for lack of better words, was just below his navel where his Immortal core had been. He did note that his aural sight was dim and cloudy. Dulled compared to the ultimate clarity he had unknowingly luxuriated in as an Immortal.

This core ... Sen's core ... seemed to be filled with unmoving mortal Essence. He prodded it with a thought and watched the Essence swirl around itself. If he thought long and hard enough, he noted he could make the Essence move in a desired direction. It followed clearly laid out meridians leading from his core to all points in his body. His torso, head, extremities, brain, and genitals. There were also meridians between all of his ... *organs.* After reaching its terminus, the Essence flowed back to his core. There was a minimal exchange of energy and ... *waste products?*

The waste was expelled through three of his organs. His lungs via the exchange of airborne elements. A looping organ that occupied most of his abdomen. And lastly, two-lobed, semi-circular organs located near his back on either side of his torso. These two organs were connected to tubes that ended in a pouch-like vessel in his lower pelvis. The looping organ seemed to have a continuous run from his oral orifice to his— *Transcendence!* Mortal life was going to be ... *untidy.*

He continued to circulate his Essence along his spiritual circuits. In response, his organs accelerated their function. The physical tube in his abdomen underwent peristalses. The pouch at the end of the chain he had noted before began filling with liquid. The core at his center also grew infinitesimally brighter when the Essence returned. As if it was collecting and consolidating the Essence through this process somehow.

When Sen finally disengaged himself from the internal observation of his core, he was covered in sweat and gasping. He was eventually able to take several deep breaths that seemed to help. After a few moments, he looked up and noted the sky had taken on the early signs of first light. Shades of dark blue were giving rise to the vague crimson lace of astronomical twilight. He was unsure exactly how much time he had been watching the cycling of his Essence. But it most likely had been hours longer than it had seemed, given the first signs of the morning ... and his physical fatigue.

The rain was long gone, and the street and walls were dry. But Sen was feeling ... cold? He wrapped his damp robes more tightly around himself with minimal improvement. There was also a pain in his lower pelvis centering on the pouch organ he had identified earlier. It was gnawing at him. It got worse when he pushed down on it. On a whim, he raised his robes and encouraged the pouch-like bladder to *release.* Amazingly, a full stream of yellow impurity flowed out, significantly relieving him and creating a small puddle that only partially drained away in the broken asphalt.

Belatedly realizing the slant of the alley was not in his favor, Senyak hastily used one of his hands to aim his genitals another way. Finally, the stream trickled to a stop. Sen again pushed on his bladder, and the pain was gone.

Hmm, maybe it wasn't going to be so hard to figure out mortal life after all—

"What are you doing?"

Sen spun, surprised at the words, still holding the tube his yellow waste had flowed from. His other hand was still poking his bladder. He stood in front of a now fully awake Joshua, shamelessly flaunting his full sun, less than thirty centimeters from Josh's horror-stricken face.

Josh's eyes widened in shock, and he moved away from Sen with his hands palm up in apparent surrender. With no way to back up, he scrambled to stand on top of the wet bags he had been lying on. "*Damn, dude!* Put your dick away! What's wrong with you?!" Josh's face puckered in distaste as he continued to try and move laterally along the wall and away from Sen's position.

Confused and momentarily uncertain of the social norms concerning genital exposure among mortals, Sen quickly pulled up his undergarments and let the top half of his robes settle back down. Had he somehow profaned a societal taboo. But how? After all, Damni didn't seem to have any objections about it.

Joshua must have reached what he considered minimal safe distance. He stepped off the rubbish bags and tilted his head slightly, spreading his hands between him and Sen to show he was no threat.

Then he interjected in the not unkind manner one would take with a child or a mentally incompetent adult. "Listen friend, there is a time and place for everything . . . even rocking out with your cock out. But . . . are you . . . *special*?"

"Special? What? Yes! Err, no! I am not mentally challenged if that is your implication, human!" Sen over-forcefully responded, shaking his head quickly in negation, causing his topknot to turn with his head.

A surge of recognition splashed over Joshua's face at the familiar movement. His eyes narrowed, and his features hardened.

"It's *you!*" Josh shouted.

All thoughts of kindness seemed to be gone as he lunged through the air for Sen's throat. Caught off guard by his internal stress over social norms and the rapid, visceral nature of the attack, Sen couldn't dodge or deflect Josh. They slammed down on the wet stones. Josh on top with both hands wrapped around Sen's throat, movie-strangling him with a fierce gleam of madness shining brightly in his eyes.

"Cease this activity now. I'm ready to explain things to you."

CHAPTER 8

———————⋆———————

Level Up or Die

A DIM blue light enveloped both Josh and Sen, and they were lifted to their feet. Looking face to face with ... well, Josh wasn't quite sure what they were looking at. A tall, powerfully built, middle-aged man, shaped out of continually involuting glowing blue lines. It was wearing what looked to Josh's sci-fi-soaked mind, like robes most properly worn by guys who fought with lightsabers and used the Force. The closer Josh looked, the deeper the lines seemed to go into infinite repeating detail. In seconds, Josh had to stop staring and turn away as his eyes started to burn from the continued exposure to the glowing fractals.

Regardless, Josh was sure he had never seen any person that the ... projection ... apparition ... was supposed to be a representation of. A quick glance over and Josh could tell by his downcast eyes that Sen had.

Senyak spoke first, or attempted to, his mouth working with no sound coming out despite what Josh could see were strenuous attempts at being heard.

Josh, whose most recent memories included—

—Having his mind and hormones invaded by a socially inept space alien who looked like a Shaolin monk.

—An elevator death match with a sixty-eight-year-old reception-ist who had almost kicked his ass. But had definitely kneed him twice in the nuts.

—Last but not least, having his face slammed into the street by a man after he had whacked that same man in the head with a half-inch steel bar so hard that had bent around his face.

Enough was enough. And this glowstick ghost was the last straw. Josh started running for his life, screaming down the alley. Or, at least, he would have if he could have moved or made sounds with his mouth. Instead, all Josh did was float there. The only seeming control he had was the ability to move his head, his eyes, and breathing.

The figure spoke. "**I am a Consciousness Clone of the perfect Immortal Zenyak Marztanak, Grand Patriarch of the Marztanak Hegemoncy, and grandfather to you, Senyak Marztanak.**" The Clone made meaningful eye contact with Senyak. "**Benefactor and potential patron to you, Joshua Elias Tanner.**" He looked Josh in the eye with a gaze that could pierce tank armor. "**And at this junction, the potential bane of you both.**

"**I am an exact representation of his mentation, persona, goals, and proclivities. I also have access to his knowledge and an infinitesimal portion of his power. I have been tasked with determining if you two will be allowed to pursue cultivation through the mortal spheres ... or not.**

"**At present, neither of you has control of your body below your neck. I have also silenced your vocalization capabilities.**

"**I assure you that Zenyak Marztanak suffers no fools. As I am an exact representation of him, down to the small mole on his left rear-end cheek, I do not either.**

"**Probability is one hundred percent that you both lack the founda-tional knowledge and wisdom to understand just how close to the end of your paths you really are. Because of this, I have mercifully limited your capabilities to act foolishly until Karma has been balanced ...**"

The words trailed off into silence. Joshua slowly ceased his head shaking, useless eye-rolling, and mental struggles. Senyak had already recognized the futility after the Clone's words several moments before.

Clone—Hegemoncy... what was that anyway—grandfather? Josh wasn't sure of anything, except strangely, the wavelength of some of the light the Clone was currently shining was very near the 400 to 405 nanometer length. His eyes hurt to look directly at it for more than one to two seconds. Josh wondered briefly how he was definite about such an obscure point, not having any science background beyond the odd show caught on the Discovery channel as a kid. But he was beyond a doubt of its accuracy. In fact, Josh was certain of it. He resolved to chalk it up to multiple head traumas in the last several hours. Then continued to steadily gaze in the neutral zone near the Clone's feet.

The Clone continued. "Good, our time is brief, and you both need to listen to me. I will allow you an opportunity to ask meaningful questions when I am confident it will be goal productive.

"I will start with you, Joshua Elias Tanner. You are the one who needs to accept a much more significant change than you were ever meant to understand concerning your concepts of the universe. What we Immortals call an iteration. Your iteration is only one among infinite others that can be traversed.

"Now, focus and follow my instructions, Joshua Elias Tanner. At the center of your spirituality, just below your physical navel, your physical being meets your spiritual reality at your core. Your core is full of spiritual Essence. You will attempt to sense this now with your mind. When you do, you will experience a gently glowing golden aura around it."

What? The insano-train he was currently riding on had just gone completely off the rails! Josh's eyes boggled at the seeming absurdity he had just heard from the Clone's mouth. His confusion was genuine. But, if Josh was honest, there was a fair amount of chosen obstinacy as well. He was at his limit with the bizzarro events that had been occurring to him since entering the elevator, up to and including being hog-tied and silenced by the blue stick man in front of him.

As if knowing every thought in Josh's head, the Clone leaned his glowing blue face, with its impossible myriad of renewing, shimmering outlines, to within two inches of Josh's eyes. **"I said . . . now, Joshua Elias Tanner."**

Josh blinked and looked away in pain as his personal space was fried with UV rads.

The Clone then continued, **"If you persist in disregarding my instructions, I will allow your elimination via spiritual expungement caused by the absorption of toxic levels of soul Essence you were exposed to during Senyak's ill-fated attempt at subduing the independent chaos actor, Hantal Brundox.**

"Your expungement, which I am even now holding in abeyance, will altogether remove you from the physical and spiritual time stream. Preventing even your soul from remerging with the mortal Essence nexus for use by future souls.

"Persist in not following my instructions, and I will allow this expungement for no other reason than so that I can focus my remaining time on Senyak.

"However, to give you an optimally informed chance to choose. And because the scales of Karma between you and Senyak still need to be balanced, I tell you that your very brief mortal existence has been adequately dharmic in my and Zenyak's opinion. I assure you, this is quite a compliment.

"Furthermore, your Karmic link to his grandson was created through your actions in helping him stop the genocidal harvester Brundox. It will be completed by my saving you from spiritual expungement. Karmic balance with you, by all probability outcomes, significantly improves Senyak's chances of success. Karmic balance cannot be achieved if I allow your soul tether to be destroyed. Karmic balance is in everyone's best interest. But . . . as with all things . . . there

are limits to what I am willing to accept from you." The Clone continued as if reading Josh's thoughts in real-time. **"Yes, Brundox is the entity you identify as the cockless wonder who ruptured your sac, killed Sadie, and curbed-stomped your ass.**

"Yes, if you are so expunged, you will never, in any way, be able to see or assist your progeny Sophie to maturity.

"Lastly, it is Karmically correct to inform you that probability predictions also show a significant increase in the success of Zenyak's desired outcomes and objectives when you and Senyak advance together to Transcendence into the Immortal Realms.

"So, Joshua Elias Tanner, choose now. You have five seconds to comply." The Clone moved out of Josh's personal space during the silent countdown.

RoboCop nightmares aside, even though this Clone could be described as a beefed-up stickman from the Lite-Brite Josh played with as a kid, the steel in his gleaming gaze was undeniable. Josh had absolutely no doubt the Clone meant what it said. Josh would be taken out if he didn't do what it wanted. No questions. Glancing to his side, Senyak's head was violently shaking up and down in a blatant attempt to get Josh to comply. In the final analysis, what did Josh have to lose dancing to this crazy man's music of madness for the next few minutes?

Eyes blinking, Josh nodded and started trying to visualize the area under his belly button.

Josh thought about what was there . . .

Then . . . as if brushing a numb hand against the side of an alarm clock before you were awake, Josh felt . . . *something* . . .

He reached for it again with his mind, and it slowly came into . . . *focus?* After a few seconds, he did see and *feel* a small marble-sized lump of . . . *energy . . . will . . . power . . .* so many things! It really felt like *life* to him. His eyes lit up, and he looked back up at the Clone's glowing outline in front of him, shock clearly registering from him.

"Yes. Of course, it really exists. I placed your core there myself. Now, it is linked with your physical body through a series of channels called meridians. These links will allow you to circulate or *cycle* Essence to your physical body as needed. You can cycle the Essence in your core through these channels by inducing a directional vector with your *Intent*. Do so now."

Not needing further convincing, Josh tried. He first poked his core and saw swirling Essence whirling around inside. Racing like gold-colored food coloring inside of a clear water balloon. He tried to push harder. Soon he started to feel a sort of pressure building up behind his eyes.

"**Proceed gently, mortal. You will rupture your cerebral vascula-ture and fracture your core with such little care. As I said, it is your Intent that moves Essence. You must *will* it to happen. Also, breathe. Until you complete your first tier of cultivation, you will continue to need oxygen as it is contained in this planet's atmosphere to fuel your metabolism and maintain consciousness."**

Huh ... breathe? Good advice.

Josh took several slow, steady breaths and reached out mentally to his core again. He thought of moving his Essence out from the core along his meridians. And saw it follow a loop up to his head and back again. When it was done, Josh noted that the pain in his head had decreased. But he did feel slightly winded from the effort.

"**Good. Yes, the micro-cerebral ruptures from your first clumsy attempt were healed by joining the spiritual to the physical. Exempli gratia, cycling your Essence resulted in restoring your body's intended form and improving your physicality.**

"**In fact, the cycling of absorbed Essence allows your spiritual and physical natures to grow closer to a unified whole. Closer to the Divine as some describe it. A more unified spiritual and physical body facilitates the transfer, storage, and use of larger amounts of Essence. Increasing your strength and power as a cultivator. Essentially an upward spiral to perfection and enlightenment, through which you will one day reach a** perfect joining of your spiritual being and physical body. Simply stated, to Transcend from the mortal to the Immortal Realm."

Josh believed he had an agile legal mind. Time and again in the courtroom he had proven himself capable of reading novel, fluid situations and applying the new concepts to get the results he needed... But here, with the Clone talking about mortal and Immortal realms, he had all of his carbon-based logic circuits engaged, and still the Clone's explanation was literally blowing his mind.

Joshua was certain the Clone could look through his eyes and see his brain accelerating in circles as it flew toward the cliff trying to understand his last explanation. The glowing blue features of his face tensed... and then they relaxed. Perhaps accepting the poor tools that Reality had bestowed on him, the Clone seemed willing to accept the poor tool Josh was and try another tack to speed his understanding.

"**Simply stated, cycling of absorbed Essence from other spiritual beings will make you better, stronger, faster ...**"

The clone closed his eyes for a moment, its brows furrowed as it decided to make one final concession for Josh's sake.

"**Yes, Joshua ... Like Steve Austin,** *The Six Million Dollar Man* **but without the bionic implants ... Now, I'm going to pretend that you are more than a prepubescent, TV-watching child and continue with the information you need to advance your understanding ...**" Energized blue arcs of sparking light radiated from the Clone's eyes as his unblinking glare drove home the point that there would be no further dumbing down of its explanations.

But that was okay ... Josh finally thought he was starting to get it.

"**Cycling Essence improves the connection between your body and soul. It also meets the purpose of purifying or distilling foreign elements from the Essence. Once cleansed, the Essence will be added to your core ... growing your cultivation and making you more powerful.**

"**Cycling Essence will also strengthen your physical movements and actions while healing associated damaged tissues and injuries.**

Mastering these two effects of cycling and cultivation will sustain you as you hunt down other Essence-containing spiritual beings. For now, and at further points in your growth, you will need to absorb the Essence of other spiritual beings to increase your cultivation." The Clone's attention turned slightly to include Senyak in its field of vision. "I know that you are already capable of cycling the mortal Essence, Senyak. We must move on to a practical demonstration... for the both of you."

The Clone waved its hand, and Josh felt a sharp pain in his left upper leg. Blood started to pool beneath his feet, which were still dangling six inches off the ground.

In a matter-of-fact tone, the Clone continued, "Now, I have severed both of your left femoral arteries. Being mortal humans with no significant cultivation level, you will most certainly die without medical intervention. I need you both to cycle your Essence to the affected area to understand the benefit of its healing effects. Do so now."

What the absolute fuck! What kind of Steven-King-hooks-up-with-Charles-Manson-and-makes-Cthulhu-babies family did Senyak come from?

Josh looked at Senyak and confirmed that he also had arterial blood pooling under him in a bright red puddle. But Senyak's bleeding was slacking off. While Josh's continued like a garden hose on a pulsatile-medium-open setting. The thought that Senyak might be better at this than Josh went through his mind and spurred him into surprisingly competitive spiritual... mental... psychic... whatever-the-heck action.

Josh again felt his core and *willed* it to move with what he considered a commanding Intent to cycle Essence to his left leg. At first, being scared out of his mind, he had poor control. His reflex response was no different from that of a squirrel stuffed in a sack and then faced with imminent demise through exsanguination. Because of this, Josh's Essence began cycling from his core in all possible directions. Only a minimal part, perhaps 5 percent, reached his wounded femoral artery.

Josh did note a slight decrease in his bleeding and pain. However, not enough to prevent him ultimately from losing consciousness and bleeding out. Josh estimated that at his standard blood pressure of 120/80, he would lose approximately one liter of blood every fifty to fifty-five seconds until he lost consciousness in about two and a half minutes. Then his blood pressure would drop as he continued to bleed until it was approximately 40/0. At that point, he would undergo ischemic and hypovolemic shock. This would lead to cardiac arrest and cascading organ failure from ischemia. First to his brain and heart within the next four minutes, then to his core organs, with death arriving minutes after that...

Josh stepped out from his own thinking. *Where did that come from?*

Josh's only medical training was self-taught by putting Band-Aids on Sophie's skinned knees ... but without question, he knew it was all accurate. No time to figure it out now. Josh only had about ninety seconds left before he lost consciousness. As his biological model predicted—*biological model?... where did that come from?*

He couldn't even talk to himself without getting all *sciency* now ... *Later!* Right now, he had to get the Essence moving in the right direction by asserting his will and *Intending* it, *for the love of little green apples!*

Cutting off his Intention for the Essence to cycle above his waist, Josh first got it to flow only in his lower extremities. This made a significant improvement. Approximately 45 percent had made it to his left leg. It could be enough to avoid loss of consciousness, as the restorative qualities were definitely noticeable. The six-inch wound began closing along with slaking of the blood flow. But, damn, man ... he could do better! Josh limited the Essence flowing to his right leg and groin and focused his Intent on a left-leg-only loop. Then the upper portion only, before it returned to his core.

After completing the first loop of Essence to his upper leg only, the bleeding stopped with a complete reduction in pain. He kept it going for a second and a third time. His leg had been completely healed after two rotations. But, after the fourth, he was able to pick up speed. He thought of the Essence cycling like slot cars on a track. How fast could he make this go?!

"Good. Stop now. You have completely recovered and avoided dying from your own incompetence."

Josh stopped and realized he was definitely out of breath. Using his Intent to move his Essence tired him out. Maybe constantly being close to death time after time in the last twelve hours also had something to do with it? But what did Josh know...

"Now that I am assured the probability models of you meeting the minimum requirements to cultivate were accurate, I will inform you of your path. Along with the expectations I have for you both."

CHAPTER 9

———————————✦———————————

Check It Out Now, Funk Soul Brothers

ZENYAK'S CONSCIOUSNESS clone continued without pause. "Senyak, you have been tasked with reaching the perfect union of the physical and spiritual, commonly called Immortal Transcendence. To achieve this, you will make your way through the five mortal levels of cultivation—foundational, physical, mental, spiritual, and cosmic.

"I will provide pertinent information predicted to enhance both the probability and degree of your success. As you have already learned this day, not all Immortals are equal. To foster your advancement through the mortal levels of cultivation, you are to be given several boons, which others do not have. Understand that your cultivation will be expected to surpass all independent mortal cultivators in this and all iterations you inhabit." The clone waved his hand in a small gesture and golden writing appeared in the air between him and them. Almost as if a legal and binding contract was being formed. "Your boons are thus—"

OPTIMAL CULTIVATOR'S PHYSIOLOGY

"All cultivators are not created equally in the mortal realms. Many physiologic and spiritual variants exist. To get both of you here at this present time, Zenyak was obligated to recreate your physical and spiritual beings from the subatomic and supra-spiritual levels. As Zenyak does nothing in less than complete perfection, you both have been gifted the optimal starting position. You would not have been able to comply with my requirements thus far if you hadn't been. It is estimated that you will be able to cultivate and grow at exponential rates with these improvements... if you are adequately motivated."

Another small wave of his hand and more golden writing in the air—

THIS CLONE

"And my knowledge concerning the foundational necessities of cultivation. My insights will be provided when I have determined you have a need. I will guide you to prevent stumbling in the dark beyond that which will benefit your growth. This is also predicted to vastly increase your rate of cultivation by at least an order of magnitude.

"You have been moved to an iteration twelve aspect doorways from any inhabited Immortal location. Immortal interference from any being from the transcended realms, beyond communication with this Clone, is prohibited. Any voluntary communication on your part will immediately place you under consideration for expungement."

The Clone again waved his hand with more golden letters appearing.

KARMICALLY LINKED CULTIVATION PARTNER

"Senyak has motivation equal to Josh to advance with him. Through his ignorant actions you will both have significant benefits in cultivation advancement while in any material-matter iterations."

One final wave and the now expected accompanying golden lettering appeared.

A CULTIVATION PROBABILITY INTERFACE

"This interface will be branded onto both of your cores. It is impossible to overstate the value of this. It will provide immediate feedback on your current physical and spiritual status. As your cultivation increases, it will also provide you with environmental information concerning the spiritual beings you are dealing with, as well as time-space locations and goal organization."

"This last boon will require another practical application." The Clone released the restraints, and Josh and Sen dropped six inches to their feet. Both stumbled at the sudden freedom.

The Clone raised his hands with its right palm facing out at Senyak's core, the left facing Josh's. Josh and Sen flinched, raising their arms in a simultaneous guarded stance remembering the last practical application. Sadly, it did neither of them any good. Instantly, Josh's mind was filled with unfiltered-solar-radiation level agony. A searing pain began at his core and spread out along his meridians. The pain pulsed in greater amplitude and frequency as the seconds ticked by. Nothing Sen had exposed Josh to had come even close to this skull-pounding, soul-burning torture. Every inch of him, including his hair follicles, hurt. To no effect, Josh grabbed his head and tried to keep it still to lessen his misery. The overload continued to steadily increase until his teeth felt loose in their sockets.

Josh didn't know how, but he knew without a doubt that Senyak was going through the same horror he was feeling. At some point, Josh lost consciousness and fell into the never-ending expanse of white noise swirling around him.

When he woke, Josh was face down over his bent knees. His face was wet and small pieces of gravel from the asphalt were stuck on his forehead. His ears were still ringing as he absently scraped the rocks off.

Rising to his feet, Josh noted Senyak also stirred. Josh's core still smoldered from the searing brand that had been placed there. But the pain receded with every second. While he had several choice words and even a few questions for Zenyak's Clone, Josh had already accepted that he would be outclassed in any confrontation.

The Clone gave absolutely zero fucks. More importantly, Josh started to believe what he was hearing. He was at the Clone's mercy for his continued existence. Most importantly, if he wanted to see Sophie again, he needed to play along. So, instead of reacting with his instincts to rage about everything that had happened to him, Josh stood there sullenly. Waiting...

Senyak had risen to his feet by then, mirroring Josh's stance. Even to the intense glare that Josh hoped he was giving the Clone. Apparently being... whatever Senyak was... hadn't made the core branding any easier for him.

"You both survived." A momentary flicker of genuine surprise seemed to pass over the Clone's face. **"Now activate your Cultivation Probability Interface's biologic assessment by Intending it to *assess*. Just as you would the Essence in your core. The interface is fueled by your Essence. Its functionality increases with your cultivation. It will serve as an assessor of your current physiologic and spiritual condition. The interface can take any visual form and notify you with auditory or ocular clues. Given the mental acuity levels we are starting with, I have set its notification level to *simple* for now."**

Josh Intended as the Clone had instructed and immediately noted the presence of a green and blue bar over to the right of his visual field. There was also a small circle at the top center of his vison. The bottom 10 percent of the circle was filled in opaquely.

"The overall status of your physical well-being is reflected by the green column on your right. Should you take an injury, it will decrease and change to yellow when in a moderate condition and red when facing critical damage. An empty black status bar means you are dead, and I have been saved the trouble of expunging you myself.

"Spiritual strength is reflected by the small figure in the top center of your visual field, along with a visual representation of the current level of dedicated Essence in your core. When the core image is full and golden, you will be ready to advance to the next level of your cultivation. You can see from the spherical shape that you both are very early in the Foundational Tier.

"How much free Essence you have use of in immediacy is reflected by the blue bar to the right of the green bar. This is the Essence you used to heal your femoral artery wounds. The Essence represented has yet to be dedicated to advancing your core and can be used at your discretion. Once used, you can obtain more from absorbing aura, which you have attuned yourself to or gotten directly from other spiritual beings."

"The interface is a ... *video game?*" Josh couldn't help but blurt out at the inanity of it.

"Yes, Joshua Elias Tanner. As I have already stated, I have set the visual clues to ones you would be familiar with to limit the conditions that will otherwise confuse your simple mind." Narrowing his gaze and looking straight at Josh, he added, "No further interruptions, or I will restrain you again. Now, for another practical application."

Josh could see Sen was as frozen in terror as he was at the words.

The Clone's smile at their response could be heard in his voice. "Fear not ... this time. A status check of the functionality of the interface is necessary. Physically striking each other one time should suffice. **No use of weapons and avoid fatal damage . . . if possible."** He chuckled smugly.

Josh took a double take at the Clone. "I get to hit Senyak? For free?" The incredulity bubbled up through his expression to place a maniacal smile on his face as the strength of promised pain flowed through his limbs.

A vulpine smile crossed the Clones face. **"Yes . . . Senyak was an Immortal combat specialist and has retained that knowledge. What should he have to fear from you, Joshua Elias Tanner? But, beware. He can strike one time as well, should he be able. Strike now."**

No further encouragement was needed for Josh. But Senyak was clearly acting first. Josh could see Sen had begun cycling Essence from his core into his hands. His opposite index fingers and thumbs were touching each other end to end in a triangle at the level of his core as a steady-golden glow began spreading out from his hands. Obviously, the intention was to cover him in some form of Essence shield. But its spread moved slowly. Much too slowly!

Josh had cycled Essence through his right arm and fist as he stepped forward with his left foot, twisting at the hip, and threw an overhand right square into Senyak's left cheek and jaw. The simple Intent of trying to punch a hole through Senyak's face like he had been taught so many years ago as a boy in Chicago's South Side. A face that Josh noted was very far from being covered by his spreading Essence shield.

Thusly smashed, Sen was lifted from the ground and hurtled into the brick wall behind him and then slid into a pile of askew limbs like a broken folding chair. His mumbling and eyes that had rolled into the back of his head while he struggled ineffectually to get up indicated he was currently at some lower form of consciousness.

Josh flexed his fingers. They didn't even tingle. Punching like that, even at twenty when he used to box, would have bruised or broken the distal ends of his carpals and possibly his proximal metacarpals. Especially if he had thrown it without gloves. Now in his forties, with

Essence, he was ready to throw down bare-fisted! *Carpals and metacarpals... what is going on with you, Josh?*

"Senyak, cycle Essence to your wounds so that we can proceed."

Josh caught the Clone's gaze lingering on him. "**Joshua Elias Tanner, you used approximately two percent of your available free Essence with your strike and suffered no damage by striking with the appendage you were cycling Essence through. Correct? Both your offense and defense were improved with appropriate economy. This result is exemplary at this stage.**

"**Please confirm that your Essence indicator reflects the two percent expenditure.**"

Josh looked at the blue bar. "Yes ... it's lower by a small amount, less than five percent."

"**Good.**"

Sen cycled his Essence, and his movements immediately began to reflect those of a creature with an intact nervous system more developed than a colony of coral polyps. He slowly rose, and Josh could see his bones reforming. His left cheek and jaw snapped and crackled as broken teeth were pushed out and new ones replacing them above! Sen bent over and spit several of the broken ones out. Rising again, he cast a wary glance at Josh. But he made no move to continue their "practical application."

"**Senyak. Just as Joshua Elias Tanner needs to learn that his universe is simply a negligible part of the multiverse. You need to realize that you are no longer an Immortal with unlimited power.**

"**Your attempted spirit shield's mortal counterpart is at least one step of advancement beyond you in the Spherical Tier you are currently in. You must learn to appreciate the immediacy and imperfection of your mortality. If you were Attuned, an Essence shield to your face and left shoulder would have countered his blow and allowed you to counterstrike. You no longer have access to the perfect completeness of Immortality. Here, in the mortal realm, there are many instances where quick and dirty will usually beat perfect and complete.**

"You lost fifteen percent of your physical wellness bar, which is now restored, and twelve percent of your Essence. Six percent in your misguided attempt to form an Essence shield beyond your cultivation and six percent for the follow-up healing. Please confirm that your Cultivation Probability Interface has reflected these changes."

"Yes. Both were demonstrated as you say."

"Good. Now we will proceed to the gathering of Essence to advance your cultivations. However, you have presently performed beyond the most likely anticipated probabilities by approximately 3 minutes and 47 seconds. I will allow you to ask any pertinent questions before we move on."

Josh stepped closer to the Clone and stared into its face even though his eyes burned doing it. "I need to get to my daughter. I need to see her. When can I do that?"

"Joshua Elias Tanner. You are four aspect doorways from your iteration of origin. Specifically, you are four dimensions away from her. Your daughter Sophie is out of your reach. Yo—"

"*What!* How can you take her from me from her like that! *What have I done to you to deserve this?*" Joshua's fist clenched, and his thoughts moved toward violence.

He specifically didn't move toward the Clone. But he did take an unconscious step toward Senyak. Essence continued cycling to his fists as if he was going to beat an aspect doorway out of his hide.

"Joshua Elias Tanner, understand that neither Zenyak Marztanak nor I have done anything to you other than save you from the complete disassociation of your soul tether from your physical body. As I have already told you, this will result in your total expungement without any hopes of rebirth. Would you prefer we allow that probable eventuality to minimize your mental anguish?"

Emotions warred for control in Josh. Anger, stunned surprise, denial, settling on abject hopelessness. His mouth worked without any sounds as he dropped to his knees, with tears running silently down his cheeks.

Essence continued to cycle through his fists faster and faster as he held them out over a head that had fallen below his shoulders. There he stayed his back slowly rising and falling with his sobs. Even the Clone gave him uninterrupted time and space.

Several quiet moments went by.

Then a hand rested on Josh's shoulder. "I can't understand the loss you feel... I have no progeny nor an overwhelming desire to protect anyone. But I know that even mortal cultivators can travel between the iterations once they have ascended through the ranks far enough. They can even bend the laws of time and space with significant advancement! It is not at all impossible for us to find a way back to your daughter as we rise.

"I recognize my part in bringing you into this... I, Senyak Marztanak, sole seeded heir of the Marztanak Hegemoncy, swear to you, my karmic brother. I will not rest until we have grown strong enough to find a way back to your Sophie."

Unbidden from either Senyak or Josh, Essence traveled from Senyak's channels into Josh's shoulder meridians. It cycled through his brain, heart, and core, where it combined with an equal amount of Josh's Essence and flowed back to Senyak's hand. Then it lit up the alley around them with a warm-golden light as it left both of their bodies and was slowly absorbed into the universe.

Josh's probability interface chimed—

Karmic link advanced. Full Karmic soul Bond formed.

CHAPTER 10

---★---

CHUD

JOSH STOOD and used the shirt sleeves on his biceps to wipe the tears from his face. Still downcast, he lifted his eyes and looked at Senyak with the faintest flicker of hope.

His mouth set in a straight line, Sen nodded back in universal, silent man-speak. *~We'll fix it.~* And, *~What tears ... I didn't see any tears.~*

"We will now move on to gathering Essence from other spiritual beings." The clone indicated a rubbish-filled and rusted-out dumpster against the wall of the alley. **"Underneath this dumpster is a series of underground tunnels and caverns housing cannibalistic humanoid dwellers. You will expunge them and absorb their Essence.**

"Furthermore, at the bottom of these caverns lays a forgotten earth temple formerly occupied by early Gaia worshippers. It is now abandoned. This temple houses several items of power specifically attuned to Earth Essence. You will make your way to the temple and acquire two.

"Being attuned to Earth Essence will provide you with advantages concerning Earth aura, including allowing you to absorb Earth aura and convert it to usable Essence to advance your cultivation. Earth

Attunement will also significantly increase your physical resilience. You will even be able to form shields to absorb powerful attacks.

"It is past daybreak, and these creatures are nocturnal. It is the optimal time to expunge them and harvest their Essence. Begin now."

Senyak lifted his brows inquisitively and looked at Josh. Still quiet but focused, Josh snapped his head up and down once, indicating he was ready for anything. Anything that was going to bring him even one step closer to Sophie. So, yeah, he was fully onboard.

The dumpster was foul-smelling, heavy, and sat on rusted wheels that hadn't rolled since the Nixon administration. Upon checking, it was also wedged between large bricks. They pulled the bricks out, and Josh tried to push it. *Fail.*

After a sharp look from the Clone, Josh cycled Essence into his legs and arms and pushed. The dumpster moved all right, a little too well. With a loud *screech*, the metal wheels slid across the ground, gouging out a two-inch trail through the asphalt and dirt and exposing a three-foot hole that had been dug out from below. Some of the still-intact bricks had obviously been pushed out from the inside. The tunnel headed down at a sharply steep angle. Down, down, and down, leading into thick, unbroken darkness.

The rear back wheel of the dumpster fell below the far edge of the hole, getting caught. Unable to take the pressure from Josh's push, the rusted-out dumpster cracked with a resounding *bong*. Putrid water spilled out, followed by bloated, gas-filled rubbish bags that burst spilling their contents on hitting the ground. And . . . big surprise here . . . among the refuse spread over the alley were many human bones in varying stages of decay.

The smell in the alley amplified. Significantly.

Josh looked around sheepishly. "Well . . . loud enough to wake the dead, huh?"

"Or at least the cannibals . . . Proceed and use whatever weapons of opportunity you find. I will join you when necessity requires.

"And this is for free, gentlemen. The hole is dark, and you have no light. Cycle Essence to your eyes and ears. You are cultivators, after all."

Josh cycled Essence to his eyes and could see Sen doing the same. What was previously a very dark and foreboding hole, was now a very well-lit and foreboding hole. Josh also cycled Essence to his ears and was surprised at what he could hear from below . . . heartbeats? Perhaps twelve separate organisms based on the cacophony of tympani. Some were closer, some louder, but all were regular rate and rhythm. Focusing on the nearest, Josh counted off between forty to fifty beats per minute. If they were human or at least followed human physiology, it meant the creatures were still asleep.

Josh caught Senyak's eye and pointed to his ears. Senyak nodded that he had already activated his ears and heard the same things. Reflecting for a moment, Josh thought that was a lot of information to get out of one nod. But Josh already knew the answer to their clear understanding of each other—the Karmic Bond.

From now on, they would have a much deeper understanding of each other. Their current actions, locations, and motivations would almost always be known information between them. Such was Karma. Josh knew it in his mind and his core, he supposed. Right now, Josh was willing to accept it as true at any rate. While he had never identified himself as an eastern philosophy guy; and all he had known about Karma was that a person lost it when they stole from blind beggars on the street. The truth of it just made a lot of sense to him right now. So, he was going with it.

Roll with it, Josh. Compared to what has happened so far . . . this is one of the easiest things to accept!

But . . . how the heck did he know what a normal-sleeping heart rate was? Josh was going to need to get some answers for how he had suddenly gone from mild-mannered lawyer to *Bill Nye the Science Guy.* But . . . right now, as they were descending to the depths of Mordor, just wasn't the time . . . so he set the issue aside and followed Senyak into the low-overhead hole.

———————————✳———————————

The tunnel had started approximately three-quarters of a meter wide and a little less than one meter from top to bottom. Senyak pulled a few loose bricks out from the sides and top of the hole to increase its opening. He still needed to crouch and drop down to his knees for some of the lower portions as he moved along the first twenty-five meters. His shoulders and bald head occasionally hit the top and sides of the tunnel. Dislodged dirt and loose stones rained down on them as they moved along. Their pants, from feet to knees, were covered in dirt, mud . . . and other things they didn't want to think about.

After fifty paces the tunnel had opened vertically and horizontally to a diameter they could walk through by keeping their heads down. They both audibly sighed with relief and continued walking. The tunnel snaked to the right and left, around unseen obstacles. Several thick tree roots meandered in the dirt sidewalls. Sen cycled Essence and snapped off a one-meter-long segment for each of them. Either to bludgeon the foul creatures they were heading toward . . . or for *anything else* they might run across. Josh took his without questioning and continued to plod on behind.

———————————✳———————————

The Clone observed from the alley as Senyak and Joshua moved down the tunnel. Both cycled their Essence in a continuous loop to their eyes and ears to enhance their senses. He also noted when they wisely harvested tree roots from the exposed walls as improvised weapons. They just might survive today.

Time will tell.

The quiet sound of heavy felt being pulled apart accompanied the opening of a portal in front of him. Intensely blue, waving fibers of order shifted peacefully past the event horizon in the opening rift. An instant later, Zenyak pulled himself through space and time to this material world.

"**Report.**"

The Clone dipped his head and allowed Zenyak to place his hand on it as if giving a papal blessing. "**The karmic link has upgraded to a full Karmic Bond already. That was not probable . . . not at this juncture.**"

Lifting an eyebrow, Zenyak reflected. "**I do good work.**"

"**Yes, I do.**" the Clone echoed.

"**Stay with them. Support them for now. Their progress is in the top three percent of probable predicted outcomes. Let's not break up the team while we are winning, hmmm.**" Another quiet tear in space-time, and he was gone.

"**I can be a right prick, can't I . . .**" the Clone said in the empty alley, rolling his glimmering eyes.

———————————✳———————————

Thirty minutes later, Sen and Josh came to a portion of the wall that had been dug out to waist height. It was filled with discarded bones, moldering shreds of clothing, shoes, and other broken pieces of outerwear, all caked in dirt and other filth. Obvious gnaw marks covered the surfaces of all the bones. Armies of ants and roaches were crawling over them, gleaning any remaining edible fibers and nesting in the larger piles. The smell was overpowering, and neither he nor Josh got very close. Josh even retched a few times quietly as they passed.

Creatures this heinous needed to be expunged. Sen moved on even more determined with Josh in tow.

With the Essence continually cycling to his eyes Sen could see as if standing in daylight. Though, it was the heartbeats he focused on. Every step brought him closer to the first cluster of three. They were going to have to expunge these creatures. Given what they knew about them, there were no dharmic issues whatsoever with that. But just being mortal now made physical death a little more real, a little more...squishy.

At least there wasn't a significant drain of Essence to continually enhance his eyes and ears. There was an initial cost of approximately 2 percent for each. The same amount Joshua had said it had taken to fuel the upper body strike that had taken Sen down.

Sen rubbed his jaw absently still remembering the pain of Joshua's strike. A decent hit to be sure—but, without doubt, there would be payback. Honor demanded it! But Sen needed to focus on the here and now if they were going to survive.

After the initial 2 percent expenditure, it didn't cost anything. Perhaps because the organs didn't have significant mass? Or, if conditions worsened, it might cost more? Senyak was uncertain about what factors were at play. But for now, he was glad for it.

After approximately thirty more minutes of continually moving down the tunnel, they came to a one-by-one-meter hole drilled directly through a massive block of stone ending the tunnel they had followed. Senyak crouched on his haunches and shuffled through the excavation's four-meter-long borehole. At the edge, he crouched, looking out on the cavernous space the hole exited into. Most likely a courtyard of what must have been the temple the Clone had told them about. The floor was laid with dark, rectangular pavers. In the center distance, Sen could see the outline of a looming structure, dark and ancient, seemingly carved from the living stone of the cavern. A tower in its center rose thirty meters into the gloom above. To Sen's sides, large blocks made up the wall he had just crawled through. They marched off to the left and right out of sight. Where the cavern ended, either ahead, above, or to his sides, Senyak could not make out, even with his enhanced vision.

Looking down, he calculated a three-meter drop to the floor. The nearest heartbeats were still a short run away and to the right.

Senyak made eye contact with Josh and pointed down. ~*I go first. You follow.*~

Then Sen cycled Essence to his hands and his legs, quietly dropping down the smooth face of stone on the other side with his cudgel cradled under his chin. Nothing stirred on his reaching the paving stones on the bottom. Sen looked around. *No immediate threats.* He signaled Josh, who came down the same way.

They turned to the right, heading wordlessly toward the first cluster of heartbeats. The partially collapsed and squarish frame of an outbuilding sat against the side of the wall they had just come through. Three smallish, bipedal-humanoid figures were curled together. Lying in tatters of shredded, soiled clothing formed into some kind of a nest.

Sen and Josh stopped a rock's throw from the sleeping forms, and Sen whispered in Josh's ear. "Let's get as close as we can. Try to crush the skulls of the two sleeping on the outside. I'll take the right, you the left. Then move on to the one in the middle. Most likely, these creatures have poor sight and good olfactory senses. If we can get to them fast enough, there may not be any kind of alarm. If there is an alarm, move quicker!"

Josh nodded and whispered back his agreement. "Go in quiet and brain the bastards." He refrained from adding that, most likely, the little monsters had advanced hearing and proprioception-based locational abilities, similar to echolocation emissions used by avian and marine mammals.

If so, the cannibals would be able to pick them up if they tried to just stand still. Unlike *Jurassic Park*-T-Rex-type hiding. But no point in bringing that up now. Josh didn't even know how he knew it. Let alone how he knew it with certainty. Sen's plan was as good as any he had. So, they cycled Essence to their arms and torsos. Raising their clubs, they slowly advanced on the sleeping forms from either side.

As Sen and Josh got within two steps, the sleeping forms' heartbeats sped up to 150 bpm. Surging up as one, they pointed straight at Sen and Josh and started screeching like extras from *Invasion of the Body Snatchers*. And very talented extras at that! Their undulating cries echoed throughout the cavern. An instant later, the standing creatures seemed to be flying through the air as two of them launched themselves at Josh, one at Sen.

The remaining heartbeats throughout the cavern accelerated to around 150 bpm as answering cries came from all directions along with the sound of running feet.

CHAPTER 11

Full

THE CREATURE flying at Sen was small compared to humans. Likely only a little over a meter tall and forty-five kilograms. It was covered in short grey hair and had straight pointed ears. No apparent eyes. Just a slightly hollow area covered in thin skin where most humanoids had them. Its mouth was filled with long, pointed teeth. Teeth Sen could clearly see because they were the part leading the creature's missile-like attack on his face and neck.

Unfortunately for the surging creature, Sen was ready. He had been cycling Essence to his upper limbs and torso during his failed ambush. Seeing the creature coming for him, he stepped forward with his left foot and met it halfway. Swinging his club in a level strike from left to right, he hit the beast with enough force to obliterate its head into a spray of blood and chunks. The cannibal's body pinwheeled into the nearby outbuilding wall. A solid *splat* thumped with its hit, reverberating through the cavern.

Sen turned toward Joshua. The man had dropped his club, catching the creatures flying at him with a hand around each of their necks. *Impressive hand skills.*

Josh was currently in the process of banging their heads together. His Essence-enhanced strength creating a heavy-hollow sound like the *thunk* of two large, thick-shelled nuts slamming together as both skulls crunched. The small humanoid bodies stopped struggling, their longish limbs limply dangling in Josh's grasp.

The immediate threat dealt with, they looked around at the sound of sharp, undulating cries coming from all directions. The nearest was approximately fifty meters away, coming from the direction of the hole in the wall they had come through.

We will have to get through them if we are going to retreat.

To keep his options open, Sen moved in their direction. Josh followed, after dropping the two now dead bodies and picking up his club.

Sen reasoned that waiting here for the approaching humanoids to come was a good way to get overwhelmed as other groups joined the attack. Better to try and face off against the group between them and the way out, expunge them, then retreat if necessary. If not, they could hide and get ready for the next group. Apparently, Joshua agreed, as he was following without comment.

The small monsters' shifting forms were visible several seconds before they were in combat range. As they came within striking distance, the next group of three were joined by two more loping over from the direction of the temple.

The monsters immediately went into action. The fangs-forward launch attack seemed to be the creatures' basic instinctual combat maneuver. Having already seen it once, Sen and Josh were better prepared. Raising their clubs and knocking the first two cannibals from the air. The monsters' small humanoid bodies spun end over end into the darkness surrounding them.

The other three halted, approximately five meters out, when the first two of their number were cut down. They vocalized, raising the pitch and increasing the frequency of their cries. Returning cries matching the increased rhythm quickly answered from farther behind Sen and Josh.

"The little cretins are calling reinforcements!" Josh hissed.

Sen kept his eyes on the three in front of them. It was evident that the current stalemate was most likely a losing proposition for him and Josh. They were going to be surrounded by hurtling-fanged death.

Nodding, Sen conveyed, *~I'll take the lead.~*

On the move, he increased the flow of his Essence to his arms and surged into action. Stepping forward, he hurled his club end over end. It blurred through the air like a buzzsaw blade piercing directly through his target's chest and slamming the still-struggling creature to the ground.

Both of its hands weakly struggled to no avail at pulling the root out.

Josh joined by launching himself into a flying tackle aimed at the humanoid immediately to the right of the one Sen had taken out. With superhuman reflexes, the cannibal turned and tried to run away. But Josh's enhanced movements were even better. He caught its foot, holding it down, as he pulled the thrashing monster one hand at a time to him like climbing a rope. Not sitting still, the cannibal's claws and fangs tore at Josh, creating deep, heavily bleeding wounds on his hands and forearms. Its fangs took mouthfuls of flesh even as Josh slammed its head against the dark tiles. The cracking sound on Josh's second smash immediately preceded the creature going limp, its skull shattered flat as a dinner plate.

With the death of its remaining companions, the last of the humanoid cannibals had fled back into the gloom. Its footsteps faded farther away in the direction of the temple. Its cry sounded different as well— more like barking with clear breaks between the vocalizations. *Run away! Run away! Run away!*

Half-laughing, half-wincing in the pain of his healing arms, Josh continued his full-body cultivation. Raising his hands from the monster in front of him, Josh was amazed to notice how fast he was healing. The gushing blood was slowing to a small trickle. Dripping down his hands and fingers as pink, unmarked flesh filled in the cuts and bites.

Sen touched Josh's shoulder to gain his attention. The group behind them had stopped advancing and changed their call to match the one that had just fled. Pulling his club from the chest of the impaled cannibal, Sen looked around for any approaching enemies.

Josh started grabbing the bodies. Holding three over his shoulder, he said, "Grab that one and follow me. I have a plan."

Sen waved his hand as if to say, *why run … we can kill these things easily?* Then a distracted look appeared in his eyes and Josh suspected he was just now noticing what Josh had already seen. A blinking warning light had appeared in his right visual field indicating that the blue Essence bar was down to less than 10 percent. Moreover, they were both out of breath and Sen was probably feeling just as lightheaded as Josh was.

Sen let his hand fall, grabbed the body, and followed Josh back to the hole they had entered the cavern from.

Josh quickly told Sen his thoughts. "These creatures are very much like bats." To Sen's blank look, Josh continued, "Bats are avian mammals from where I come from. They are very territorial creatures. If we stay here, they will regroup and likely come to get us. I can count at least five left, including the one that got away. I can also feel that your Essence is bottoming out like mine is. I doubt we can fight them off without our Essence to enhance us. They are way faster than I am without it."

He raked his free hand through his hair. "But … if we head back up through that hole … I'm betting they don't consider that as their home territory. It is probably just a place of transit in and out. At least, it appears so based on where they dumped the bodies we found. They won't likely follow us up there … Worth a try anyway." Josh nodded up toward the hole in the wall. "Worse come to worst, we can get them one at a time as they come out of the hole."

"Good strategy and plan. Know your enemy. Know yourself." Then, looking at the bodies they were carrying, Sen added, "These bodies are for us to restore our Essence?"

"Got it in one. Now let's get up through that hole. Cycle what's left of your Essence and help me throw the bodies up first. Then we can jump up, assuming we have enough Essence left."

Between the two, they had enough Essence to get the four bodies through the hole. The last one they had to throw a second time as it was tossed too wide and splatted against the wall to the side. Jumping up was a bit beyond them, though. They were both well below 5 percent, lightheaded and woozy. Josh felt the start of a migraine coming on. In the end, Sen stood on Josh's shoulders and pulled himself through the hole. He then took off his Kasaya and tied the top and the bottom together ... braced himself against the lip of the hole's exit and tossed the makeshift rope down. Josh struggled back up the three meters from the plaza's floor to the opening.

Using unaugmented strength, they dragged the bodies one at a time through the tunnel uphill. They stopped, exhausted, at about twenty-five meters back up, and stooped in silence. No cries from the cannibals ... but their hearing was only the mundane variety. For reasons they couldn't explain, their enhanced hearing had failed. They could no longer hear the cannibals' heartbeats, and neither had enough Essence to restart the hearing enhancement.

As the last body was brought up, both collapsed on the ground gasping for breath. Josh had some theories about why their enhanced hearing had quit on them. But he was very grateful that their enhanced sight had continued. Why it did, Josh had no idea. He was out of Essence ... very out, in fact. Less than 2 percent if he was gauging it right based on the thin blue line at the bottom of his interface. If meridians acted like a battery, then his sight should be fading in and out, at the very least. But it was still rock solid ... These were questions for later ... or for the Clone, if they ever saw him again.

———————————✳———————————

Five minutes later, after catching their breath, they stood and looked over the bodies.

"Okay, let's get the Essence from these things and get back to it." Josh said, gesturing for Sen to take the lead.

"Yes, let's do that." Sen looked at Josh, also motioning for Josh to take the lead.

Josh's eyes narrowed, and his tone sharpened. "What! Are you telling me you don't know how to gather Essence from these bodies?" He canted his head at Sen.

"Well, it's obvious you don't either! This is mortal Essence. You are a mortal. You should know more about it than me!"

"Yeah, well ... I'm not invading people's brains to fight it out with Immortal dominator ... dudes ... am I?"

They eyed each other for a long second, jaws working, fists clenching.

Sen finally blew out a breath and looked down. "It's my first time. Okay ... I suspect it is a lot like moving our own Essence. We just have to identify it and move it into our core ... or something similar ..." He trailed off.

"Something like that, huh?" But Josh looked down as well without any heat in his words. "Okay ... I'll go first ..."

Josh reached out with his hand and placed it just below the creature's umbilicus. He tried to sense Essence like he would his own. He did feel ... something ... a small, dark muddy ball of turgid Essence sitting near the thing's navel. He prodded the Essence with his mind. But not his whole mind. He had targeted it with what felt like the *center* of his mind. The place his mind was touching the Essence from was ... the pineal gland ... his recent onset wealth of scientific knowledge told him.

At his prodding, the Essence moved ... but it was weird. It was like trying to pull a three-foot water balloon by grabbing the center and dragging. It wasn't connected to anything. Just dead weight, like an unconscious body, twice as heavy as an awake person and always trying to flop away. Josh focused his mind. Concentrating on the very center of his brain. The place where he was sure his spirit and his physical body met. He then *Intended* for the cannibal's Essence to join his.

Sweat broke out on his brow. He saw the Essence line up like iron fillings in the strange tiny, dark core. Then, similar to a line of ants moving in single file, it slowly left the core and crossed over to his hand. Once in his own meridians, it started to move faster. Not as quickly as his own Essence did, but three times faster than in the dead monster's body and with much less concentration than it had required to instigate his Intent. The Essence moved into his core and plummeted to the bottom of it like a fifty-pound barbell dropped into a swimming pool.

Josh drew in a sharp breath. Crouching on his knees, his upper legs wobbled under him. He went back to his haunches, then fell flat onto his backside. His eyes glazed over, unfocused. He marveled at the strange feelings running through him. It wasn't exactly like being stronger because he couldn't really use the Essence yet. It was more like being malnourished and having his stomach filled in one second. There was also an intense sensation of iron or dirt—*Earth*—in his ... *spirit*?

"Good, Joshua Elias Tanner!

"Now that you have begun to absorb Essence from other spiritual beings, we can proceed with your growth. You will need to absorb a second cannibal's Essence to adequately stretch your core. Then you will begin your purification cycles. This will increase your core's capacity and the strength of your meridians. You will be able to carry and use greater amounts of Essence faster. Do so now."

I was wondering when you would show up. Josh decided the price of saying his thought out loud would be too high. Judging by the Clone's expression, it knew exactly what Josh was thinking. But the Clone wouldn't call Josh out on it if he kept it to himself.

Silently eyeing the Clone, Josh pushed himself back up to his knees, Like a man whose coordination was slowed through drink, he reached out to repeat the process he had just undertaken ...

And then something that hadn't happened before occurred.

The Clone reversed itself ... partially ...

"Ahhh ... but first ... please share with Senyak the details of your first experience and what he can expect when absorbing the mortal Essence. With your Karmic Bond, it should provide meaningful information for him ... Please do this ... first."

The Clone finished, eyes blazing at Josh. Wearing a smile that sane people could only describe as *pure malice*. Flashes of Jerry Robinson meets Heath Ledger meets Joaquin Phoenix haunted Josh's mind. *I'm fucked, aren't I?*

The Clone's smile only widened.

So, Josh did it. He explained what he experienced with the pineal gland in the center of his mind. The need to truly focus from there. Josh also went over the floppy, unhelpful nature of the Essence outside of his body. And how it was not useable in his core after being absorbed.

The Clone had been correct. Senyak was getting meaningful information about the process. It seemed Sen was actually feeling what Josh described. That somehow Sen was getting the firsthand knowledge necessary to absorb Essence from outside of his body through their communication and joint efforts in understanding.

Then Josh knelt back to the second cannibal's body. The Clone nodded as if Josh's compliance with its commands were the only possible result in this or any other iteration. Josh reached his hand out to the core and *Intended* ...

This time he was able to get the Essence lined up and moving through on its way to his meridians in about half the time. But that was the good news. It was another story when it crossed over to his home-turf meridians.

His first feelings were—*Full . . . Full . . . Full! Full! I am sorry! There is no room in the inn, Baby Jesus!* He tried to reverse the flow with his mind and, instinctually, his hands. Any possible thing he could in that millisecond of its first entering.

But it was hopeless. Josh's spirit welcomed the Essence with open arms regardless of how excruciating it would be for him at some detached physical level.

So, the Essence flowed into his meridians. His eyes bulged like he had just swallowed a flaming bowling ball, and he suddenly knew what *The Little Prince's* boa constrictor felt after it had swallowed its elephant. Then the Essence moved into and expanded his core.

Instantly, Josh felt a stretching, tearing, and burning pain that went from his core to the center of his brain. A trail of *gasolinas*, lit by a Mexican match on a Tijuana Street during Grito de Dolores. The tiny green sphere in the center of his interface's display started blinking. A dotted-red outline appeared outside the spherical dimensions and began flashing. A detached part of Josh's pain-soaked brain noted it apparently indicated the new-expanded dimensions of his core. After a few seconds, it steadied to solid green. A wide smile spread across his face as Josh looked up to the Clone and then Senyak, who smiled back, and nodded in a terrified but encouraging manner. Then Josh's eyes rolled into the back of his head, and he fell forward face first onto the dead cannibal's mangled chest.

So ended the first day Joshua Elias Tanner spent as a cultivator.

CHAPTER 12

---*---

Exploding Cortexes

CONTRARY TO what Josh had been afraid of when he passed out, his head was still attached to his shoulders upon waking. He checked his interface and noted that his core was now approximately 25 percent full. There was no numeral next to the icon, just his eyeballing it. *Numbers would be greatly appreciated.* Sadly, no number appeared after his absent thought.

He also noted his green health bar was now full again, and his blue free-Essence bar was sitting at 25 percent as well. It was much higher than when he first absorbed the cannibal Essence into his core.

He prodded his core. There was still a pronounced difference between his pure Essence and the foreign Essence he had absorbed from the cannibals. But it was more like peanuts in chunky peanut butter than the rocks and water it had been before he passed out.

Sitting up, he noted he had been laid out in a straight line with Senyak's crumpled top under his head. Looking over to Sen's sprawled form, Josh felt a twinge of unspoken gratitude. The kindness of moving Josh to a more comfortable position after he passed out spoke volumes for an unquantifiable reason. Senyak was lying on the ground, slightly more spread out than Josh had been. He was also right next to one of the dead creatures from yesterday. Clearly, after witnessing Josh's psychedelic experience, Senyak had been smart enough to absorb the second core while lying down. But there had been no one to help him afterward or move the dead thing away from his prone body.

"All right. That is enough rest. Rise to your feet and be about your continued cultivation."

Josh looked to the left, down the roughly carved tunnel toward the opening to the plaza they had barely escaped from the day before. The Clone was standing there. Had he been guarding them? Given what he had done to them in the past, Josh thought that was unlikely... but he couldn't argue with the Clone's chosen position.

The Clone was readily glowing a vibrant blue from the inversion, emergence, and resolution of countless fractal lines. Yet it wasn't his glowing that was lighting up the area. There was almost no light down here. Josh's sight was still dependent on his enhanced vision. How had it continued after he slept? After he was so low on Essence, he could barely stay conscious... and then after he was unconscious?

And what the hell do you know about fractals? He asked himself the silent question... *Just that they are a geometric figure or curve, each part of which has the same statistical characteristic as the whole. Useful in modeling structures in which similar patterns recur. Like snowflakes, crystal growth, and galaxy formation...* Josh's thoughts trailed off. *Something is seriously wrong with me...* He didn't understand where all these stray thoughts of scientific certainty were coming from.

The Clone looked directly at Josh. **"Yes, you have questions. I will answer some of them as you need answers to increase your productivity. I will address yours first, Joshua Elias Tanner, then Senyak. Though you both share many of the same questions.**

—Your free Essence has increased. Even unconscious, your cultivator's core will work to convert foreign Essence already absorbed to Essence for its own use. This process's speed can be vastly improved

with conscious effort. And yes, we will do that as soon as we finish twenty questions.

—Yes, there is something different about your ability to apply scientific principles to your everyday activity. No, it has nothing directly to do with starting cultivation. I will let Senyak go into more detail with you about this . . . as he is the reason for its development. But note that this increased application of scientific knowledge saved your life yesterday . . . Didn't it?

You next, Senyak . . ."

Josh had jumped up to confront Senyak at the Clone's confirmation that he was at least partly responsible for what was going on with Josh's mind. However, as the Clone slowly turned his gaze back toward Josh, its mouth in a firm line, Josh suddenly realized that, in this case, discretion might be the better part of valor. Instead, Josh stood, mouth hanging open, waiting for a chance to speak, with all the tension of a runner on starting blocks waiting for the pistol to go off . . . But a *quiet and non-interrupting* runner. Seeing what was waiting for him, Senyak looked like a caged rat that knew it was about to be fed to a hungry python.

Seeing Josh's mutiny had been aborted, the Clone continued, "**When you dedicate Essence to a process that incurs no further cost, Essence, which is eternal, will continue to serve that purpose. Exempli gratia, your continued visual enhancement despite no additional Essence dedicated to it. Also, please note that your enhanced hearing has ended. That is due to having spent all of the Essence to repair microdamage done to your ears by the cannibalistic humanoid's sonic emissions. Exempli gratia, more was demanded of the Essence, and it was consumed. No further Essence was dedicated. Your audio enhancements then ended. Rededicate Essence to restart your enhanced hearing. It was this enhancement that gave you both significant advantages yesterday. Do so now.**"

They both did.

Having finished speaking, the Clone nodded once to Josh.

And Josh flew the last two steps to Senyak, who was standing in the small corner of the tunnel they were in. "Dude, what's going with all of these thoughts about science. Just by looking at the rocks in this hallway, I can tell you with absolute certainty that we are in the continental crust, far away from an oceanic subduction zone. The rocks here are composed of all three primary crust components—sedimentary, igneous, and deposits of metamorphic silicate. There was a flood around here over twenty thousand years ago based on the thickness of the layers on the far wall..." Josh squeezed his head between his fists. "I never even played in the sandbox when I was a kid! *What is going on with my brain?*"

Senyak spared the Clone a glance that spoke of wounded betrayal.

He couldn't look Josh in the eyes as he wheedled, "Err... well... ahh... you remember when I needed you to save the physical functions of the Ka dominion the independent chaos actor had invaded... and *Damni* sent you the information about cardiac resuscitation so you could do it? Well... as it turns out, she didn't think there was enough time to pare down the transfer to just the packets of information necessary for resuscitation..."

"So, you sent me more? How much more? I can tell you are hesitating through your inverted body language and the gaps in your speech. Along with the fact that I *know* it through our Karmic Bond! *Spit it out, man!*"

Sen's Asian features turned a very bright shade of red, "Well... *Damni* might have sent all of the knowledge packets concerning medicine up to the current place in your time stream. Including all of the related physical sciences that could impact them..." Sen finished in a quiet voice.

"*You put the entire* Encyclopedia Britannica *in my brain?*"

"Ahh... well... um... *vastly* more than that... All scientific discoveries that had been then presently known in the time stream of your home iteration. So, yeah... *vastly more*... You were lucky that your cortex maintained cohesion... I'm... um... *sorry*..." Sen finished quietly with his eyebrows raised and his teeth clenched in a pained smile.

Face as red as Senyak's, Josh slid from seriously concerned all the way up to ready to tear Senyak a new orifice or three.

Raising a clenched fist, he pushed his index finger at Senyak's face. *"You almost blew up my brain, and you didn't think you needed to tell me about it?"*

Senyak began jabbering. "Well, youcameoutofitfine ... And there has been somuchgoingonsince ..."

"Hmhmm-hmmm." Chuckling, the Clone finally interceded, the mirth evident on his face. **"As entertaining as this truly is, gentlemen, we must get back to our schedule today. Do understand, Joshua Elias Tanner. This egregious act, obviously lacking in judgment on Senyak's part, is a factor that probability models hold as giving you and Senyak one of your most considerable advantages. This is true for advancing your cultivation and successfully transcending to the Immortal realm."**

Josh, opening his hand, looked at the Clone nonplussed. "How can being the world's greatest high-school science teacher help us reach the Immortal realm?"

The Clone looked at Josh and Sen consideringly for a moment, then adopted a resigned expression. **"Very well. Now is the time for this discussion. Your knowledge of all physical sciences, up to that point in your time stream, is significant regarding *material-matter iterations*. To understand how significant, you need to consider what Essence really is. Regardless of the basal origin of the iteration, exempli gratia, negative energy, antimatter, Polar Neutral, tidak ada, etcetera.**

"Essence is a thing or entity's true center nature or most important quality.

"In a *physical-matter iteration*, such as this one, or the one you come from, Joshua Elias Tanner, what is the true center nature of Essence ... exempli gratia, the paramount qualities of Essence?"

Narrowing his eyes, Josh had a good guess. He didn't, however, say it out loud.

"Yes, Joshua Elias Tanner . . . The laws of physics, such as you know them, that is. After all, at this point in the time stream, your mortal scientists are barely more than hairless apes trying to make themselves fly by swinging a thigh bone over their heads with reckless abandon.

"However, even this limited knowledge is confirmed on probability predictions to be of significant assistance to you both. It will help you make the necessary connections to understanding how to cultivate and use your Essence. Significantly speeding up your cultivation and assent by greatly limiting the trial and error that most cultivators must go through to properly absorb and apply Essence. You will be able to perform cultivation functions right on the first try . . . and be perfect at it! This is no small thing, Joshua Elias Tanner.

"Understand this."

The Clone looked Josh square in his eyes, the constant involuting blaze of his stare burning through any attempt to resist total focus on his words.

"While I am guiding and keeping you accountable for your progress, this will not advance your cultivation. It is the spiritual connections you make in your understanding of this iteration and its physically attuned Essence. Along with how these things bond with you . . . how you fit with them . . . that will trigger the unification of your spiritual and physical being. Your relationship to time, space, spirituality, and how well you unite them is what cultivation ultimately is . . . what leads you to the perfect union of the physical and spiritual.

"You must also understand that for all mortals, the multiverse-wide, cultivation is a singular journey that every spiritual being must walk alone. The Path of One, it is called in virtually every iteration.

"Throughout this sole journey, they build their own unique experiences, which, upon reflection, leads them to an increased understanding of cultivation, Essence, iterational truths, and how these apply to them as individuals. These understandings can never be fully explained in any meaningful way to other cultivators. This is because all epiphanies of cultivation are based almost entirely on feelings and intuition as opposed to facts and probabilities. A truth discovered by one person, based solely on their unique experiences, cannot be a light on the cultivational path for others. Every individual cultivator must stumble in the dark alone and make their own novel connections to enlightenment based on their unique experiences. Even when someone standing right next to them may have just discovered an epiphany about the same nuance that very instant." A feral grin appeared on the Clone's face. "But . . . you and Senyak have found a very uncommon loophole in the Path of One. Your Karmic Bond allows you to share feelings and information with almost perfect clarity.

"This is a very rare thing!

"Being so joined, your understanding will also become the understanding of Senyak. Hence, when you make rapid leaps in cultivation as we fully expect you to, so will Senyak.

"A reality you have both shown me by enhancing your core after less than twenty-four hours as cultivators. This is adequate progress toward our goals." Turning his head, he gave Josh a sidelong glance. "Very adequate progress."

More than anything, the positivity and hopefulness in the Clone's countenance and tone drove the significance of what he was saying home to Josh. For a moment, youthful joy overcame the usual rock-hard and calloused presence. Half a moment later, the Clone returned to its usual reserved and sour demeanor.

Josh and Sen looked at each other. Not sure if they completely understood what the Clone had just told them. But without question, both knew they needed to grow in strength and cultivation to get where they each needed to be. Based on what the Clone had said, it looked like they were getting on this ride together. They gave a side nod to each other as they faced the Clone. For the first time as a team with joint goals.

Recognizing that his words had had the desired outcome, the Clone nodded to both of them and spoke again, "Very well. Now, you must solidify your gains by purifying the Essence you have absorbed. This is achieved by cycling the Essence through your meridians. Mainly, your lungs, kidneys, and bowels ... Yes, Senyak, you have identified them correctly.

"You will know that the Essence has been purified because, at that point, it will feel like it is yours. This is a general cycling pattern for purification. There are others that you will learn and use as you advance and have need. For now, focus on this. Begin."

They did. The cellular processes from their first hours in the alley repeated. Josh also saw his meridians gaining in strength, volume, and seemingly ... ease of passage? The more he cycled the Essence, the faster it seemed to be circulating for the same amount of effort. It was getting slightly *easier*.

"Okay, you have both purified your Essence. Note that your free energy bars are full. Also, note that your Essence is racing through your meridians and core. Please Intend the deposit of all Essence not needed to fill your Free Energy bar in your core. Yes, Joshua Elias Tanner, it will be something you can *feel*. Do not be overly concerned with the need to objectify the endpoint. It will occur instinctively. Do so now."

They both moved the Essence to their cores and experienced a slight sensation of fullness. Nothing compared to how they had felt the night before. Then the core indicator of their interface registered an opaque level of 24 percent. An actual number this time. Not bad for absorbing two scruffy bats. The Clone had also been correct. It was instinctual to stop adding dedicated Essence to his core before they started to deplete their free Essence. Sen and Josh, finishing approximately the same time, looked up to the Clone from their seated position.

"Good, now you need to expunge the remaining creatures below, as well as obtain the items of Earth Attunement from the temple.

"First, however, several points in evaluation to improve your rather pathetic performance yesterday.

"Aside from constant observational enhancements, constantly cycling your Essence is wasteful. You would have had sufficient stores to eradicate the creatures below yesterday if you had only used Essence when needed. Not flooding your channels and using it with every twitch of your hand and blink of your eyes. You must improve your actions in this regard.

"Secondly, be prepared for significantly improved performance compared to yesterday. You have increased your capacity to use Essence in speed and volume by at least twenty percent. You have also increased the free Essence available in your meridians by approximately fifty percent. This is a vast improvement. The terrestrial creatures below were no match for you yesterday. They are less so today. Essence users are dangerous when they utilize their powers appropriately. Act accordingly. Expunge these foul beasts with expedience. Aside from Essence, time is the most valuable resource. Do not waste mine."

Clearly dismissed, Josh and Sen picked up their clubs, walked down the tunnel to the hole, and dropped down to the plaza floor. The five remaining heartbeats were now all clumped together, approximately a bit more than a football field from where they stood. Their heartbeats were again in the 40-45 bpm range, indicating they were sleeping.

Josh leaned over to Sen and spoke in a low voice. "Okay, sneaking up on them won't work. They can obviously feel our electromagnetic fields or our Essence or are very sensitive to micro-movements of air. The possibilities are limitless... The point is we need to move in fast, brain these fuckers, and move on to the temple. As much as I hate to admit it... the Clone is right... We're stronger... My Essence pool is *supersized* today!"

Sen nodded. "I agree. Strike first. Strike hard. Show no mercy."

Moving to within a short distance from the sleeping forms, Sen halted them with a raised fist. From there, they could see the beasts were sleeping in another collapsed outbuilding approximately a stone's throw from the looming temple and its rising tower. All five were curled up like dogs on the ground. Thin rib cages rose and fell with their shallow breaths.

Sen held out his hand with three fingers extended. They both cycled Essence to their legs, upper body, and torso ... basically, the whole body. Sen lowered his fingers one at a time ... three ... two ... one. They exploded into motion. Anyone with human eyes would have seen two streaks as after images blazing across the intervening space from where they started and ended. Striking quickly with their clubs to the monster's skulls, they each eliminated one on the opposite edge of the group. Before the other monsters could react to their presence, they moved on to their next targets.

As the other three were rising from their sleep, but before they could act, Sen executed a front snap kick and sent the one on the middle right spinning off into the darkness. Josh swung his club from right to left, all but decapitating the middle left and caving in the skull of the center one.

All five creatures down! They hadn't even had a chance to screech! Looking to the right and left, seeing all the creatures accounted for, they stopped cycling their Essence. Josh had only spent about 7 percent of his current free Essence.

Obviously, the Clone had been right again. Properly applied cultivation left standard-terrestrial creatures no chance at all. He felt like a wrecking machine.

Josh felt drawn to reach out and absorb the Essence of the downed cannibals. From Sen's body language it was obvious Sen felt the same way. After the improvements they had gotten from just two, this stuff was money. Neither Josh nor Sen would waste it. Through silent agreement and a little dance of *you or me first*, Sen stood guard and let Josh go first. He absorbed the turgid earth-flavored Essence in less than thirty seconds. His core was not significantly filled by the first one.

However, Josh didn't purify it. He knew it had taken hours to cycle the Essence this morning, even if it hadn't felt that way. And this was not a safe place. Still, the funds were in the bank so to speak. The foreign

Essence sank to the bottom of Josh's core with an imagined *thunk* as it had the night before.

Then the real question... could he get the second one now? Josh wasn't sure. Holding up two fingers in a *V* to Senyak, Josh raised his eyebrows for Sen's opinion. Sen shrugged, unsure if Josh could handle two right now, given what had happened last night...

Knowing this wouldn't be the last time he was going to push the limit to get back home, Josh went for it. He needed to get back to Sophie. To do that, they needed to advance. He and Sen couldn't afford to leave cash on the table, so to speak. Not if they wanted to get where they were going. Reaching out to the second downed creature, its neck bent at a ninety-degree angle, Josh repeated the process. The Essence lined up and funneled into his meridians through his hands. When the Essence hit his channels, Josh felt like two pounds of sausage in a one-pound casing, as his grandfather used to say about girls in tight shorts. But the non-purified Essence made it to his core and *kerplunked* down to the base of his committed Essence. The terrible feeling of overstuffing was gone when it all migrated to his core.

Josh shared his experience and Senyak repeated the procedure. Josh smiled slyly when Sen's eyes bulged out of his skull as the Essence entered his meridians. Sen smirked at him. Josh would have to teach Sen how to give him the finger in moments like this.

They stood up and turned to face the temple. Stark and brooding, its walls lay a short distance ahead of them in the darkness.

The ten-meter-high wall around the temple was built with square corners and watchtowers at each. As far as Sen and Josh could tell, the central building and its looming tower filled most of the courtyard within the temple's walls.

"Let's find a door?" Sen suggested.

Josh nodded in agreement. They walked around the temple wall counterclockwise, away from the opening they'd crawled through to get into the plaza. The towers didn't appear occupied. No lights shone in any of the wall sconces they could see when they got within shouting distance. There were no heartbeats or any noises to be heard. Upon rounding the second corner, however, things soon changed.

In fact, everything changed.

CHAPTER 13

---★---

Family Drama

JOSH AND Sen stood and blinked their eyes at what was materializing in front of them. Like heat waves on the horizon over sunbaked sand, the walled structure they had been walking around seemed to waver from existence. In its place stood a classic Greek temple in the Corinthian style. Gigantic, shining white-marble columns reached to a rectangular roof. A low triangular peak at either end.

To Josh, who had only ever seen pictures, the temple looked like a restored version of the Parthenon in Athens. There were burning bronze braziers with what was likely olive oil set aflame. They were placed at even intervals along the colonnades supporting the overhead roof. A series of broad, low-rising marble stairs surrounded the building. Leading up to its singular open-floor level.

In the center of the temple was a woman wearing a white toga which was presently stripped down around her waist. She was chained by her forearms to stone posts rising about seven feet above the floor. She sagged between the chains as she was scourged about the back and shoulders by a dark figure in classic-Grecian armor. The woman, with multiple lash marks on her back, upper shoulders, and neck, was not reacting to the lashes. She lolled unconsciously in her restraints.

The enforcer with the whip looked up at them as the Grecian Temple finally "miraged" itself into focus. Red eyes swirled in an empty space where a living human would have a face. Black smoke in the shape of arms and legs gave it a roughly humanoid form. The same smoke somehow held up its helmet, black-iron cuirass, and what appeared to be greaves and bracers.

"How dare you interrupt the Judgement of Zeus! Prepare to die!" With nothing more than that, the figure started marching with an even tread at them. Its scourge, with three thick leather straps and what was likely sharp metal bits embedded in them, whirled around its head as it prepared to strike. A long spear with a leaf-shaped head appeared in the other hand.

Yes, so . . . this is actually happening! Incredulity surged through Josh's mind as he instinctively moved to the left.

Sen, taking a wide-based, defensive stance, shifted to the right.

Coming from both sides is what smart guys would do in this situation, right? Josh asked himself.

Sen nodded affirmatively as if he had heard him.

Bracing himself, Josh remembered what the Clone had advised them about only cycling the necessary amount of Essence. But he still figured that fighting ancient-Greek spiritual enforcers probably qualified as a full-body-cycling kind of event. Sen obviously agreed and was also cycling Essence to his whole body.

Josh's strength and speed increased as he settled in to see who the specter would go after first, Sen or him. He was right both times.

The whip lashed out at Josh's feet, and the spearhead shot out at where Sen's face had been an instant before he dropped to his knees and pivoted away. Spinning on his haunches to the armored enforcer's back right. It looked like a very cool way to avoid getting speared through the head.

With much less flair, Josh jumped over the three lashes of the scourge. Their counterstrikes hit almost simultaneously. Sen's went to the back of their attacker's head, and Josh's overhead strike to its left shoulder. Golden light erupted from the impacts forming what looked to Josh like large round shields in both places. The attacking spirit continued, unfazed by either strike.

"The shield is an innate ability of this creature! We can overcome it by striking a strong enough blow to break through. Keep hitting it!" Sen shouted to Josh as he rolled out of the way of a follow-up spear strike to his chest.

"Not like I was going to do anything else, Captain Obvious!" Josh yelled back. Though, it was good to know this wasn't some sort of impervious-to-physical-harm ghost thing or something.

Josh dodged an overhead strike of the scourge, only to have it wrap around his hip and dig into his upper and midthigh through what was left of his pants. The specter's strength was incredible as it pulled the whip back, flipping Josh off the ground in a 1080-degree spin and flaying the skin from his leg. Josh was still holding his club when he landed, slightly dizzy, on his face and chest. His left pant leg was shredded, and large chunks of his thigh were missing.

"Ahhhhkk! This hurts!" Josh shouted as he diverted all his free Essence to his wounds for three cycles.

With alacrity, the wounds healed to a point where the bleeding had stopped, and raw red skin overlaid the intact muscles. Checking his interface, Josh had 65 percent of his free Essence and about 75 percent of his health. He considered healing for one more rotation, but Sen needed help . . . and he needed it fast!

Sen had managed to strike the enforcer twice while Josh was down. At the same time continuing to dodge and roll out of the way of its counterattacks. Sen's club produced resounding *bongs* against the specter's shield ability each time . . . but the golden barrier continued in full strength.

Unfortunately for Sen, with Josh out, the dark spirit was free to focus on him. It didn't take him long to entangle Sen's feet with the scourge and yank him down, dragging Sen along the ground as he slowly backed up. Sen struggled frantically, trying to sit up and reach the lashes entangling him. He was dragging his arms and even kicking with his other leg to reverse enforcer's momentum. But, given the enforcer's greater strength, Sen was only delaying the inevitable, even with full-body enhancement.

A sudden jerk from the dark spirit put Sen flat on the ground. The back of his head slammed hard off the marble. The specter somehow held Sen down while lining up its massive thirteen-foot spear for a thrust to Sen's chest.

Josh was out of time but had an idea. Instead of fully enhancing his whole body, he would only enhance what he needed to full effect. Starting with his legs for the speed to close the gap. In a fraction of a second, Josh was immediately behind the creature, moving so fast his eyes felt dry from the wind resistance. Unfortunately, he hadn't entered the momentum of such speeds into his quickly formed plans. So, while still being carried forward by inertia, Josh diverted his cycling to his upper body. Swinging his club in a horizontal line through the specter's back. Its shield ability flashed brightly but immediately shattered at the force of Josh's momentum and fully enhanced swing. Once through its shield, the club continued through the dark spirit's body, crushing the iron cuirass, and sending it flying into the plaza. As if dispelled through this disruption, the specter dissolved in wisps of rising-black smoke, weapons and all.

Following the hit, Josh's body continued several yards before smashing into the ground, where he rolled several times in an unplanned and painful manner. The rough, white marble grated off of his shirt, pants, and underlying skin. Josh's full-body skid also left a widening red streak five yards long.

Josh lay where he finally slid to a stop, panting and trying to get his frazzled brain to triage where he needed to heal first. His right shoulder was broken or dislocated. A lot of skin was missing from his face, chest, abdomen, and upper legs. Not to mention he had seriously bruised and fractured ribs, skull, and both knees. He cycled Essence to his shoulder and the areas with missing skin first. Remembering the benefit of focused cycling as he checked his interface. His health was at 57 percent and rising. Free Essence was down to 35 percent and dropping. Hopefully, enough to heal him to a point where he could start cycling the Essence he had absorbed from the cannibals earlier.

Sen rose and walked over to Josh, holding out a hand to help him up.

With a shallow look of shame on his face, Sen mumbled abashedly, looking down at his own feet. "Thanks for saving me, Joshua."

A pained and slightly sarcastic smile stretched the still-healing skin on Josh's face. "Don't mention it . . . seems like a habit I'm having a hard time breaking!"

Sen turned a darker pink as Josh took Sen's offered hand and rose to his feet.

Then Josh grasped his partner's forearm and looked him straight in the eyes while coming clean. "Seriously, Sen, I'm sorry I got taken out of the equation so fast. It would have been different if I had been helping the whole time."

Josh then informed Sen of the benefits of focusing his total enhancement in the last fight. Sen agreed. In this case, it was undoubtedly the right course. He also admitted that he should have adopted it. Talking through the melee, they acceded that it was still early days in their understanding of mortal cultivation. They needed to keep an open mind about what to do and when to do it.

After a minute, Josh reached a point of healing where his shoulder popped back into place, and his skin had regrown, pink and angry. He walked with Sen over to the temple to check on the woman hanging from the stone posts. Looking up, they noted that she was still tied but fully healed. She was naked from the waist up as well . . . and smiling at them. They both immediately turned red and looked directly in her eyes!

"Stars, it's been so long since I had a chance to heal. Thank you both for that. Can I get one of you to unlatch these ties for me?" she said, rattling both of the large iron bindings and chains on her wrists. "It's been five thousand years since my grandson gave me a chance to sit!

"Oh . . . I'm Gaia, by the way! Welcome to my temple!"

———————————✷———————————

Josh and Sen had silently agreed that releasing her was the right thing to do. They could have acted paranoid and kept her there for a round of questioning. They probably would have if they were uptight asses. But they were both tired. And there was something in Gaia's sincerity that made them not want to live in a world where they couldn't trust a beautiful woman they had just saved from being chained to two posts while being whipped by an evil specter for five thousand years. Guys were generally dumb that way. Enough said.

Needless to say, they quickly released Gaia. Freeing her was as simple as lifting the large, looped chain from a hook above her head, then sliding the holding bolts on her wrist cuffs. She adjusted her now pristine white toga to cover her previously exposed bits, mainly to make them more comfortable. It was obvious she seemed not to be uncomfortable with her body. Nor did she seem ill at ease with them looking at it. She then gave each a genuine hug of gratitude.

Three low-to-the-ground sitting cushions appeared with a wave of Gaia's hand. And she guided them to sit down. She explained how she had ended up in the position they had found her in.

"It all started with my youngest son Cronus's bad habit of eating his own children."

Sen's eyes screwed up.

Gaia nodded enthusiastically, confirming what she had said and continued. "I know, right! I tried to talk to him about it. But would he listen? Of course not. It finally got him in the end. Zeus, my only surviving grandson at the time, made Cronus throw up his brothers and sisters. They then proceeded to wipe out Cronus and all of his siblings ... How was I supposed to take that? I was okay with rescuing the trapped ones. But I draw the line at killing the ones I still have ... they are all my children, after all. My first set of kids, anyway. The ones I had with my son-husband Uranus. He is my heaven! It's such a shame I had to have him castrated ...

"Anyway ... to show Zeus how unhappy I was with him, I had my last batch of kids, the Gigantes ... Boy, were they cute! To try and teach Zeus a lesson. Did that go wrong!? It sure did, I tell you! The rest is history. So, for siccing the Gigantes on him, Zeus has punished me for the last five thousand years with a never-ending lashing. Mr. Overkill, I used to call him when he was a baby ..."

Josh looked at her, his mouth slightly agape. "You are a god?"

"Oh, silly! Of course not! I'm a Star Child. We come from deep in the galactic center and find planets where we can get the ball rolling for everyone. We gave birth to the gods, the Titans before them, and ultimately, everyone else here. We were the first ones on this planet. My cousins Vishnu, Shiva, Brahman, and myself, that is. Some distant relatives we didn't know very well went to what you humans call Egypt and got things going there."

She took a small sip of water and smiled warmly at them again. "Now, I can tell that you, and you ..." She smiled at Josh and Sen, respectively. "Aren't really two of mine. Josh ..." Gaia thinned her eyes for a second focusing on him. "You are from one of my iterational sisters. I owe her a debt for bringing you into existence. And you ..." She made the same expression looking at Sen. "You are from very far out of town. Unless I miss my guess?

"And not that I am in any way ungrateful to you for saving me from that"—Gaia pointed at the seven-foot posts behind them—"but why are you here, if you don't mind me asking?"

Josh and Sen explained that they were cultivators looking for items of power in the cavern. And that they were still hoping to get two of them.

"Ahhh..." She touched her index finger to her lips and then continued speaking. "You are looking for the Earth Attunement crystals. I understand. They are down in the catacombs below this temple. I can guide you to the door. But every cultivator is obligated to get their own. Or I understand the attunement wouldn't work as well... perhaps not at all for the cultivator if they aren't earned appropriately. Karma is so closely tied to cultivation, after all... What can you do?

"There is also a guardian you will have to defeat, a chimera. She is another grandchild of mine. Believe me, she's never listened to me. What can I say, her being a child of Typhon and all... but do watch out for the fire!" Gaia laughed in sincere humor.

Truly grateful for her goodwill but feeling the exhaustion of heavy activity and decreased Essence, Josh and Sen could only manage a few suppressed chuckles at the thought of being incinerated by an ancient-Greek-mythological creature.

Taking on the expression of a concerned mother, Gaia spoke again. "I suggest you eat and then rest up for now. I can tell that you are still wounded, and your Essence is low. Furthermore, you both need to cultivate to restore your Intent. Please consider this temple a refuge of safety until the morning."

Two divans appeared in an empty space with a low-profile table between them. The table was laden with fruits, nuts, a moist goat cheese, unleavened bread, several bowls of washed olives, and one large decanter of olive oil. There were even two jugs. One of wine. The other of cool water. Each pitcher came accompanied by small-earthen cups.

Josh couldn't remember the last time he had eaten. He had skipped lunch the day this had all happened to him. He couldn't even remember if he had breakfast that morning.

But before Josh could even thank Gaia, Sen's eyes had bulged out, and he had lunged for the things on the table.

If Josh had given it any thought, he might have realized that Sen had never eaten physical food in his entire three million years of existence. He also would have realized the brand-spanking new mortal was having the same edgy, hollow feelings chewing at his abdomen for the last several hours as Josh had. Where Josh knew these feelings as hunger and had no fear of them, this was certainly not true for Sen. Upon seeing the food, the novice mortal obviously couldn't help but be drawn by his instincts. Sen surged to the table. He started shoveling food into his mouth, apparently not even looking at what he was cramming in while barely chewing. When he tried to swallow with an open, full mouth, he gagged and choked spewing a fountain of food all around himself.

Gaia raised her brows and stifled a nervous laugh with a polite hand.

Somehow knowing that Sen had lost all reasonable perspective, Josh held up his hand to get his Karmic brother's attention. Grabbing one olive and a cracker, he showed Sen how to eat without dying. Then washed it down with a sip of water. After that, things went much smoother for everyone, including Sen's GI track.

CHAPTER 14

---★---

Hearing Is Not Everything

SEN AND Josh finished everything on the table. Including the little pinch-dish of sea salt Gaia had put out for them. Sen kept licking his finger, dipping it in the bowl, and then putting it in his mouth when he thought Josh wasn't looking.

Lifting the last of the nuts to his mouth, watching Sen out of the corner of his eye, Josh mumbled as he chewed, "For a guy who was an Immortal until two days ago . . . you're like a kid, you know that?"

Cheeks turning red at being discovered, Sen couldn't help but admit, "That's . . . that's true, Joshua. In many ways, the things that we are encountering are much newer to me than you. Eating! Wow! Who would have thought so much delight came from something that outwardly seemed so banal?" He patted his full belly in contentment.

Smiling, not in an altogether kind way, Josh replied, "Heh, true . . . but you will see the banal side tomorrow when you're finished with it."

Sen narrowed his eyes, wheels turning, obviously using his Essence to track his digestive system. His eyes widened with a brief look of abject horror. Josh could tell through their Karmic Bond that Sen had understood Josh's comment and stalked his alimentary track to its *prosaic* ending.

"I had forgotten about that . . ." Sen said almost to himself with eyes narrowed.

Josh chuckled. "Yeah, I can see you got it now . . . Listen, I'm going to start cycling the Essence we picked up this morning. Give me two hours, then rouse me so that you can cycle. We can stairstep until we both finish. I trust Gaia . . ." Josh looked over his shoulder in the direction the Star Child had walked off to after leaving them with their meal. "But if that specter comes back or has friends that come to check on him, it would be best to have a lookout, right?"

"Agreed, Joshua."

Josh settled in to cycle the remainder of the cannibal Essence he had collected the morning before. When Sen gently shook his shoulder, he had reached what he thought was about 95 percent conversion, the approximation being necessary as there were no numbers for this.

Josh blinked and nodded that he was back from *cultivation land*. It had literally seemed like only fifteen minutes for him. But he could tell from the candles on the table that much more time had passed. He also felt restored and fresh-minded. Like he had received a restful night's sleep. He shared his findings, then let Sen repeat the process.

Josh checked his interface as Sen was cycling. His health was fully restored during the cycling. He checked his shoulder and leg through his shredded clothing and noted intact skin and a full active range of motion for abduction, adduction, forward flexion, and extension . . . *Stop the science jargon in your own head, Josh . . . your shoulder is fine!*

Josh darkly chuckled. If Sen could put things inside his head, why did he turn me into a *Farmer's Almanac* instead of *The Kurgan*? If it came up, he would have to ask. But Josh was suspicious that there was no minimum safe amount of information to put in someone's brain. Sen had likely taken a chance with *decohesion of his cortex* even if they had only given him the CPR info.

Josh noticed his core on autopilot converted 1 percent of the remaining unpurified Essence to his own every fifteen minutes. He couldn't identify any foreign Essence remaining in his meridians after about 1.5 hours. He also had instinctively converted the excess free Essence to cultivation dedicated Essence in his core. The numeric indicator read 49 percent, and his free Essence bar seemed full. Like breathing and digesting his food, some aspects of cultivation were now a part of him and would, seemingly, function on their own.

Two hours later, Josh roused Sen. After a quick debrief to confirm they had consistent experiences, they were ready to head down for the Attunement crystal. As if on cue, Gaia rounded a colonnade holding some white linens in her hand.

Smiling and waving to them, she said, "As much as I love the rough and tumble, fresh-from-the-field look you guys are putting out, these are for you." She placed the white linens on the edge of the richly covered divans they had slept on.

"Go ahead and change. You can leave those..." She pointed to the rags hanging from their bodies in tattered, blood-soaked, and muddy strips. "Over there... for burning."

Looking down at their clothes seemingly for the first time, to realize that the articles had seen much better days, they nodded their thanks and reached for the fresh set.

Sen rushed to take off his rags but, seeing Josh was just standing there looking at Gaia, he stopped pulling off his upper garment halfway over his head, leaving it at the midway point.

Josh looked pointedly at Gaia and raised his eyebrows...

Gaia looked back with a prurient smile on her face. "After all, you already saw mine!" She winked lewdly at them.

"For the love..." Josh mumbled, turning around and pulling what was left of his clothes off.

Soft undergarments went on first. Next were the pants—a sturdier linen for the britches type of lower garment. It was pleated between the legs and ended just above the knees to allow full movement. Next was an off-white upper garment that reminded Josh of a tank top. Last was a rectangular cloak; Gaia showed them the proper way to wear and fasten over their right shoulders with a solid bronze brooch.

"I remember putting my first kids in their chlamys..." A sad smile touched her eyes for the briefest of moments. Then she straightened their outfits out with a few quick, well-practiced movements. Like any good mother would for her children on their first day of school.

"Now, boys, the Earth Crystals are down there." She pointed to a closed door between two nearby columns.

Josh would have sworn it wasn't there even thirty seconds ago. Braziers on either side lit up, strengthening his suspicions.

"No one has been down there in a very long time. Watch out! In the old places of the Earth, lost Essence from the fallen can become corrupt and attract unfriendly things. I also told you about the chimera guardian outside the chamber with the Earth Crystals, didn't I? Be ready! I don't want this to be the last time we meet." She smiled a warm, caring smile that lit up her whole face.

At that moment, Josh believed, without a doubt, she was the mother of the whole world.

"And one more thing..." Gaia made no effort to hide the fact that she was eyeing the root clubs Sen and Josh were carrying.

Partial cracks and large divots from forceful strikes were present and telling on both... They wouldn't last much longer for either of them.

"Before you get to the Crystal Chamber, there is a sort of... *storage room*. Uranus and I... we moved a lot of old things down there when all the kids and grandkids had moved out of the house and were living on Olympus most of the time. If I remember, there might be some old training weapons from when my first kids, the Titans, were just learning to use their training xiphos and dorys. They are yours if you want them. Just tell the custodian I said so... He'll know what to do."

"But... weren't Titans gigantic?" Josh blurted out before he could help himself.

Gaia smiled her motherly smile for Josh again and waved her hand dismissively. "Oh, silly! Not all the time ... only when they wanted to be."

———————————————✳———————————————

The door closed behind Josh and Sen. Gaia waved her hand from right to left as if opening a sliding window, returning her temple to its normal state. Attendants waited in the eaves of the colonnades. Flute and harp music could be heard sifting through the smoke of burnt offerings. The chanting of supplicants murmured from the far reaches of every side. Her many guards stood at attention around the perimeter.

She raised an eyebrow and glared to the right of the door the two young cultivators had just walked through. A second later, the Clone appeared, causing the classic white marble setting to glitter with his pulsating ultraviolet.

"You were not instructed to give them weapons, Gaia."

She glared at the Clone's accusation. "And *you* said they were warriors on a hero's journey to collect their first Attunement! These were children armed with sticks! It was all we could do not to kill them by accident!" Her voice rose at the end as she glared accusingly at the Clone and called for her guard captain. "Machitis! Attend me!"

The specter who had stood over Gaia several hours before with his scourge appeared instantly.

Without hesitation, he dropped to a knee, fist over his heart. "Mother." His red eyes were downcast.

"Assess the strength of the two men you fought."

"Disorganized. Noneffective. Pathetic. While the last blow had some modest strength. They were prey, not fighters."

Raising a scornful glance to the Clone, Gaia more accused than asked, "How long have they been cultivating, six months? A year?"

"Thirty-two hours ..."

Gaia's eyes widened in shock as she gasped in surprise at the Clone's impossible statement. Even Machitis's swirling red eyes turned toward the Clone as if seeking confirmation that he had heard correctly. The Clone looked away briefly and sat on the edge of a divan.

Appearing weary from his choices, he raised a hand to Gaia as if to hold her off. **"I know ... believe me, I know ... We have no choice at this point. Things are even more dire than you know. There is no time for them to acclimate to cultivating in the usual or even an accelerated time scale. Zenyak needs them as immediately as possible! Thus, I have created this fiction to attain their first Attunement. They need to make their own connections and still advance, with us spoon-feeding them from the shadows as much as possible. To fail them ... is not an option. Believe me, Gaia, the remainder of their Attunements in the Spherical Tier will be significantly more dangerous."**

------------------------✶------------------------

The door closed with a finality that Josh hadn't anticipated. Looking around with darting eyes, there was no sign of abandonment, no thick layer of dust or piles of long bleached bones in the corner. Still, the air in the winding stairway was stale and stifling. It gave the impression that the passage had been empty for an exceedingly long time.

By unspoken agreement, Senyak walked down first. He held his root cudgel tightly in his right hand. Josh did the same. Burning braziers lit the winding hall as they proceeded down. Thick, black smoke rose to a ceiling that was unseen above them.

Their enhanced hearing gave them the first warning they were not alone. The sounds of heavy clacking from far below echoed on the thick-marble walls. It grew louder as they continued down. It was hard to tell exactly what was causing the sounds, but no heartbeats could be heard.

Josh's thinking shifted to an undead creature or some kind of automaton. *Who am I kidding? I'm a total newb in this place. It can be anything. For gods' sake, we just met the mother of the Earth.*

But Gaia's final and very cryptic warning about corrupted things coming from, or being attracted to, lost energy made Josh think about shambling, undead things. So, as unpleasant as those were, that was where his thoughts remained.

The clacking continued to get closer as he and Sen descended. There was no indication that they had been detected. No sound of claws, undead or otherwise, rushing up the stairs at them. Finally, after what Josh thought was thirty minutes of steady walking down, they reached the bottom of the stairs. A wide hallway opened up before them with two open doorways on either side. A fifth and final doorway held a barred, wooden door at the end of the hall opposite them, about thirty yards away.

The clacking was coming from the first room on the left. But that wasn't what concerned Josh at the moment. Approximately twenty yards from the winding stairway's last step, five zombies with black skin, all emitting the blue-green glow of foxfire, quietly stood at the center of the landing. The zombies were dressed in rotting leather armor with rusted iron weapons in their hands as they started to move forward toward Josh and Sen.

Without much need to overly reflect, Josh decided they were a much greater concern than anything else presently.

CHAPTER 15

---★---

Profaning the Ritual

THE THREE undead warriors standing in the front rank moved to immediately to intercept them. *Moved* being the right word, they walked as if alive. No shambling gait, no flesh dropping off. Upon reflection, zombie might be the wrong way to describe them. Their black or very dark-blue skin was desiccated like a tight-fitting husk over intact but shrunken muscles below. They maintained at least a collective intelligence, given their coordination and ability to brandish their very real-looking short swords. The two in the back were each holding bows with a quiver full of arrows which they were already nocking.

"Move back! Up the stairs! Now!" Sen yelled.

Cycling their Essence to their legs, they turned and ran back up the stairs two complete 180-degree turns, which was twenty steps in their count. Sen put his hand out, signaling Josh to stop. Two arrows hit the curving wall down several steps in front of them. Shattering against the marble and launching splinters up the stairway that showered over them.

"We'll meet the first draugr here; defeat him then we move back up ten more stairs, another 180-degree turn. We are as good as dead if we don't stay ahead of those archers!"

"Draugr?"

"Yes, they are the risen dead. Formed by spirits drawn to the bodies of those who are unjustly killed. If they touch us, they can leach our Essence. Don't let them do that. And we will need to destroy their heads. They feel no pain and are only stopped through crushing their skull, decapitation, or destruction with fire."

Josh's enhanced ears heard the draugr's even steps about to round the corner into their sight. He raised his club overhead to bring it down on the first one that showed him the blacks of its eyes. If they wanted to attack at the same time, which Sen said was their plan, they needed to stand on the same stair. Josh, poised on the hub's narrower inside, Sen taking a wide-based and more vulnerable stance on the broader outside.

A black and desiccated foot, immediately followed by the tip of a sword, rounded the bend of the spiral stairs. Josh and Sen both swung their clubs down from overhead. They were fully cycling Essence to their arms and upper body. Both clubs struck true. Sen's hit first, with Josh's piling on a close second later. A burst of moldy green air and stinking moist leather-like scraps covered them as the draugr's head exploded into foul-smelling bits. Its body was driven to the floor in a twist of legs, arms, and moldering torso. The incoming draugr behind extended its arm and slashed at Sen with its rusted sword. Sen pulled back, narrowly avoiding the blade as it whistled through the air, then clanged off the marble wall. Spraying chunks of marble filled the air around them, scoring bloody tracks on their faces and exposed skin.

Josh stepped forward with Essence cycling to his legs and sent a kick to push the defeated draugr's freshly re-killed body down the stairs and into the next attacker. Both undead and re-dead tumbled back down. An arrow shot from below skidded around the rounded outside wall of the stairs. It missed Sen's bent head by a fraction of an inch, him still crouched down to avoid the previous strike. Josh was pretty sure the archers would have had to advance up past the first turn to get that arrow to graze the wall like that.

Grabbing Sen by the collar, Josh pulled him up as they ran to put a few more bends in the stairs between them and the pursuit. Two more full 180-degree turns and they stopped, waiting against the hub of the stairway to repeat what they had done. They waited in silence while breathing deeply. They waited and listened ... and listened and waited ... and ... the draugrs obviously weren't coming!

Still listening, Josh heard dry feet rasping on the rough steps, heading back down.

Josh looked at Sen and pointed down the stairs. The question was evident on his face and through their Karmic Bond. *Why aren't they coming?*

"They are risen undead ... not stupid. They are waiting for us."

"Zombies are smart enough to play a waiting game with us?" Josh asked, simultaneously checking his interface. Ninety-one percent free Essence remaining; 100 percent health.

"Not zombies ... remnants. They are *the spiritually risen undead*. They are not the reanimated meat puppets of the Necrolon. Draugr are most commonly raised when a portion of a spirit that hasn't made its migration to the mortal soul nexus lingers in the place of its death with an empty vessel nearby. Because of that, they have a rudimentary intelligence. Which is obviously enough to thwart our plans ..." Sen trailed off.

"Well, *run, Forest, run* isn't exactly an amazing strategy to begin with," Josh said almost to himself. "But when you say *intelligence*, do you mean sitting around chatting about the current selection on the book-of-the-month club over a cup of Darjeeling or something similar to *insect cognition* level intelligence. Such as moving from the light to the dark, avoiding large overhead predators, following attractive smells to food kind of intelligence?"

Sen's mouth made a straight line as he thought about Josh's question. "Most likely the second one ... Why?"

"I think I may understand why they retreated. They aren't *waiting for us*. They are following their *draugr-cognition* and returning to their *home range*."

"What..." Sen looked blank-faced at Josh.

Josh then spent the next fifteen minutes explaining to Sen about the concepts of agro, threat generation, pulling mobs, and home range computer models, along with the general *play nature* of video games.

———————————✳———————————

"So, I'm not saying we are in a video game. Or anything like that. I'm a million percent certain that we are not. What I am saying is: I recognize this behavior model. We should be able to predict the aggressive actions of these draugr based on what I have seen so far. *In this particular set of circumstances.*"

"So... Joshua, if I understand you correctly, to properly enact the ritual of *the agro,* we have to get close enough for them to see us. Thereby generating *the agro.* Then we need to run. But we must stay close enough for *the agro* to continue. Or, as you say, *hold.* If we go too far, we will defile the ritual, and the draugr will return to their reset point. The center of the landing at the bottom of the stairs. Then we will have to perform the ritual all over again? Do I have it right, brother?"

Josh had been through this with Sen about ten times. He had actually encouraged the conceptualization of drawing agro as a ritual because it helped Sen grasp the concepts and his mental acceptance.

Josh grinned to hold back his laughter. "Yes, you have it very well."

Pursing his lips, Sen could sense the sincerity through their Bond. There could be no deception between them. "All right. It is worth a try."

Josh looked up at Sen from the position he had propped himself against the wall during his explanation. "How is it that you know so much about these ... draugr, but nothing about so many other things, like eating, for instance?" The question had been nagging at him.

"I'm a combat specialist who studied mortal physical combat for over five hundred years. Studying battle tactics against draugr was a part of that. They are one of the most common mortal undead forces encountered in the multiverse. There are even Immortal counterparts." Sen said, nodding.

Josh nodded, pursing his lips in agreement. *That makes sense.*

✦

After creeping down the stairs to where they had defeated the first draugr, they took stock of the situation. Its sword was where the body had fallen initially before it had been kicked down the stairs. Josh picked it up and handed it to Sen without a second thought. There was no doubt between them that Sen was more battle capable and could put it to better use.

Sen inspected the weapon. A thick, double-edged short sword of seventy-five centimeters. It was made of iron and blunt on both sides. Its rusted and pitted surface was a far cry from the well-cared-for weapons he used as an Immortal. But, compared to a stick he had dug out of a dirt wall ... it was a significant upgrade.

Sen's interface flashed.

Weapon Equipped: Short sword. Quality poor. Damage increased from negligible to poor. Cleave and dismemberment options are available for physical combat. Do you wish to continue with this as your new weapon?

A little box even popped up on his interface when he thought *about it.*

Weapon: Short Sword	Quality: Poor Increasing quality of weapon will increase damage.
Skill Level: Advanced	Allows interface guidance for optimal usage.
Damage: Average mundane	97% probability of 865% increased damage vs. open hand damage. Increasing skill level will increase damage capabilities.

Sen, used to over three million years of choices offered by his Ethos Combi, responded immediately.

Yes! Transcendence, I have missed you.

The interface responded with more information.

Optimal strike opportunities during battle will be highlighted in your visual perception.

Sen filled in Josh about the interface's expanded capabilities. Josh looked at his root club.

Frowning, he muttered to himself. "I don't have a little box. Maybe I'd like one too, huh ... but no little box for me." He looked at Sen. "The next one is mine!"

"Of course, brother!" Sen laughed. "Of course."

They also inspected the gear. Dirty and rusted. Pre-owned by a vile, rank-smelling undead. But much better than what they had been dealing with ... which was nothing! Looking over draugr's gear, the bracers and greaves were salvageable and split between them. Sen took the greaves, Josh the bracers.

———————✳———————

Josh eyed the thick, dark, and pitted metal on his wrists. The leather straps were moldering but still supple enough to open and attach over his forearms. "You are so getting boiled the very first chance I get ..."

Despite Josh's greatest hope, no boxes popped when he donned the armor. The Clone had said that its function would increase with their cultivation. Perhaps weapons were all that it could support at this point? Time would tell.

Josh pointed to the draugr's deformed and now looted body. He moved his hand in its direction, indicating to Sen through their Bond that Josh was going to collect the Essence.

Sen grabbed Josh's hand and pulled it away from the corpse. "We can't do that! Undead are not spiritual beings that cultivate Essence. They consume it, much like your version of vampires. Damni had me watch several historical records called ... movies ... I think ... Draugrs with skin that shined in the sunlight ... Anyway ... they do not carry or cultivate Essence as we do. They consume it to perpetuate motion after the spark of most of their soul has returned to the mortal nexus. If you gathered enough of their *energy*, you might start becoming one of them. I was not on the path of an Atalmon or a Vitalist ... but these facts are well known."

Josh scurried away from the corpse as if suddenly afraid it would grab his hand and feed him its undeath.

Without taking his eyes off it, he spoke. "Thanks for the tip ... Don't take Essence from undead things ... got it!"

Josh's conversion to undead avoided, it was time to get to work.

Sen patted his shoulder, and a dangerous gleam came into his eye. "Let us begin *the agro!*"

Josh smiled at Sen. "For sure, brother!"

———————————✳———————————

They returned to the landing after dragging the defeated draugr's body up ten 180-degree rotations and placing it on the outside of the steps. As Josh had explained, they would likely have to run up and down a few times if their plan worked. But Sen pointed out that the body might get in the way. He didn't want them to trip over it and "profane the ritual."

Once at the bottom, they saw, as before, that the melee draugr stood in front of the archers. And, again, the undead moved to intercept them. The draugr clearly had learned from past events. Instead of walking, they started running *very, very fast.* The immense strength of their undead bodies gave them incredible acceleration, which they seemed eager to use.

Fortunately for Josh and Sen, upon showing their faces, they had already started running to the planned ambush point where they had killed the first draugr in the last battle. Or, as Sen had learned to call it, they *pulled* the melee warriors. The ambush point was two complete rotations up the stairs. Sen was their rear guard. Even with fully enhanced legs, he sensed he would be overtaken approximately two-thirds of the way up.

But . . . things were a little different for Sen this time as well. After ten stairs, he turned, placing his feet in a wide stance to intercept the first draugr. He ducked under one arrow skidding along the rounded wall as well as the shattered shards of another that hit farther down. While partially crouched, he raised his short sword and straightened up, waiting for his target to round the corner.

Fully vertical, Sen adopted the high-held roof stance to attempt a decapitation. However, his interface had another recommendation, demonstrating a flashing yellow upswing line from his right to left. Using the fool's stance, his blade would start in a low position and build momentum.

47 percent more likely to disable pursuing draugr.

It added no additional explanation.

Sen blinked at being vetoed. But after eons of trusting his Combi, he quickly adopted the stance and swung his shoulders and hips to affect the strike. The first attacker rounded the corner, sword drawn, chest and head leaning forward. Sen's enhanced strike took it, slicing through the left shoulder and chin, finishing with cleaving its head on a diagonal. The top portion of its skull followed the course of Sen's sword, smearing the sidewall with black blood and the putrescent foulness inside the draugr's cleaved skull. The now *dead*-dead draugr's body continued with its momentum and crashed into the wall behind Sen as it collapsed to the floor.

Sen redirected his enhancement to his legs and cleared the still-falling body with a single leap. He continued to the planned ambush point, where he sensed through their Bond that Joshua was waiting as planned. The pursuing draugr did momentarily slow down to get over the fallen body of its undead companion. But it still, very kindly, followed *Josh's draugr-cognition theory of agro* by continuing up.

<hr>

With his enhanced hearing, Josh heard Sen confront the draugr and hightail it out of there. He could also tell the archers had continued to advance their position as their arrows kept skidding along the rounded walls from behind Sen. Things only picked up speed from there.

In less than a blink, Sen flew past Josh and nodded. ~*Incoming! Your turn.*~

The sounds of dry, undead feet scrabbling up the stairs as the first draugr cleared the last bend in the stairway came to Josh's enhanced ears. As the tip of its sword came into sight, Josh brought his club down in an honest attempt to smash its helmet straight through its navel. Josh's enhanced strength provided more than enough power to end the draugr's final existence. Still, even after the enemy was dispatched, physics weren't on vacation. The draugr's body continued moving forward under the power of its rapid momentum and slammed squarely into Josh, bowling him over. Ultimately the re-killed body of the draugr came to a rest against the wall covering Josh's prone form. Its shattered head dribbled fetid fluids into his face, hair, and eyes.

The stairway went silent. The footfalls of the remaining two draugr archers the only sounds Josh's enhanced ears could hear as he struggled to push the rotted husk off him. Sen flashed back down the turns in the stairway that separated them and offered him a hand up.

Despite the stinking undead sap that had soaked into his hair and linens, Josh couldn't keep the smile out of his voice as he rose to his feet. "I love it when a plan comes together!"

CHAPTER 16

---✦---

Nothing Stings Like the Truth

JOSH HELD the looted short sword in his hand. Rusted, dull, and pitted with a mostly moldered and rotten leather handle. He couldn't keep his smile from stretching ear to ear as he inspected his first box.

Weapon: Short Sword	Quality: Poor Increasing quality of weapon will increase damage.
Skill Level: None	-
Damage: Poor mundane	92% probability of 236% increased damage vs. hand-to-hand damage. Increasing skill level will increase damage capabilities.

They also looted the salvageable armor from the two downed draugrs. Now, they each sported bracers and greaves, a studded leather cuirass, and a studded pauldron covering the left shoulder. The pair then endured ten minutes of small-volume breathing caused by wearing the extremely fragrant gear. It smelled of rotten mayonnaise and sunbaked roadkill. But, as with all things ... after a relatively short period passed, Josh had to admit he was getting used to the smell. After donning the chest gear and pauldron to complete the set, Josh was overjoyed when a second box from the interface popped up.

Armor equipped. Draugr studded leather, quality poor. Protection increased from negligible to poor. Partial blocking options available. Do you wish to continue with this as your new armor?

After mentally picking *yes*, they received a second text box.

Armor Equipped: Draugr Studded Leather	Quality: Poor Increasing quality of armor will increase protection and probability of damage reduction.
Skill Level: None	Increasing skill level will increase probability of interface guidance for optimal usage.
Protection: Poor mundane	54% probability of 15% damage reduction from physical attacks from mundane weapons. Increasing skill level will increase probability of damage reduction capabilities.

Sen, having skill in wearing armor, received the same text box with slightly enhanced probabilities of protection.

Armor Equipped: Draugr Studded Leather	Quality: Poor Increasing quality of armor will increase protection and probability of damage reduction.

Skill Level: Advanced	Increasing skill level will increase probability of interface guidance for optimal usage.
Protection: Below average mundane	99% probability of 25% damage reduction from physical attacks from mundane weapons. Increasing skill level will increase probability of damage reduction capabilities.

Josh couldn't help but feel pretty badass despite the smell of year-old, slow-cooked, dead ass lingering in his nose. For the first time since this had all started, he wasn't wishing he could be *anywhere* but here ... just *most places* instead of here. For instance, Josh would much rather be here than at Miranda's mom's house for lunch ... he considered it a start, at least.

Wrapping up the archers was anticlimactic following the melee encounters. Having grasped the *ritual of the agro*, Sen had lured them into the blind stairway with another classic line-of-sight pull. He then sprang back down the stairs as the archers were reloading. Two decapitations later, they had free reign of the landing and the five doors surrounding it.

A quick check of their interfaces showed their free Essence levels—Sen at 54 percent and Josh at 64 percent. Both of their health bars were at 100 percent after a few cycles to heal several minor scratches and one streak on Sen's back from an unlucky arrow ricochet.

Josh was a bit taken aback when he looked through the open doors, and there was just a kind of white and shimmering barrier instead of rooms. The mercurial apertures constantly rippled like the surface of a still pond after a rock had been tossed into it.

"Portals." Sen had said and then looked around as if it was the most normal thing in the world to have a doorway filled with rolling quicksilver.

"Portals?" Josh repeated. "What do you mean, *portals*? Portals are small doorways through walls in buildings and boats! These weird glowing barriers could lead anywhere or electrify us as we pass through or give entry to thousands of grasping appendages from a groping tentacle monster or . . . a million other things!"

Sen must have sensed through their Bond that Josh was strangely thrown off by the dimensional aspect of the passageways. He explained. "Relax, Joshua . . . these are just like portals that lead through walls in buildings and boats. But instead of leading into an adjacent room, they lead to other nearby pocket dimensions attached to this iteration."

Sen narrowed his eyes and added slyly. "Really . . . if you were going to lose it, I would have thought it would be against the undead remnants, the dark specter, or the furry-cannibalistic humanoids . . . not the dimension ports."

"Really! You're shaming me like a thirteen-year-old at the skate park?"

Sen's smile reached feral proportions. "Whatever works, brother . . . whatever works!" Leaving Josh to accept that he wasn't in Kansas anymore, Sen stepped away and began inspecting the doorways more closely.

Seeing Sen had moved on, Josh lowered his raised index finger and chased after him. But whatever Josh was going to comeback with remained unspoken when he noticed the title's etched, boldface script above the mullion on three of the doorways.

The first one on the right side, where the clacking had come from, was: TARTARUS.

The next on the right side: ELYSIUM.

And the first on the left side: OLYMPUS.

The last portaled door, farthest on the left, had no title.

The doorway at the end of the landing was still closed by a thick wooden door banded in iron and barred by a sturdy beam bolting it from this side. No other locking mechanism could be seen.

Josh looked to Sen. "So, these portals go to mystical places and even . . . *the home of the Greek gods?*"

With the patience of a mother toilet-training a toddler, Sen spoke with a small smile, "Yes, brother . . . it would appear so."

"Well . . . okay then . . ." Finally accepting the dimensional aspect of the portals, Josh mentally moved on and reengaged his brain. "I bet that the storage room Gaia mentioned is the one without an ancient mythical title."

Sen nodded. "Agreed."

After discussing the titles, it turned out that even Sen had heard of all three places and that the ancient-Greek mythical locations had almost complete multiversal penetrance. Furthermore, all three were associated with robust warrior traditions, and he had studied them at least in passing.

The tapping restarted from the door marked Tartarus. For an unaccountable reason, Josh felt compelled to go through that portal. Something was calling him from the other side. Thinking about it, Josh wanted to go through and see what was over there. Something motivated him to walk through the shimmering portal . . . and right an injustice that had been done . . . he could *only* set it right on the other side—

Stepping back, clearing his mind with a quick head shake, Josh refocused while stretching out his arm to pull Sen back. It disturbed him to realize they had both been slowly edging toward the open portal . . .

Sen looked up at Josh with appreciation.

Josh nodded back. ~*I got you.*~

Sen inclined his head. ~*Gratitude.*~

Josh narrowed his eyes at the portal. Some very shady mind games were afoot at the Circle K . . . bad things were sure to follow if they went through there. If their path took them through the Tartarus portal . . .

they would go. If it was accurate that a great injustice had been done that they could right, they probably even wanted to go ... but right now, he didn't want to go enough to ignore the possibility of better weapons and obtaining their Earth Attunement.

Without better weapons, he and Sen were going to eventually be overwhelmed. Without an Attunement to keep their Essence filled, they would need to constantly kill spiritual beings and absorb their Essence. An option to do that without having to stalk prey unworthy of continued existence would be invaluable. So ... these two things needed to come first before any extracurriculars.

Josh realized more and more with every step he took that getting stronger and *advancing* his cultivation was going to have to be his way of life. That meant putting its goals first above what he merely wanted. In short, he needed to take care of business before he looked behind the Tartarus door. It needed to be that simple from now on.

Nodding to Sen, they stepped up to the unmarked door. Sen walked through first, and Josh followed. No doubt Josh was less skilled with the sword and armor. Sen with an *advanced* skill and a *below average* protection rating meant he was their *tank* for now.

Phasing through the portal was a nonevent. It didn't feel any different then walking through any standard doorway. Being on the other side, however, definitely gave Josh the feeling that he was somewhere more than one doorjamb away.

The immense space they found themselves in was filled with tall, wooden shelves that marched off into the distance—way beyond what they could see, even with their enhanced sight. The marble floor was gone. Replaced with dark, polished stone. The blue and green of mother of pearl flashed to their eyes when the light from the lit braziers struck it at the right angles.

And directly in front of them, seated behind a small counter blocking the narrow entryway to the wide-open spaces of the room behind, was a man in the same chlamys they were wearing ... and wearing his much better if Josh was honest. His body was well-muscled in classic heroic proportions. A suit of armor, similar to the one worn by the enforcer they had fought, could be seen poking above the low top of the counter. The long shaft of a dory leaned diagonally against it. The man behind the counter set the cooked leg of the humongous bird he was eating down and pulled what looked like a flat carpenter's pencil from behind his ear. He finished chewing and pulled a clipboard from the countertop.

Flipping through several top sheets, he raised his eyes to Josh and Sen and said, "I'm Achilles ... you guys looking for the storeroom?"

Josh's mouth hung open, and he said the first thing his knee-jerk reaction brain forced out of his throat. "You ... you are ... *the* Achilles ... from Troy ... *that* Achilles?"

Achilles stood up so fast that his stool shot out from under him and flew off into the distance. Then out of sight.

Pointing his finger at Josh, waves of force seemed to radiate from its tip. "Listen, mister..." A pained look of remembrance came over his face. "Troy was a low point and a long time ago for me... okay? Gaia pulled me out of there and gave me this gig protecting her storeroom..." He looked around at the vast spaces around him. "For which I am very grateful... so..." He pursed his lips and made a fist with his right hand that space seemed to shrink and solidify around. "What can I do you two for?"

Realizing that he was on the verge of pissing off, past the point of no return, an immensely powerful demi-human hero that could likely turn them both into grease spots without even breaking a sweat, Josh reapplied the capacity of intelligent thought to his mouth—or at least he tried. "Ahh... sorry about that... *really... really sorry!* Gaia sent us to get some things that her kids used... when they were kids. Swords and things... said to tell the custodian Gaia said so... I'm guessing that's you... um... Achilles..." Josh trailed off, squinting his eyes and ever-so-slightly turning away in preparation for the pain that was sure to come.

But Achilles . . . apparently placated by the apology—and the fact that they had real business there—pursed his lips and nodded.

Snapping his fingers, he sat back down on his now rematerialized stool. "Why didn't you say so in the first place? Let me scan your tags . . . one sec." He held his hand up to the bronze brooches, clasping their capes, and flipped through his clipboard again. "Okay . . . that's a box that has been down here for a while. It's in the back . . . I'm uploading its location into your interfaces. Take a look at your interface map. But . . . are you sure about this? For two guys . . . with your . . . limitations . . . it might be tough."

"Tough?" Josh and Sen both said in unison.

"Hey . . . listen, it's not my place to tell you guys your business . . . but take a look over my shoulder . . . there is a kraken loose five aisles down." He pointed over his shoulder with his thumb to a mass of giant tentacles waving over an impossibly high self, grabbing things at random and in an alternating pattern of crushing them and flinging them over the horizon. "A flock of Badger-Phoenix got loose this morning, and the animal guys haven't gotten them under control yet." Another thumb over his shoulder, and they saw faint lines of smoke rising even further in the distance than the tentacles. "And we've been having a rash of draugr popping up all over the place the last few days. On top of that . . . everything in this place *can,* and many *want* to kill you . . . dead."

Josh and Sen blanched at the picture Achilles had just painted for them. But there was no question they needed the weapons if they were going to face the chimera.

Sen spoke first. "We really need what is in that box . . . without it, we will likely fail against the chimera . . . and I will break a promise to get my friend back to his daughter . . . we have to try. Is there no way . . ."

Achilles scowled and seemed on the verge of sending them packing when he puffed his cheeks and blew a breath out, tossing his clipboard down on the countertop. "Cry me a pota'mi, why don't you. His kid?" He pointed at Josh.

When they both nodded, he shook his head once.

Sighing, he said, "Let me see what I can do..."

A map appeared of a vast area, seemingly taken from a satellite in low orbit. It zoomed in, zoomed in, and zoomed in again until Josh and Sen could see city-block-sized areas of shelves. "Your box is here... I can get you here..." Two points of golden light appeared approximately two blocks apart. "I'm going to color code the area based on Essence density... anything in red is a no-go zone for you guys... guaranteed *Thanatos*... you get me?"

They both nodded.

"Anything in yellow... I would really avoid. You want to stay in the green areas... believe me on this. I can leave the temp portal up for twenty minutes... you guys gotta be quick, right?"

Sen and Josh swallowed a hard lump in their throats and nodded again.

"Here... I'm sending it over to your interfaces. Good luck." He waved his hand, and their interfaces chimed.

Color-coded Threat Assessment Map Received. Display?

They both selected *yes*. And true to his word, Achilles's map showed a very narrow and winding path of green through an ocean of red with what looked like small islands of yellow across the two blocks of shelves. They would have to pick their way through the middle of the stacks in one place.

"Guys! The clock is ticking on this maintenance portal... get a move on!"

A miniature portal appeared to their left, and they both jumped through after fiercely thanking Achilles, who smiled warmly at them. "I'd do the same for my kids, go be a good dad."

And then they were in the stacks of shelves. The wild cry of animals could be heard in the distance, and a humid pressure settled around them like it was going to rain. Before looking around, they noticed that the interface had shrunken Achilles's map to one-eighth of their visual field and decreased its opacity so it could be seen through. There was also conveniently located a timer counting back from twenty minutes, now at 19:45, and dropping.

Finally, looking around, they were standing in a narrow green area, and their trail led off to the left and around the corner of a large shelf. They followed it, tensing up at every sound and expecting the group to swallow them . . . nothing jumped out at them. Soon, they were moving quickly along the path laid out.

Myriad items lay on the shelves, from the normal to the seemingly impossible. Rows of simple glazed terra-cotta pottery that Josh had seen Miranda use in their yard in Florida. Others with pottery of every color, highly detailed with intricate inlaid mosaics that shifted as he and Sen passed. The scenes changed from green pastoral vistas to raging seas with sailors struggling to overcome the tempest in their single-masted, oar-driven vessels. Some others had mundane but elegantly painted scenes that Josh had seen on display in museums.

There were tools of all types, made from all metals, for all purposes. Topless boxes filled with heavy bronze needles for sewing. A stone bench littered with worn iron adz. Off to one side, there was a solid gold mining pick displayed on a stand that gave off a ringing crystal sound that seemed to be warning them away. It rose as they neared it. Lessened as they backed away.

There were entire sections of sculptures. From tiny soapstone figurines to what might have been a bronze foot from the Colossus of Rhodes.

At one point, they had to go under a gap that appeared between the shelves . . . like a massive beast had crawled out of its resting place on ground level and taken to the sky. Coincidentally, they were also at the closest point they would come to a red area. And it was no secret what it was. On its own shelf thirty yards off the ground, seated upon a pedestal, was a vague face carved from simple volcanic stone. It radiated menace in a visible black hue from its crudely carved eye sockets. Even at this distance, considered green by Achilles, it made their ears and eyes bleed. Cycling Essence to repair the damage, they fled at double time. Once they were 100 yards away, their sense of doom faded as they were hurrying past a pantheon of greater-than-life-sized gods and heroes carved to fine detail in the purest white Carrara marble. The statues' faces and eyes seemed to follow and track Josh and Sen as they sped past.

Ducking under the rowing oars of a Viking longboat hovering above the center of the last aisle they had to pass down, they came to the blinking dot Achilles had placed on their map. Still, it was an astronomically vast space, and they weren't even sure what the box looked like. Hopefully, it was on the bottom level... or they would have to climb, and the clock was ticking down. 14:58 as Josh checked his interface.

They spread out and hectically looked at everything in their eyesight. Sen spotted it first. A high-quality closed wooden box sat alone on a bottom shelf to their right. The items above it were a rack of paintings from what must have been renaissance masters and a hutch containing tableware. The plates looked like they had been shattered and glued back together with iridescent gold. They glowed along their repaired cracks even in full light. The knives and forks in the set rose up from the trays they lay in and assumed defensive positions as Josh and Sen walked up.

Backing away from the sapient utensils, the men instead focused on the box.

A single line was written on its top in English, plain as day.

CHILDREN'S THINGS

Josh asked about the words being in English. Sen said it was written in Polar Neutral cuneiform for him, settling the issue of whether or not their interface was translating for them.

Sen lifted the lid on the large rectangular box. Inside was what one would expect to find in any parents' attic whose children had grown and moved on. Old clothing, some thick for warmth, some thinner for summer use. There were pastel-chalk pictures of the sky and the earth and twelve children running through fields of waving grain. There were several wooden toys, models of boats, and carved animals. In a smaller separate box that Josh lifted out, there were the heads of twelve throwing spears, each in its own felt-laden indentation. They were much narrower than the heads of the dorys seen so far. Their bright bronze tips with serrated teeth on the bottom gleamed from the overhead sunlight. Josh and Sen felt a strong sense of destruction and unmatched sharpness emitting from the weapons.

Urged beyond temptation by the strength of the weapons, Josh picked one up ... "*Yaoooowwww!*" He immediately regretted it.

After touching it, all of the free Essence in his meridians siphoned into the spear tip. In the one second it took him to let go of the weapon, he had also lost 2 percent of his dedicated core Essence. The central figure now read 47 percent, down from 49 percent.

One side benefit of this debacle was the confirmation of his thoughts about the possibility of withdrawing Essence from his core in an emergency. The event also raised his free Essence from 54 percent to 89 percent through the forced transfer. But the loss of the dedicated Essence still stung. On top of that, his hand had suffered second and third-degree burns, and he started circulating his free Essence to the charred and throbbing appendage.

Sen, who had also been reaching for another spear tip, saw what happened to Josh and pulled his hand back like it was on fire. It almost had been, Josh thought darkly as he laughed through the pain.

A fearful look of realization came over Sen. "These are enhanced weapons of power for warriors who have advanced their physical and spiritual unity much farther than we have. Perhaps the Titans' second weapons as teenagers? Regardless, these weapons require a constant stream of Essence to function and are beyond our ability to use now ... and perhaps for quite a while."

Josh agreed as he related to Sen what he had discovered about Essence withdrawal from his consolidated core. Sen nodded in appreciation, confirming what he had been expecting as well.

They quickly checked the timer showing they still had 13:21 to return to the portal and kept looking through the box.

The weapons they were looking for were in the bottom corner, carefully wrapped in individual linen squares. Twelve swords and twelve spearheads. Largely blunted and dulled with age, their color long ago faded from bright to blotchy dross and nothing compared to the throwing spears. But, compared to the draugr weapons, they were a definite improvement. Neither the swords nor the spearheads radiated any sense of damage, death, or unearthly sharpness.

Sen picked up one of the swords and executed a mixture of quick foot forms and blade maneuvers. "These are perfectly balanced. Furthermore, the upgrade on my interface..." Sen smirked in satisfaction. "Is telling."

Weapon: Titan Short Sword	Quality: Mundane masterwork. Increasing quality of weapon will increase damage.
Skill Level: Advanced	Allows interface guidance for optimal usage.
Damage: Superior mundane	100% probability of 1500% increased damage vs. hand-to-hand damage. Increasing skill level will increase damage capabilities.

Josh related his upgrade, too.

Weapon: Titan Short Sword	Quality: Mundane masterwork. Increasing quality of weapon will increase damage.
Skill Level: None	-
Damage: Low mundane	100% probability of 480% percent increased damage vs. hand-to-hand damage. Increasing skill level will increase damage capabilities.

There was also a bag with a single shoulder strap made of faded-black leather, but it was still serviceable. Not wanting to leave a possible needed weapon behind, Josh also put two of the spearheads inside the bag. He then placed it over his head and under his left shoulder. There were no shafts to affix them or tools to do it with. But it just seemed stupid to leave them behind as Gaia had said they were welcome to them.

Finishing with the chest, Josh picked up his sword with a slight sense of awe. A Titan had used this … "Not bad!" Josh said to himself.

He started brandishing the sword with increasing exuberance. Josh even began to take some practice swings with the weapon. Sen backed out of his way to avoid having his limbs severed by the apparent ineptitude.

Screwing his courage to the sticking point, Sen stepped forward and bowed to Josh. He waved for Josh to stop.

Then, Sen spoke difficult words. "Brother, we are in a rush now, and there is no time. But as soon as we get out of here, I will teach you the basics. Just promise me you will never swing a sword in front of anyone but me until I do. I would spare you that shame."

Josh cast a sullen glare at Sen. "…"

———————————✶———————————

They retraced their steps to the portal without further incident. Josh silently fumed from Sen's well-meaning rebuke. Upon returning to the portal with 2:45 left, they went through and noticed that Achilles's post was empty. A small sign on the countertop read—

Back in 15 ... Dealing with Kraken.
Please wait here.

They could no longer see the tentacles above the shelves ... but the sounds of crashing and the heavy distant thuds of large objects impacting the ground after a high fall filled the air. Silently wishing him luck ... but doubting he really needed it ... they exited through the entry portal they had first entered and reentered the landing where they had faced the draugrs.

CHAPTER 17

———————✦———————

A Rose by Any Other Name...

HIS PRIDE stinging more than his recent third-degree burn, Josh demanded that Sen show him the very first basics any child would learn during their first hour of sword instruction, right there and then. Partly to say he knew something about the sword. But mostly because they would face a chimera in the next room. Perhaps any knowledge Sen could impart in that time would be better than Josh fighting like a currently seizing epileptic having a fit while holding a sword in his hand. Sen had agreed to the demand.

They stepped out through the door, and the foyer was the same as when they had left save the fallen draugr archers were now gone. If the bodies had faded as a property of undeath, or Gaia's basement had some supernatural cleaning function ... or, perhaps, they had gotten up and walked away. Josh had no clue. Sen showed no sign of concern, so Josh didn't worry about it.

The Tartarus door was no longer clacking and banging. But there was still a low-level calling, which Josh appreciated more than Sen. Josh was still able to tune it out and turned to Sen.

Josh started their lesson with narrowed eyes and a sullen expression. "Okay, Zatoichi... start teaching!" He stood with his feet apart, white-knuckling his sword in a closed fist.

Sen looked confused for a second at Josh's words. "How do you know of Zatoichi, the Blind Swordsman? The multiversal weapons master of all arms, renown even in Immortal circles ..." Sen saved any further quandary for later and stepped into the role of a teacher as Josh remained silent and stared intensely at him. He kneeled; opening his hands in a welcoming gesture, and said, "Put your sword down and kneel with me."

Josh hesitated, waving the sword trapped in his death grip back and forth as he shuffled to a place in front of Sen.

Sen raised his eyes to pierce Josh's without moving his head and spoke clearly and loudly again. "*Kneel*... Using a sword is a sacred art! Not one to be taken lightly! If you insist on being my student, you will show me the respect I've shown my instructors for millions of years."

It was Josh's turn to feel Sen's intensity through their Karmic Bond. This was obviously something he believed in down to his core. Josh would, of course, respect it.

Setting the sword down, he kneeled in front of Sen. His head and eyes were downcast out of respect, and he was a bit ashamed of having driven Sen to raise his voice to get the respect he deserved.

"Understand. I have approximately ten years of study with the weapon you call the sword. I have also trained the same amount of time in most of your hand-to-hand martial styles, small blades, polearms, firearms, energy weapons, and neural infusers. Some of these are after your time in the local cuboidal's time stream.

"But I can teach you the basics. To master the sword, you must use it as an extension of your body. Just as you would your arms, legs, hands, or other parts. Now, I have seen you use your fists well. As well as swing your club and even your ... *case of briefs* ... when it counted." He looked Josh straight in his eyes and cocked his head to make his point. "Would you wave your arm, leg, or case of briefs as you have that sword?"

"No, I wouldn't . . ." Josh said, feeling more embarrassed than he had expected.

"Good! This is the right way to start!"

———————————✦———————————

Over the next hour, Sen instructed Josh on the proper way to hold his sword as an extension of his body. To keep his sword in a rigid line from his hand to its tip. Josh learned what the basic stances were and how to use them. *Plow.* The middle stance for a general approach to all fights. *The Ox.* Outside high horizontal pointing for shorter targets. *Fool.* Low stance for taller targets and low blocking from compact targets. *Roof.* High for blocking high from all opponents and those who simply preferred holding their sword high. Josh also learned how to position his feet during each of these stances. And, until they had more time, Josh would be best served to keep his feet shoulder-width apart while wielding his sword. He should swing his sword in the mid-range or with an upswing to handle all targets as tall or taller than him.

After their session, sweat soaked Josh's linens. Small puddles had collected under him on the marble floor. But now, instead of shame when he looked at his sword, he felt a growing challenge to master it. That, and gratitude towards his Karmic brother for dealing with his arrogance and wounded pride. Josh bowed deeply from his kneeling position at the end of the lesson.

Bowing his head in return, Sen replied, "Well done, Paddle Juan."

"Paddle Juan?" Josh cocked his head to the side like a confused pigeon trying to make the connection.

A worried look came over Sen's face and through the Bond. "Do I misremember the historical records I watched with Damni? If I did, I'm sorry . . . It was from a long time ago in a galaxy far, far away. It involved young students under powerful mortals learning to use plasma blades along with telekinetic and other mental powers. They dressed just like my father and grandfather... so I watched all eighty-six records from the time stream of your iteration?"

Through their Bond, Josh could feel Sen had meant what he said as a term of respect for his progress in so short a time.

Josh replied with a crooked smile. "No, Sen. You remembered it perfectly." Josh rose as a student, again bowing at the waist. Once on his feet, he grasped forearms with his brother. "I am very grateful for what you have taught me ... but I will need more."

"And I will teach you. You will grow in your knowledge and skill ... and we will reach Sophie. I know it weighs heavily on you. But we will." Sen spoke aloud, leveling as resolute a look at Josh as he had seen on his Karmic brother's face.

Josh's interface pinged. Checking it revealed a happy surprise—

Weapon: Titan Short Sword	Quality: Mundane masterwork. Increasing quality of weapon will increase damage.
Skill Level: None → Junior Basic (2%)	Allows interface guidance for optimal usage.
Damage: Below average	100% probability of 685% increased damage vs. hand-to-hand damage. Increasing skill level will increase damage capabilities.

The upgrade was significant. Furthermore, Josh's life had no room for wounded pride any longer. Certainly not over snippy titles for skill levels coming at him from out of the ether.

"I'll take it!" he said with a full smile.

———————————✳———————————

Standing together on the landing, they looked at the barred door. Behind it was their Earth Attunement. They knew it ... and they needed it.

The plan was for Josh to lift the bar and open the door. Sen would move in first and confront what was in there. If there was a chance to talk, spy, creep around, or reach a diplomatic solution over limoncello—great! Sen would be ready to "tank" whatever was facing them if not. Josh would strike at every opportunity until it was dead.

Reaching out with both of his hands, Josh moved to lift the crossbar... and the clacking from behind the Tartarus portal erupted fiercely. On top of that, the *draw* calling Josh to walk through the portal doubled. Josh honestly believed something very wrong would happen unless he went through the Tartarus portal. They didn't need to just go there first... they needed to go there *right now*! Sen, who had been less sensitive to its calling, seemed significantly more affected now. Josh had his hands on the crossbar when Sen looked up at him with a worried expression.

"Brother... should we at least check?"

"I don't know, Sen. Tartarus is described as a place like ... hell ..."

Sen looked confused, clearly not aware of the concept. Josh also got the same feeling of unknowing confusion through their Karmic Bond. *Weird to have no concept of hell. Just imagine it.*

"It's an awful place where only terrible people go. The Titans, Gaia's first children, were held there for a long time. Gaia's grandson, Zeus, eventually let them out ... I don't know who could be calling from there."

As Josh stared at the portal, for a reason that he couldn't explain, one of his favorite lines from Tolkien crossed his mind. *"A chance for Faramir, Captain of Gondor, to show his quality."*

Josh remembered reading Tolkien's trilogy when he was thirteen years old. One of the very few things that his father had encouraged him to do. Reading the *Lord of the Rings* was one of the few good things he associated with his father ... consciously putting his daddy issues aside, he refocused on Faramir ...

Faramir had been in a position to further his own cause. To make things significantly better for himself. But he would be screwing everyone else in the process, and Faramir knew it. There he sat with his choice. With absolutely everything up to him ... and he made the right one ... and it had made all the difference.

In his heart, Josh didn't compare himself to an epic hero in a tragic tale of good versus ultimate evil. Yet, Josh was here, hanging out in the downstairs landing of the mother of the Earth after raiding her basement for the Titans' first baby weapons. Maybe it wasn't that much of a stretch after all ...

He and Sen needed the Earth Crystals behind door number one. It was step *numero uno* for him to get back to Sophie and for Sen to make it back to Transcendence. Yet Josh could not shake the certainty that *everything right to do* was behind door number two.

What the hell ... he probably should have been killed by Brundox ... or against the cannibals ... or by the draugr ... What did he have to lose now?

Nod. ~*This is probably going to bite us on the ass, Sen.*~

Nod. ~*Agreed.*~

Turning ninety degrees, they went through the portal to Tartarus.

The portal trip this time was decidedly different. Instead of feeling no discernible change from one step to the next, this trip was more like being strained through a colander with holes lined with razor wire.

Sen had stepped through first. To Josh, it seemed as if Sen's body stretched out from where it crossed the portal's threshold into infinity. His leading leg accelerated at incredible speeds while the rest of him stayed behind on the landing until that part passed the portal's sill. The theoretical model of an object passing the event horizon of a singularity came immediately to mind. Then Josh felt an aching pain in his core and the center of his mind ... along with, for lack of better words, a sense of dread for his Karmic brother.

Without thinking, Josh jumped through behind Sen. Whatever it was would at least have to deal with Josh's short sword upside its head as it took them both down. But they would go together. Upon crossing the threshold, the problem immediately made itself apparent. Not only did it look like passing an event horizon. It *felt* like going through one and still being alive. As if he was being pulled through the eye of an infinitely long needle.

Josh immediately cycled Essence to his whole body to help deal with the strain and heal his wounds. The difficulty was compounded by the fact that it was taking a much longer time to transit this portal than it had the storeroom. Whatever spiritual machinery was running the Tartarus portal was on its last legs.

What felt like an hour and ten minutes later, but was likely only a fraction of a second, had Josh getting spit out onto a barren landscape with dark and forbidding shadows at every corner. There was no discernible light source to be seen. Just a low-level illumination from everywhere and nowhere. After being forced out of the portal, Josh was sent tumbling over shards of igneous rocks like broken glass. Ultimately, he came to rest by crashing into the rising form of Sen.

Sen again pulled himself up and lent a hand to Josh. A stabbing pain told Josh he had gotten a twisted ankle rolling across the ground. Sen looked like he was in about the same shape.

While panting and cycling Essence to heal their wounds, they looked around at their surroundings. Several things came into sharp focus. Multiple shield volcanoes dotted the landscape in front of, to the sides ... and in fact, all around them ... *Everywhere*! And worse, said volcanos were *all* simultaneously going through the final stages leading to pyroclastic eruption. Multiple dome failures were evident, with sporadic ash and magma explosions above many rims and visible clefts in the volcanos' sidewalls. The air was already thick with dust and ash. It was getting harder to breathe by the second, and Josh's super-science-know-how was telling him in no uncertain terms that it had been a nice trip ... *but it was time to go!*

A deep voice spoke from behind them. "This pocket is ending ..."

Josh and Sen spun together as one. Seeing first, immediately behind them, a large cage. It was one hundred meters to the side and fifty meters high. Thick, overlapping iron bars ran horizontally and vertically, creating squares along the cage's faces. A shining steel door five meters wide sat court in its center. The cell was built into the corner of a cliff with perpendicular angles to the rear.

A man of solid build and average height stood facing them from the middle of the cage. Appearing to be in his late thirties, he wore his dark hair short, had a well-trimmed beard, and clothes that were similar to theirs. But it was impossible not to notice that his vestments had gold trimming in all the right places. He was also sporting a gilded laurel wreath tucked behind his ears as a crown.

But most notable was that despite standing amongst the end-stages of ... well ... *everything* ... the man was poised as the very image of calm and collected. His hands were held behind his back. His face had a superior expression, and he seemed to be entirely at leisure.

"I am Cronus. It appears my children have forgotten me after releasing my brothers and sisters ... it must be several millennia ago at this point ... would you be so kind as to pull that lever to the left and release me. The glyphs on this cage are preventing me from otherwise evacuating." Cronus raised his hand and waved nonchalantly to the numerous early-stage pyroclastic eruptions.

Simultaneously, a long string of icons lit up on either side of the door's frame, glistening green and gold as if to make his point. Josh had no idea what the sigils meant individually. Translating them was most likely beyond his interface's current abilities.

Sen straightened and started walking over to the massive lever. It was topped with a large gold ball attached to a bronze rod rising directly from the ground. Josh also couldn't help but notice it was just out of arm's reach of someone trapped in the cage. Some sadistic piece of work had built this thing.

Josh held up his hands to stop Sen. "Whoa, whoa! Sen, this is Cronus! You know, one of the classic bad guys. Child eating ... father maiming ... we should think about the ramifications of letting him out ..."

A small smile touched the corners of Cronus's mouth. "You know your history very well. But, please, do remember that history is written by the victors. I'm not as bad as all that. People are never as good as they say they are *or as bad* as you are led to believe by their enemies ... I would think that a young vampire who just finished raiding my childhood toybox would be well served to keep that in mind." Cronus finished with a superior expression, cocking his right brow.

"Gaia gave us permission to take these." Josh pointed at the swords. "And we are cultivators, not vampires."

"Tomato ... tomahto ..." Cronus's smile grew slightly, knowing his point had been made.

Before Josh got to unleash what would certainly been a multiversal devastating reply to the king of the Titans, the air pressure noticeably dropped around them. As if the whole dimension was inhaling an immeasurable breath. Then the ground shuddered in every direction as a loud and steadily increasing rumbling sound filled their ears. All three of them looked around for the causative source. With wide-eyed horror, they watched several of the more advanced and, unfortunately, closer volcanoes starting up frank pyroclastic eruptions. For the first time in a while, Josh was decidedly unhappy with knowing what he knew about the basic science of such eruptions.

For instance, first, there would be a rapidly expanding and superheated gas cloud, greater than 752 degrees Fahrenheit, moving toward them faster than Tomahawk missile. He, Sen, and likely Cronus would be incinerated a long time before the much slower-moving tsunamis of lava got to them. But they might last long enough for the overhead-rocketing boulders to crash into them and the surrounding area, obliterating everything larger than a pocket watch. Josh could see that many such boulders above them were the size of aircraft carriers and already arching through the air to detonate the entire area where they stood.

Even Cronus's ice-cold demeanor was slightly shaken at the new circumstances. With his smile faltering, he started speaking marginally faster. "Very well. I, Cronus, King of the Titans, promise to do no harm to either of you, your families, clans, or city-states."

Josh's eyes narrowed.

Cronus quickly added, "And to do no injustice to those who locked me up and left me to ultimate destruction."

Sensing the Titan's desperation, Josh knew that was as good as any promise they would get if they were all going to get out alive.

Sen must have felt Joshua's agreement through the Bond, because he pulled the lever, straining with his fully enhanced strength. As it locked into place, the bronze gate ponderously started to slide from the left to the right along a track on Cronus's side of the bars. It took two full seconds. A length of time that all three of them felt was intolerably long as the sky grew darker and darker, obstructed by gas clouds and hurtling debris. The launched rocks, trailing burning pitch and smoke, were well past the peaks of their arcs when the door opened enough for Cronus to step through sideways.

But, once through, Cronus's return to full Titan power could be palpated. Even against the raging destruction all around them, Cronus's aura emitted what could only be described as a gravitational pull. It was almost more fearsome than the falling rocks above their heads. He seemed . . . *more real* than the failing dimension they stood in.

Still, Josh met Cronus's eyes while Sen pulled Josh back to the wavering portal exit thirty feet away. "See that you keep your word to us!" Josh yelled over the deafening sounds of the continued explosions.

Cronus, who was in the midst of performing a series of complicated hand movements, warping space around himself in concentric circles, stopped and shot a piercing glance at Josh through the shockwaves and ash. *"You stand before Cronus. First and last of the Titans. I swear I will honor my word by my father the sky and my mother the earth below him."* He continued to speak as he made a quick gesture of rolling his right wrist toward them. "Take this as a sign of our covenant!"

Josh partially saw a flash over his right shoulder, then Cronus finished with a brisk clenching of his right fist and was gone from the world. An instant later, Sen managed to push both of them through the flickering portal. At the same time, the first of the volcanic detritus crashed and starting impact detonations where Josh and Sen had stood a microsecond before.

No one remained in Tartarus to see the portal they had fallen through, along with everything else, destroyed by the crashing of mountains and fire.

Wherever he was, Cronus did take the time to send one last message directly to Josh and Sen. *"Test me again, young vampire, and there will be an accounting between us ... Joshua Elias Tanner."*

CHAPTER 18

---★---

Hegemon-4

FOR THE second time in five minutes, Sen and Josh were rolling across the ground together. A cloud of dirt, ash, and stinging rock shards caused by the impacting explosions on the Tartarus side of the portal followed them through transit. Hazy dust lingered in the air of the landing as they slid across the floor and impacted the wall on the far side of the portal. Shakily, they rose to their feet, checking for missing appendages and other signs of the cataclysm they had just escaped. With a dim flickering, the Tartarus portal guttered and ... went out? In its place, only a solid white marble wall remained. The lettering above the door had vanished as well. Like it had never been there.

Still catching his breath, Josh grunted incredulously at what could have been their fate if they had been even one second slower. Eyes wide and stupefied beyond the ability of coherent speech, Josh nodded jerkily to the missing portal. ~*You see that?*~

Sen nodded. ~*Way too close, brother ... way too close!*~

Achilles stuck his head through the storeroom's portal, fully armored, with dory in hand. After a quick glance at the empty wall where the

Tartarus portal used to be, seeing that the only remaining ruckus was Josh and Sen on the floor among the rocks and ash, he closed his eyes and shook his head once. Turning in a blur of steel, he went back to his post . . . clearly deciding he didn't want anything to do with whatever they had been up to.

Josh couldn't disagree with his discretion . . . very wise . . .

Continuing his pat down of himself, Josh touched the brooch on his right shoulder that held his cloak—his chlamys—in its place. Cronus had . . . changed it. Josh then recalled the flash on his right shoulder as they ran for their lives for the portal.

His hand nudged the deep orange crystal embedded into the gold of the new clasp—and his interface chimed.

Item of Power obtained.

Item of Power:	100% probability of increasing your
Gaia's Earth Crystal	health status by 5,000%.
Quality:	100% probability of increasing the mo-
Unique	lecular density of your connective tissue
Will provide:	by 780%.
Earth Attunement	An increased probability of being able to
of your core.	manipulate Earth Essence outside your
	meridians.
	Further increase your health status
	and density by increasing your level and
	cultivation.

You do not yet have this Attunement. Do you wish to absorb Gaia's Earth Crystal?

Josh looked to Sen. ~*Did you get a notice for the Earth Crystal?*~
Sen smiled back. ~*Yes, I did!*~
"That arrogant prick Cronus wasn't such a prick, was he?"
Sen smiled and spoke through a chuckle. "I kind of liked him!"

"Right now, he's one of my favorite people too! Let's absorb this thing in shifts."

"Do not attempt to absorb the Item of Power here. Your Attunement will require many hours of cultivation, expansion, and augmentation of your core.

"Yes, Joshua Elias Tanner, you are damn lucky you didn't have to fight the chimera guardian to access the Earth Crystal cave. Probability predictions only granted you and Senyak a twenty-two percent chance to succeed based on your current cultivation, equipment, and skills."

The Clone had appeared directly in front of them. The ultraviolet fractals providing its form and facial features continued to twinkle and resolve infinitely, creating endless cycles of growing and simultaneously diminishing lines. And he was, as usual, answering unspoken questions from Josh's mind. When he chose to . . .

We must away.

———————*———————

Sen and Josh reappeared seated in firm but comfortable chairs in a compartment the size of a minibus. Two seats at the front and several fold-down jump seats lining each of the opposing walls filled the remainder of the space. But that was where the resemblance to any Earth-bound vehicle ended. The two seats at the front of the compartment were obviously for a pilot and copilot. Both were filled by spirit beings sitting in them and making adjustments to instruments while taking orders from the Clone. The pilots were dressed in blue and silver with a body habitus that reminded Josh of the flashes he had seen of Damni. Their telescoping necks waved as if pulled by an invisible, gently surging tide, and they had slim frames with long, weedy limbs to work the consoles.

I'm in a spaceship! A deduction Josh couldn't miss given that the forward view screen showed the shuttle they were in accelerating past

Jupiter and three of its larger moons. The celestial objects crossed the screen in less than five seconds.

Given how fast Jupiter left the viewer, the shuttle had to be traveling a fraction of the speed of light. A significant fraction of the speed of light! Josh looked at Sen seated across the shuttle opposite him and couldn't keep the childish smile from his face. "Space, Sen! We're in space!"

"Yes, Joshua . . ." He stifled a yawn with the back of his hand. "This is where I spend most of my time in mortal iterations . . . until recently, anyway." He showed a definite lower index of excitement compared to Josh's glee-faced goggling.

The pilots executed a sequence of instrument commands, and the forward viewer went from the fixed light of stars piercing the black veil of the surrounding space to streaks of light all around them.

"Light speed! Did we just jump to light speed?" Josh blurted out, reaching across the aisle to violently shake Sen's knee, forcing him to open his eyes and respond.

"Most likely, Joshua. It would take forever to get anywhere without it. Let's talk more when we arrive—" He yawned . . . again. "Shall we?" Sen closed his eyes and turned toward the back of the shuttle.

Josh was already back to intently staring out the forward view screen. Too excited to notice Sen's brushoff. Well, they could be anywhere now . . . Who knew how many multiples of the speed of light they were going. Were they outside of the solar system at this point? It would take light roughly five and a half hours to leave the solar system from the sun . . . about five hours from the location near Jupiter where they started.

For the first time, Josh consciously delved into his scientific mind boost. Current Earth theory was that it would be almost impossible to see anything when traveling beyond light's speed. Because . . . refracted light off an object couldn't reach your eyes. It would require overcoming or intercepting a stream of reflected photons to actually see anything . . . but that didn't stop Josh from looking. Maybe he could pick up some random space creature's Essence-trail outside the theories of particle and wave physics ... *Then again, maybe humans at my place in the time stream don't know squat about speeds greater than light speed, and I should keep looking to check for myself, huh?*

His brain told him that if they were outside the solar system, it would be next to impossible to see anything at any speed other than the periodic comet orbiting in the Ort Cloud every five to one hundred years ... approximately. The nearest star to the sun was Alpha Centauri, more than 4.367 lightyears away after all ... there was just not much going on outside Pluto's orbital ring ...

Josh let out a frustrated breath. Now, he wished his science brain would just shut up. Shut up and let him be excited about being in space!

C'mon! Let's see some giant space manta sailing along the solar winds. Maybe some lost civilization living on undiscovered asteroids hurtling through the darkest parts of the cosmos ... A never detected dark-matter oasis, carrying unknown kinds of life!

In minutes, they dropped out of light speed. The view screen went back to the usual glistening star dots. And Josh was pretty sure they were back to normal, sub-light speeds. At this point, the view screen confirmed that Josh's mind had been right. Presently, the only thing moving into view was a growing speck of light against the constant and unchanging star-studded background.

Josh was hardly disappointed, however. The light was steadily growing larger ... and larger ... into a spaceship of absolutely massive proportions. Taking the ship in as they drew nearer, it had an overall sleek design. If something the size of Africa could be considered sleek. Five engines, arranged in a circular configuration, and gigantic on a scale Josh could not wrap his head around, glowed electric blue at the stern of the ship. The color made Josh think of the engines on a Star Destroyer. Just ... much larger.

Moving forward toward the bow, the next section was the wide end of a *V*, narrowing down to a waistline near the center of the ship. From there, the ship's body formed into another *V* with the wide end at the bow. On either side of the bow were moderately sized bulky forward sections about half the size of the forward *V*. Both were mounted on the top of the forward section's superstructure.

The shuttle started to decelerate as they neared the ship. Josh could see the ship's name, *Hegemon-4*, written in neat block letters along the port wall. They pulled up onside and got in front of the line with tens of thousands of other ships moving to enter one of the thousands of hangers that Josh could make out from his position. His line of sight along the ship stretched until the entering shuttles, and other vessels, were tiny dots of light moving like gnats under a porch light. All the ships seemed to be scurrying in simultaneously to get back aboard.

The Clone had been speaking to the pilots. Now he turned and joined Sen and Josh in the middle of the shuttle. Electing not to sit, he stood several feet in front of them.

"We are boarding. The *Hegemon-4* will be underway when all support staff have boarded. Once aboard, we will begin attuning your cores to the Earth Crystals you have obtained. We will use our time now to review your performance in Gaia's Temple.

"Your mission was a success." The Clone rolled his eyes. "Barely . . . More due to your logical reasoning and just plain dumb luck than any prowess as cultivators or warriors. Whoever said it was better to be lucky than good was wrong. You need to be both lucky and good if you want any chance to survive your ascendance.

"Your Essence application and prowess as combatants is disorganized, noneffective, and pathetic.

"However, now that you have proven worthy of the investment by retrieving your first Attunement, we will advance both here enroute to your next Attunement.

"And yes, Joshua Elias Tanner, this is the fourth produced Hegemon-class ark-cruiser. Zenyak has created over two thousand of these ships in the mortal iterations. They were constructed and used prior to his

Transcendence. The vessels of the Hegemon fleet have varying levels of cultivation aptitude. The *Hegemon-4* is an entirely mundane category vessel. You two are the only active cultivators aboard."

The Clone took on a whimsical air as he tilted his eyes to the heavens. "The multiverse is a vast place. Some trinkets, even mundane ones, come in handy here, given the requirements of actual physical bodies in the prime material iterations. The Hegemon-class cruisers have been reactivated of late as Zenyak spends more time away from the central Immortal iterations. This one was detailed to us as it was closest.

"On the seats in the rear of this shuttle is proper attire. Change and discard what you are wearing. Keep the brooches, your swords . . . and . . ." The Clone hesitated for the briefest of seconds as he scrutinized the bag. "And that bag. You earned the swords. That bag will be useful. Do so now."

Josh and Sen disrobed as the shuttle went through its final docking procedures. Each donned a one-piece jumper in blue and silver like the pilots. The jumpsuit zipped up from the side under their left arm and had built-in, rubberized-padded soles, obviating the need for independent footwear.

There was one spare onesie for each of them. Josh put them in his leather bag.

They left the still fragrant armor on the seats as the Clone had instructed, but Josh stuffed the linens Gaia had given him into the shoulder bag. He had thought that the linen would end up trailing out of the bag. But they seemed to take little space once he got them in. *Hey . . . waste not, want not!*

With a small metal-on-metal *clonk*, the shuttle landed, and the side hatch lifted for them to board the *Hegemon-4*. Behind them, Josh and Sen could see the myriads of support vessels lining up to dock.

They followed the Clone at several paces, which he seemed to prefer.

Josh leaned over to Sen with upraised hands, encompassing everything around them. "This is really all for us?"

"Yes ... my grandfather is one of the most powerful Immortals in Transcendence. This here is nothing to him. I assure you. I suspect it is more a lesson to me to understand the importance of mastering my mortal cultivation than anything else."

Josh could only raise his eyebrows at that. Gestures in relationships were important and gave meaning to one's efforts. Miranda hadn't even gone through the trouble to cook dinner for him in over two years. But he had to hand it to Zenyak. The grandeur of the *Hegemon-4*, and the unbelievable travail involved in making it a living, breathing, moving reality did impress Josh with the importance of what they were doing. Though he didn't really understand *why* Zenyak thought it was.

The Clone continued to lead them through long passageways. Up lifts at incredible speeds and on moving sidewalks that left the beings walking outside of it a blur. They even boarded a small flying craft at one point and flew over an internal rainforest that reached as far as their eyes could see.

They passed many crew members, in their blue and silver, manning consoles, security stations, and flight-necessary positions. Like any massive government facility, and this was the most massive Josh had ever seen, civilians were always needed to support the duty forces. They passed many humans, as well as humanoids with animal-like characteristics.

Sen told Josh they were Beast Affins. Many of them passed by. Some with rhino horns. Some with fox ears. Even some with fish gills. At least one with thick elephant-like skin on an otherwise human-looking man. And most had any number of sharp and pointed teeth on the smiles thrown his way.

There were also many more classically alien sapients and sentients going about their businesses, including tall, dark-skinned, thin-limbed beings. Turning large heads and eyes as big as baseballs toward Josh and Sen while they manned their carts and shops along the never-ending passageways.

There were short grey and green-skinned aliens who always traveled in groups of four or more. Josh was sure he had seen beings very similar on some random Area 51 show playing in the background somewhere he had been.

There were short beings with large, egg-shaped heads and no apparent necks on small bodies. They chittered to each other like insects as they walked down the passageway, carrying various items back to their restaurants or bars or, from what Josh had seen on several occasions, bordellos. He even saw a group of over 100 members, consisting of multiple visually different species in full coats and tails carrying what looked like the instruments for a complete symphony orchestra. Josh recognized some of the musical devices. Others that required multiple members to handle, he had no idea what they were.

Lastly, he noted several close-knit groups that varied in their species. But all with some type of uniting external accouterments. There was one definite group who wore robes similar to the Clone. They all donned a glistening silver ring around the back of their head that aligned with their temples. They also seemed to have the same metal covering over what might have been neurovascular pathways. Josh could see the thin-metallic lace on the exposed skin of their hands and feet. For some reason, they were all barefoot. Faintly glowing lights of different colors traversed in seemingly random pulses along the length of their neuro-conduits. Red, blue, teal, and lavender were the most common hues.

"They are the Techno Lords," Sen whispered to Josh as he noted Josh's interest.

Another group sported a glowing gem or crystal in the center of their foreheads. Whatever species they were, they all seemed to be in incredible physical shape. Muscles rippling, zero body fat, heads of glossy voluminous hair, and age-resistant, wrinkle-free skin.

"The Biologics," Sen whispered.

On three separate occasions, there were individuals surrounded by a quiet crowd of moving corpses. The nonliving beasts were harnessed with thick electronic collars connected to metal implants on their necks. Despite Josh's amazement, the shambling dead were treated with complete disinterest and accepted with no eyebrows raised by anyone.

"The Necrolons. Accepted as regular members in many mortal societies ... as long as they are collared." Sen pointed his index finger at the metal ring around the undeads' necks.

Finally, the Clone went through a security checkpoint with several heavily armed and armored crew. Sen had already told Josh they were the Jaralon, the favored race of his grandfather to crew his starship fleet. In their own communities, they lived their entire lives, from birth to death, in zero gravity. Unless they were on formal employment as here on the *Hegemon-4*.

Their surroundings began to increase in creature comforts and overall poshness. Richly carpeted floors with artwork adorning the walls. They went through a door on which the Clone placed his hand to activate some form of fractal-bio-scan. The door silently slid to the right, and they walked into what could only be described as a gymnasium. Two hundred yards to the side.

The floor was padded, with several areas marked out for differing activities and martial styles. Among them, Josh noted some areas that reminded him of boxing rings and mats for grappling. Several weighted bags hung from the walls for striking with fists and feet. Lastly, there were two cots. Each bore a thin folded silver sheet at its end with a small ten-inch pillow sitting on top.

"We shall begin."

CHAPTER 19

★

Face Hugs Anyone?

"LIE DOWN on the cots and absorb the crystals to attain your Earth Attunement."

They both lay down. Josh using his pillow, Sen not. Each reached for the brooch they had attached to their jumper and their interfaces responded.

Do you wish to absorb Gaia's Earth Crystal?

Not really a question, is it? Sen mentally selected *yes. Josh must be rubbing off on me.* His last thought as things began . . . happening.

His skin tightened and became rigid. He tried to open his eyes to see if there was a color change to his skin, but his eyelids were stiff and unyielding. His heartbeat slowed down. Breathing became impossible. His heart, lungs, and other organs became stiff and concrete in his chest and abdomen. Then he was . . . *different.*

Sen was grand and majestic. Standing in a vast field of summer flowers, bushes, and trees. Other than the sun shining down, Sen towered above all before him. Rivers flowed from him bearing salmon that jumped only to be caught by hungry bears who had been waiting. Herd animals grazed on his lower reaches. Winds howled above him, freezing the ground, along with the plants and beasts foolish enough to venture there and try to grow and live. The moon reached overhead, and bats flew from his caves to scour the night for insects and small rodents. Lions sought unwary prey on his slopes. Seasons, years, millennia, millions, and billions of rotations of the sun and moon overhead. He was unchanging, and this was as it should be. He was Earth.

The scene shifted. Sen was strong and undeniable. The mighty sea rested its great weight on him and raged as it frequently did for reasons uncertain. Always trying to escape him and his bounds. Sen easily kept even that monstrous power in its place. He was undeniable, and this was as it should be. He was Earth.

Another shift. Sen was unstoppable. It was dark, and the pressure and temperatures built to levels that could not be contained. Sen was going to move, and nothing would prevent him. He erupted from the ground announcing himself to all with the devastation of massive clouds of ash and raining boulders. He was there, first in a shower and then a wide molten river. Surging from below to cover everything and everyone who stood in his way. He was unstoppable, and this was as it should be. He was Earth.

The scene changed again. Sen was eternal. Rising from the depths, he allowed the lesser powers to wear away at him over time. He would evolve as all life did. But he only separated from his larger self in tiny fragments at a time. Even when he allowed it, this was all any of the other lesser forces could change him. Minuscule traces of him circled the world in the streams of the air and the currents of the water. Only to ultimately rejoin himself by rising once again from the core of the world. This time even more glorious than the last. Sen was everlasting. And this was as it should be. He was Earth

Yes, I am! I'm unchanging, undeniable, unstoppable, everlasting... I am Earth!

Sen sat up with a start, covered in sweat and panting.

How long have I been gone?

Assuredly his change had taken the life cycles of several iterations.

I am different.

How could he not be, given what he had learned and experienced? He was *Earth!*

Sen had learned of the perpetual nature and the unstoppable forces of Earth Attunement. He had never experienced anything that made such an impression on him while an Immortal. And this gave him pause. His grandfather was right. Knowledge of the mortal foundation of Immortality was irreplaceable and invaluable.

Josh was there and looked over in concern at the sudden angst in his Karmic bonded brother. ~*You all right?*~

Sen widened his eyes in amazement. ~*Better than all right! You?*~

Josh broadly smiled. ~*Same!*~

That was enough confirmation for Sen that he and his brother had had similar experiences in absorbing the Earth Crystal. He raised his hand and looked. His soft, pink skin was unchanged from before the Attunement. Fingers moved. Muscles and tendons flexed. But the strength he felt, along with increased resilience, was undeniable.

"Yes, Senyak, changes have occurred. Along with significantly increased physical attributes. Your core and free Essence capacities have also increased. Moreover, your Cultivation Probability Interface has matured alongside your increased spirituality.

"Inspect it now."

Body	Earth Attunement: 100% probability of increasing your health status by 5000%. 100% probability of increasing the molecular density of your connective tissue by 780%. Further increase your health status and connective tissue density by increasing your level and cultivation.
Psyche	Mortal level.
Spirit	Spherical cultivation level 48% of stage 2/7.

Weapon:
  Titan Short Sword
Skill Level:
  Advanced (84%)
Damage:
  Superior mundane
	Quality: Mundane masterwork.
	Allows interface guidance for optimal usage.
	100% probability of 1500% increased damage vs. standard hand-to-hand.

Armor: None	Standard Earth Attunement resilience.

Physical Health Status:	100 → 5000/5000 Spherical cultivation units.
Free Essence:	60 → 1200/1200 Spherical cultivation units.

Significant improvements! Sen's *health*, as Josh called it, had increased by fifty times from what it had been. And his free Essence had increased by a factor of twenty. But remembering back to his ... *vision*—seemed like the only way to describe it—he wasn't surprised. Earth was indeed mighty and glorious. The descriptor *unchanging* surfaced in his thoughts and mind ... absolutely!

The molecular density of his connective tissue was ... well, 780 percent greater. He guessed this was a lot as well. But, without his Ethos Combi, he was having trouble qualifying this quantification ...

"We're as dense as iron, brother!" Joshua shouted with the slightest gleam of madness in his eyes. "Look at this!"

And without preamble, he picked up a handheld firearm. One that Sen had actually trained with, a Glock 19, 9 mm. Sen didn't get the chance to see which generation Glock it was, as Josh had immediately jammed the pistol's muzzle in his mouth and pulled the trigger rapidly five times before Sen could get a good look. The gun's discharges echoed to the ends of the training room as Joshua, with gun smoke coming from between his teeth, smiled and spit out the flattened slugs.

"We're bulletproof, Sen! *Bulletproof*...Okay, okay! The science side of my mind is insisting I point out that armor-piercing, large caliber, and very fast-moving rounds could still penetrate through to our organs and ruin our day...But for god's sake, this is awesome! What will we be like as we continue to advance—"

"That is precisely what we are going to find out. It is time to further your spherical cultivation capacity. As you noticed, the Earth Attunement is primarily a boon to the physical side of your spiritual-physical bond. It will increase as your cultivation increases as well. The first step is to continue your core's expansion by absorbing Essence from defeated spiritual beings.

"Joshua Elias Tanner, despite your apparent shortcomings in combat capability, probability predictions are definite that your surest success will be achieved, working to increase your cultivation synchronously while Senyak instructs you with the sword. You will be continuing both.

"Your rapid response to Senyak's brief instruction was not probable. It has been determined that your shared Karmic Bond has increased your learning quotient while training under him. This will continue. Do so now."

Josh followed as Senyak rose and walked out to a marked-off area in the shape of an octagon approximately thirty feet in diameter. Sen stepped on a floor switch, and a glowing-translucent green screen closed around them. A rack of training weapons also materialized with metal handles, leather grips, and translucent-green energy blades. Josh kept all of his light-saber jokes to himself. To Senyak, weapons training was a sacred art, and Josh now paid it the respect it was due.

Sen kneeled, and Josh didn't need to be told to follow. For the next ninety minutes, Sen reviewed what they had gone over previously. Then they covered basic lunges, thrusts, and accompanying footwork. Because Joshua had absorbed what he had been shown, Sen also introduced him to the concept of leverage for the sword fighter individually and against opponents. They also covered several techniques in creating the space required for the adequate usage of leverage in various situations.

They even got into some light sparring. Sen repeatedly demonstrated in what areas Josh misunderstood the concepts of the space needed to create fighting leverage. Not only to launch his own attacks but to control his opponent's weapon. By the end of the lesson, Sen had made it painfully clear to Joshua that these skills were indispensable if he ever wanted to defeat an armed combatant.

All the work and effort was to improve Joshua's skills so Sen could help him get back to Sophie. Senyak's gleeful and repetitive sweeping of Josh's legs out from under him with the extended reach of a bo staff to ensure Josh didn't miss any of the finer points had nothing to do with their first confrontation in the alley. That would be childish and counterproductive now that they understood each other. So, Josh took the beating silently and with the sharp-eyed good nature that someday his payday might come back around ... after all, payback was a bitch, and even he acknowledged that Sen owed him one after Josh's abrupt introduction of his overhand right.

The session eventually ended with Josh on the ground panting, bruised, and aching pretty much all over, despite being bulletproof. Sen helped him up, and they concluded with a bow of student to sensei.

Josh checked his status, walking back to the front where the Clone had appeared at the close of their session.

Body	Earth Attunement: 100% probability of increasing your health status by 5000%. 100% probability of increasing the molecular density of your skin by 780%. Further increase your health status and connective tissue density by increasing your level and cultivation.
Psyche	Mortal level.
Spirit	Spherical cultivation level 47% to stage 2/7.

Weapon:
  Titan Short Sword
Skill Level:
  Junior Basic (10%)
Damage:
  Below Average
	Quality: Mundane masterwork.
	Allows interface guidance for optimal usage.
	100% probability of 865% increased damage vs. standard hand-to-hand.

Armor: None	Standard Earth Attunement resilience.

Physical Health Status:	5000/5000 Spherical cultivation units.
Free Essence:	1200/1200 Spherical cultivation units.

The Clone wasn't alone. **"This is Lieutenant Commander Naron Shamla."**

The Clone indicated a small humanoid with moist-green skin wearing the blue and silver of the crew and carrying the rank insignia of four silver bars on his left shoulder. A large, toothless mouth gaped at them, and a forked tongue shot out and licked his green and bulbous left eye. The lieutenant commander bowed slightly and blinked nervously at Sen and Josh.

Sen whispered in Josh's ear, "His species is vergei. An amphibious people who have made homes of most wetland planets in almost all mortal iterations."

"He is the officer in charge of maintenance in the forward sections of the *Hegemon-4*. There is a problem with invasive organisms near a maintenance area in an infrequently used section of the *Hegemon-4*. Expunge the beasts and expand your cultivations.

"And this is for free, gentlemen. The *Hegemon-4* is an expansive ship for mortals of your limited capacity. Bring any necessary supplies with you.

"Lieutenant Commander, please take them to the Quartermaster of the Forward Section."

Naron Shamla bowed deeply to the Clone, and in a voice so deep that it shocked Josh, he said, "By your command, Lord Clone."

The Clone disappeared without further comment, and Josh and Sen turned to the lieutenant commander.

Still wiping sweat from his face, Josh asked, "How can we help, Lieutenant Commander?"

"Please, call me Naron. Neither of you are crew. Formalities are not required." Naron walked them out the door and led them down a passageway they hadn't arrived through.

Naron spoke again once they entered a lift. The vector of the elevator moving in what felt like a 45-degree angle to Josh's proprioception.

"Well, this whole mess started about two Ka nexus cycles ago when we got the *Hegemon-4* out of its cradle for active duty." Despite his small size, Naron spoke with grand gestures of his hands and arms, reminding

Josh of his Italian uncles after they had had several beers and were excited about the ballgame.

Josh looked to Sen. "Ka nexus cycle?"

"It is an Immortal timescale that Zenyak must be having the crew use. A Ka nexus cycle is approximately twenty-five earth years."

"So, it was about fifty years ago ... okay." He turned back to Naron.

The vergei continued. "You know"—Naron lifted his left-hand palm up—"up until then, the ship had been in its stasis cradle for ... well ... longer than any of us has been alive. Maintenance logs indicate several billion years if that makes any sense."

Josh blinked, and Sen nodded for Naron to continue.

"Right ... now the *Hegemon-4* is still staffing up to its full complement of two billion crew and two point five billion support staff. We are at about seventy-five percent, presently. A long way of telling you that there are still parts of the ship not reconnoitered and that have lain unoccupied for as long as ..." Naron held his thin green hands palm up and shrugged.

Sen and Josh nodded for him to continue.

"Anyway ..." Naron circled his hand to include the whole world in his talking. "As we expand the crew, we populate these unused sections. Before we open them up, we send scouting crews of four ship-certified space marines. These are some very tough hombres if you don't mind me saying. Some of the toughest we have aboard. The section in question, Epsilon 97, has swallowed eight of these scouting crews over the last Ka nexus cycle. This is further complicated by the fact that the area in question is very near one of the Stargen Tier power conduits. You know, one of the big ones that power the main engines. Its shielding must be damaged because the electromagnetic fluctuations from there are interfering with our communication and sensor data from most of this section. So, we don't know what happened to these eight teams. Now, I need you to go in there and eliminate the problem so we can reseal this conduit breach and reclaim Epsilon 97. But, because of the lack of sensors and communication capacity... when you go in there... we won't be able to help you." Naron finished with an embarrassed toothless smile on his giant mouth and his hands held out to his sides indicating his helplessness.

Sen spoke, "I understand the difficulties of communication you are having because of your exposed power conduit—"

"Stargen Teir conduit! The big, *big ones!*" Naron waved both hands around his body to indicate as-far-as-he-could-reach big.

"Yes, *the big ones*... but despite that, is there anything you can tell us about what you or the space marines *might think* is going on?"

For the first time in the conversation, Naron looked ashamed and became subdued in his talking and gesticulations.

His tongue flicked out and licked both eyes before he spoke again. "I wasn't going to show you this because I didn't think it could help you much. But if you insist... one space marine was tough enough to make it back to a checkpoint and was picked up on sensors. When the checkpoint detected him, a search and rescue team was detailed to go in and get him, as sensors showed he was still alive. He was unconscious by the time they got to him. As they were evacuating the section, while the marine was in the back of the rescue unit... *something*... something killed him. We don't know what it was. But I can assure you. The records are clear that the vehicle was sealed, and nothing got in there with him when he went in... but something sure came out.

"These are the pictures taken by the autopsy team." Naron flicked his wrist three times like a Las Vegas dealer.

Large digital images appeared in front of Josh and Sen. Josh's eyes bugged out when he saw the second picture. A Beast Affin with a very lion-like appearance and a full mane of golden hair. He had large fangs and claws and was wearing what looked like a suit of modular kevlar-plate armor. Only much larger than the ceramic and kevlar plates that most US Army soldiers wore on deployment.

But what caught Josh's attention, and was likely to give him nightmares for the foreseeable future ... was the entire chest cavity of the marine had been ruptured from the inside out. The kevlar plates over his chest were chewed through with the metallic portions bent back on themselves toward the outside. Several of his splintered ribs were jutting out, and only a fragment of the sternum and xiphoid process remained. The rest ... gnawed off and eaten.

CHAPTER 20

---★---

Search and Rescue /
Seek and Destroy

JOSH'S EYES almost burst out of his head. "What do you mean you don't recognize this!"

Sen stood in the isolated passageway with Josh where Naron had displayed the images. Josh's hands were frantically waving at the center of the three showing the unmistakable xenomorph eruption from the space marine's chest.

His voice became increasingly more animated as he spoke. "This creature was shoved down his throat by a . . . *face* . . . via an organism grappling his head and forcing its way down his throat. It gestated inside of him." Josh's face showed disgust as he spread his hands in front of his chest and moved them apart, demonstrating growth. "And then, when it was big enough . . . *Bam!* It clawed its way out of his chest. This is a real big problem, Sen! A real big problem! Didn't you review any of the movies . . . *the historical records* . . . with Damni about this particular type of space monster?"

Sensing his Karmic brother's sincere distress, over what Josh believed was an emergency, Sen shrugged and went into a deeper explanation. "Well, honestly . . . we regularly reviewed the historical records for entertainment purposes. If there was a particular one addressing a topic that was an everyday occurrence ... *well* ... what was the point of reviewing it, really? Internally gestating xenomorphic creatures are hardly something to get excited about. Sorry, brother ... I just don't see the reason to get all worked up about another bug hunt." Sen pointed at Naron.

The vergei was defensively crouched on his haunches and actively looking up to the corners of the passageway for something about to drop on him. His tongue took turns swiping each of his eyes.

"Now, really, Josh, you are scaring poor Naron ..." Sen reached out and pulled the vergei to his feet, dusting off his shoulders and smiling at him. "Come over here, Joshua, and I will show you ... if I still can, that is ..." Sen walked over to one of the wall consoles and placed his hand on the biosensor used by the crew.

To his surprise, the scanner recognized him in his new mortal form.

"Greetings, Senyak Marztanak, sole-seeded heir of the Polar Neutral Marztanak Hegemoncy. How can this Intelligence serve?" The console spoke in a cultured but cheery tone with an androgynous voice.

Sen smiled at the greeting. "Greetings, Intelligence ... please display records of the last five recorded fatalities involving internally gestating parasitic xenomorphs outside of this ship. Please also include how long ago each event occurred."

"Complying . . ." the ship replied.

"Gratitude, Intelligence." Sen slightly bowed to the console.

———————————✦———————————

Pictures sprang up all around Josh.

Intelligence narrated each in its crisp, mid-ranged voice as they did. *"Today: Parallel Iteration Seventeen, local cluster. An elderly Rodocon was reported to have been parasitically invaded with complete internal-xenomorphic gestation. Local exterminator forces hunted and killed the organism to confirm that it was a Centropa."*

The two pictures displayed a thin, four-legged creature wearing a homespun shift with a small skullcap covering its furry, dog-like head. Its chest burst from within, similar to the space marine's. The second picture showed five heavily armed members of the same species, all smiling doggy grins. They were posing in front of an obviously dead centipede monster. It was ten meters long or longer, and its pincers were sharp as steel if the score marks on the local exterminators' armor were any indication.

"Today: Parallel Iteration Nineteen, local cluster . . ."

Two similar graphic photos appeared next to the first set. This time a gelatinous-like victim. The perpetrator was a leathery-skinned, flying monster with sharp, bony ridges on its twelve-meter wingspan. The victim was identified as a Glimenot, and the monstrosity was a Chiroptour. There was even a ground vehicle in the background of the kill picture with a painted side panel image of a large, dead roach with *X*s over its eyes. The logo under it read—

Jack's Extermination Service. We Kill Bugs Dead!
Call us for all your extermination needs.
20% discount for repeat customers!

"Today: Parallel Iteration Twenty-Four, local cluster . . ."

This time the victim was one Josh recognized. A Jaralon, the species that made up the majority of the crew, its long and lanky body defiled as the others had been. It was floating in orbit above a blue-green gas-giant planet that reminded Josh of Neptune. The parasitic organism was a Cebolar, a chlorophyll-using space plant that had matured into a three-meter sphere. It reminded Josh of an immense and terrifying onion. Several sharp, root-like projections in the shape of buzzsaw blades were growing from its sides.

"Yesterday: Parallel Iteration Seven—"

Josh, with his head hung low, raised his hand in a stopping motion to admit defeat. "Okay, Intelligence, you can stop. I get it. This is more a rat infestation than a civilization-ending issue. Thank you for setting me straight."

"You are welcome, Joshua Elias Tanner. And please allow me to formally welcome you aboard the Hegemon-4. Be informed you have been given access parallel to the seeded Hegemoncy heir for the duration of your stay."

Josh nodded to the console.

Sen quickly wiped the smile off his face when Josh spoke to him with a sheepish look.

"All right . . . it's obviously my turn to be the country bumpkin out of his depth. I'm sorry for overreacting."

Sen nodded through their Bond. *~No need for apologies. We're in this together.~*

Josh nodded. *~Thank you, brother.~*

"But you are right about one thing. Whatever is killing the scouting teams is a more challenging organism than the average internally gestating, parasitic xenomorph."

Josh smiled wickedly. "I'd like to think that is an accurate way to describe us as well."

———————————✦———————————

With the end of all life as they knew it on the *Hegemon-4* averted, Naron spun on his heels and continued to lead them down two more lifts, several walkways, and a zip-line across a dark chasm they couldn't see the bottom of. Apparently, a facility shortcut for the maintenance crews. He finally stopped at an open door and turned to them, his hands raised at chest level in an I-surrender-motion and his eyes, possibly, opened even wider than usual.

Speaking fearfully in his deep, resounding voice, he cowered away from the door. "This is Symbal's place. He's the quartermaster for the forward section of the *Hegemon-4*. Aside from being difficult for everyone to deal with ... he's specifically pissed at me right now. I got drunk and forgot to detail enough men to support his last cross-ship convoy of supplies during our outfitting last week. We're still working it out. But ... I think you should probably go on your own from here. I'll be more of a ... *hindrance*, than anything—"

From the other side of the open doorway, a high-pitched and nasally sounding male voice shouted in what sounded to Josh like very thickly accented Chinese yet was still somehow in crystal-clear English. "*Is that you, Naron?* May the Tan Lao thorn monks nest in your rectum! Your ham-fisted goons still haven't fixed my transports. Half of my supplies are rotting at random places around the ship!"

Naron's tongue spasmed as it cleaned his left eye. Then he was off like a shot down the passageway, bowing his farewell to Sen and Josh as he ran backward the first few steps.

Sen and Josh waved a slightly surprised and tentative goodbye. They had already asked Naron all the pertinent questions they could think of. Among the information they had gotten from him was the number of missing space marines—thirty-two over the last twenty-five years. The most recent group to be sent was a joint team of eight. They had gone into Epsilon 97, 1.5 Ka nexus gyra ago. Sen calculated this for Josh as approximately six Earth days. Naron confirmed that the double-squad of eight space marines had also suspected an invasively gestating, parasitic creature.

Furthermore, standard procedure in areas with limited ship sensors would necessitate leaving a clear trail for rescue teams to follow. Also, the space marines were to leave cached-log entries of their findings. Naron had given Josh and Sen master codes to the recording devices the marines had taken in with them.

They had also confirmed with Intelligence the extent of the internally gestating parasite issue. Josh, using his hand on the biosensor at another terminal, had opened that conversation with Intelligence.

"No, Joshua Elias Tanner. No other episodes of internally gestating parasites have been reported or observed on the Hegemon-4 since it came out of its stasis cradle 2.01 Ka nexus cycles ago. Of course, the sensor block in Epsilon 97would prevent any detection of such gestation attacks in that location."

"Thank you, Intelligence."

"Glad to serve, young cultivator. May your spiritual growth be without bounds!"

Josh couldn't help but bow at what seemed like a traditional farewell among cultivators.

Based on this information, it was unlikely that these parasites had migrated outside the blacked-out sensor zone within Epsilon 97. Ridley Scott would have been aghast.

Nonetheless, there was still a sense of urgency for Josh. They could rescue some or all of the double-team of space marines if they were on time. After all, the marines had only gone in six days ago. Josh had a growing feeling, not too different from the Tartarus portal, that it was necessary for them to try and save any they could. He couldn't explain why it was imperative. But that didn't matter. It was a top priority to him and Sen on their Path of One … or Two in their case. They would move into the zone today… after they got what they needed from Symbal, that was.

Nod. *~You feel it too?~* Josh queried through their Bond.

Nod. *~Yes, this is important.~*

They entered the door that the yelling had come through and were greeted by several assistants working a front counter. However, the enormity of the room that spread out behind the workers was what caught Josh's attention. It stretched as far as their enhanced eyes could see and then continued reaching off into the distance, out of sight. Row after row of shelves not much shorter than the ones in Gaia's storeroom. All were neatly laid out and filled with sealed containers bearing *Hegemon-4's* identification printed on all sides. It was almost a flashback to the massive storeroom they had met Achilles in. Almost . . . but Josh was certain Gaia's room had been bigger . . . and much scarier!

The crew were dressed in the standard blue and silver onesies as they milled about behind the counter. After the initial mind-explosion of walking through a regular door and unexpectedly finding himself standing in a space with more area than the Grand Canyon, Josh's attention was drawn to an unassuming figure sitting dead center at the counter. He was slim, human with Asian features, and had been eyeing Josh and Sen without blinking since they had walked through the door. He was wearing a well-made, but faded with age, grey sweater over his onesie, and what looked like four silver bars on his shoulder, placing him at equal rank with Naron.

Lieutenant Commander, it is.

"Yes, how may I help you both?" the man said politely.

Several assistants nearest the man acted busy without really being so. They absolutely wanted to hear what was going to happen but didn't want to attract more of Symbal's attention than necessary. Josh was reminded of a *Seinfeld* episode he had seen where George Castanza demonstrated how to look busy in front of his boss without actually being. These guys were masters of George's techniques.

"It's a pleasure to meet you, Lieutenant Commander—"

The unassuming man's eyes thinned, and a slight tilt entered his neck as he spoke over Josh in a pleasant voice. "You can stop blowing smoke up my Chinese ass right there, Joshua. I'm Symbal Nang. Symbal to the people who want to get along with me. I know that you are here for supplies to go into Epsilon 97 . . . *this is a critical mission* for us in the supply depot . . . one of our friends is on that last scouting mission. You are our only hope to get them back. *Agreed?*"

Josh and Sen nodded in agreement.

"Well, then . . . we understand each other. Please, this way." Symbal jumped down from the stool he had been leaning forward on and lowered his head in welcome as he flipped over a section of the counter to lead them back into the warehouse segment of the supply depot.

On the ground, Symbal was even shorter than Josh had thought, placing him around five-one or five-two at the most.

Symbal walked ahead of them and began speaking and pointing. The fleet of assistants behind them began moving forward and gathering equipment in a coordinated activity that would make German watch-makers weep with envy.

"You will take the standard field-pack for our special operators. Tents, cooking equipment. Standard rations for eight weeks. Water purification. Weather gear. Submersion gear. Radiation shield array and generator, radiation gear, and detoxification units. Advanced first-aid kits. Advanced communications rig. *For all the good it will do for you.* Utility knives forged from neutron-impregnated steel. Timekeeping gear. Portable atmospheric units, along with a portable air purifier. Sonic, infrared, and motion-based sensor equipment effective up to five hundred meters . . . again . . . *for all the good it will do you—*

"Do either of you have any special needs? Handicaps not obvious, food allergies, required medications?"

Both shook their heads no, and Symbal moved on.

They came to a massive section of the warehouse containing racks upon racks of weapons going on as far as their eyes could see. Of course, there were firearms—handheld, rifles, carbines, automatic, fully automatic, and long-range weapons for snipers. There were also mounted firearms of all forms. Mass-weight projectile, energy, plasma, and even one that Sen couldn't identify, when Josh asked about it. Josh was sure he had also seen crates identifying grenades, landmines, and even marine-drop-deploy mines for large, water-going vessels.

The immediately adjacent section displayed suits of compound, kevlar-metallic body armor that Josh had seen in the picture of the space marine. The same armor that had been chewed through by the para-site. There were energy-shield versions of the same armor. At least Josh thought so based on pictures accompanying the crates. Josh could also see racks of what could only be described as full-on, mechanized-power armor. The kind that he had only ever seen in video games.

Symbal stopped and faced them there. Holding his arms out from his sides as if barring them from proceeding into the section.

His face contorted in pain as he was clearly about to say something his heart was at war with, and his teeth ground on every word as he spoke with them clenched. "Concerning weapons ... our Lord Clone ... *in his infinite wisdom* ... has strictly forbidden me from offering you anything more than a sharpening stone and these leather scabbards for your already possessed ... short swords ..." Symbal reached down to a small desk hidden in the shadow of the shelves they were standing under and handed them the sharpening stones and scabbards. "Please know that if it were up to me, I would provide you with anything up to and includ-ing the R and D prototype Mobile Stargen conduit plasma cannons to roll in with you at Epsilon 97!" He sighed, closing his eyes tightly for a moment. "Beyond this, I offer you my daily prayers for success."

He leaned down to the desk, grabbing a photo in an 8x10-inch frame. He kissed his finger and placed it over the face of the young girl holding the hand of a much younger Symbal.

Tears glistened in his eyes as he looked up at Josh and Sen. "Bring my little girl back to me, gentlemen."

A large pile of gear waited for them near the front counter they had passed through on the way in. Much more than they could put into any standard backpack. Backpacks that Symbal had insisted they both carry to have the standard survival package of food, first-aid, utility, and communications gear they would each need in case they were separated. Beyond that, they looked at the tents, weather gear, purification equipment, etcetera ,,, and weren't quite sure what to do.

"What are you waiting for, sherpas from my home world, to carry it? Put it in your aspect facet!" Symbal pointed to the bag dangling under Josh's left arm.

Symbal then picked up the largest item, a quick-erecting, two-person tent. No less than four feet long. Pulling the black leather bag's top flap up, Symbal neatly dropped it into the opening, no muss, no fuss. The mouth of the bag expanded to encompass the ten-inch wide square of the tent's frame and immediately returned to its normal dimensions.

Josh eyes almost jumped out of his skull. He and Sen immediately started putting things in the bag. Soon the 3x4-foot pile was neatly put away.

Josh had many questions to ask Symbal about the bag but held back for now. More important things to do. And after the faith that Symbal had placed in them, he couldn't bear to show the man his lack of knowledge about something so simple. Symbal needed to see hope. Josh understood that better than most concerning a lost child. For now, Josh would hide his feet of clay from the quartermaster.

On the way out, just to be sure, Josh flipped the loose flap of the black leather satchel that still weighed no more than when he first had put it on. He held his hand over the opening and a portion of his interface silently sprang up offering him the option to summon the bag's contents by name and by graphic interface. All the items were there, up to and including the two spearheads they had placed inside first. Leaving it at that for now ... they quickly left the depot, heading to the entry of Epsilon 97.

CHAPTER 21

---✦---

"Oops..."

SEN AND Josh moved with a purpose down the passageways through the ship. Sen could feel the pressure that Josh was taking upon himself through their Karmic Bond. Their thoughts were shared so rapidly it was difficult to tell whose was which.

Nod. *~Symbal's need is a mirror's reflection of our goal for Sophie.~*

Nod. *~There is no question that we need to save this girl so we can save Sophie.~*

Blink. *~Agreed without doubt!~*

Blink. *~If Symbal's daughter is alive . . . we have to do everything possible to bring her back.~*

Head shake. *~To fail her is to fail Sophie!~*

As ridiculous as this seemed, it felt right down to the bottom of their cores. The girl needed to be saved at all costs. Karma demanded they achieve this to reach balance. Either for what they had been given . . . or, more likely, what they would be given . . .

Sophie's safety.

Sen and Josh started walking faster. Transcendence help them should they fail.

Nod. *~Yes, she must be saved!~*

Epsilon 97 was located almost in the center of the *Hegemon-4*. Perched on the *Hegemon's* upper-surface decks, it sat toward the bow just past the waist of the ship. It was a vast free space with an open range for fostering forest habitats and growing crops. The area was primarily used for research by investigators looking into organismal growth in space environments. Knowing all these things helped Sen understand how an invasive species found its way into Epsilon 97. And why they would have wanted to stay. Sen could also understand why it had never been an emergency to make it available for the expanding crew. It was primarily an area for "egg heads" as his father would have described them. They were usually the last aboard a duty vessel.

Sen and Josh arrived via monorail at the midship junction. From there, they would catch a skin-to-skin shuttle flight to the main airlock of Epsilon 97. Their last leg of the trip was the longest in distance but the shortest in time. They were only 20,000km from their insertion point, which would take less than one minute of flight time. Typically, a shuttle wouldn't be used for such a short intra-ship hop. But Symbal's influence was anything but ordinary. Just a digital order with his name on it was enough to make the crew snap to attention and ask if there was anything else they could do to facilitate their travel.

Josh smiled and nodded to Sen. *~It is the small things in life that make it fun.~*

Smile. *~I'm learning this every day.~*

It had taken them three Earth-hours on the monorail to get from the center mass of the *Hegemon-4* to its surface. Sen had used the time for his personal training with the short sword.

As was right, he spent the first minutes training for continued perfection of his basics. He started with blocking maneuvers and footwork.

Focusing on the head, shoulders, abdomen, chest, legs, and the basic guard. He then moved on to attacks, thrusts, lunges, and parry maneuvers. Parrying was very limited with a short sword, but such was Sen's lot in life right now, as enforced by the Clone limiting their offensive capabilities.

After this, Sen grabbed one of the practice long swords and spent the remainder of his time focusing on dual-wielding attacks and blocking.

Sen was playing a losing game. He would eventually have to find a new way to apply the mundane acts of sword usage or find a grandmaster to further his knowledge. This was a problem for tomorrow, though. For now, he could still slowly but steadily improve what he knew. So, he would.

As he finished his last sequence of dual-wielding figure eight passes, his probability interface chimed—

Advancement.

Even this little bit was enough. He and Josh would figure something out. Of that, he was sure.

Josh's instruction came after. For him, just a review of the basics still yielded significant results, which was what they did. Sen was encouraged that Josh's retention was phenomenal. It even showed in his sparring. He lacked the skills to stop Sen from overpowering him with strength and speed. But he never fell for the same trick or feint twice. This was truly remarkable for any student.

After their session, Josh stood for several long moments looking at his sword and focusing his Essence in his right hand to swirl it around the pommel.

Sen had finally taken note and asked Josh what was going on. "Troubles, Josh?"

"I'm just thinking about the first tenet of sword usage you taught me." Then in a meek, slightly Asian accent, Josh repeated, "The sword is an extension of your body ..."

Sen rolled his eyes at Josh's weak joke.

Josh quickly changed the subject back to what he was doing. "So, anyway ... I cycle Essence through all the other extremities of my body. So why not this extremity?" Josh slightly raised his short sword to make his point. "By applying the concepts of EM fields to how our Essence flows through our meridians, I'm almost certain that I can get Essence into this sword under the same physical principles that arcing electricity does when it ... arcs." Josh started repeating complicated mathematical formulas under his breath then looked up and waggled his eyebrows at Sen. "Simply apply these electrical formulas to our Essence ... and I should be able to do the same with this sword as I do my hand. And ... viola—"

At that point, they both felt Josh's Essence break the barrier between his hand and flow into the pommel of the Titan Short Sword. It took on a golden-orange hue, like Josh's Earth-Attuned Essence. The sword immediately began imposing sensations of sharpness and durability.

Josh's interface chimed.

New Earth Attunement skill created:

Weapon enhancement: Invest 200 units of Earth Attuned Essence into a weapon for 100 percent probability to increase weapon's durability by 1000 percent and damage rating by 500 percent. Duration dependent on use. Increase your cultivation to increase this Earth Attuned skill.

Check your status for details on current weapon enhanced.

Weapon:
  Titan Short Sword
Skill Level:
  Junior Basic
  (10% → 20%)
Damage:
  Superior mundane
	Quality: Mundane masterwork.
	Allows interface guidance for optimal usage.
	100% probability of 915% increased damage vs. standard hand-to-hand.

Body	Earth Attunement: 100% probability of increasing your health status by 5000%. 100% probability of increasing the molecular density of your skin by 780%. Weapon Enhancement: Invest 200 units of Earth Attuned Essence into a weapon for 100% probability to increase the weapon's durability by 1000% and its damage rating by 500%. Duration dependent on use. Further increase your health status, connective tissue density, and Earth Attuned Skills by increasing your level and cultivation.
Psyche	Mortal level
Spirit	Spherical cultivation level 47% to stage 2/7.
Weapon: 　Titan Short Sword Skill Level: 　Junior Basic (20%) Damage: 　Superior Mundane 　(Earth Enhanced)	Quality: Mundane masterwork. Allows interface guidance for optimal usage. 100% probability of 865% (x5 while Earth enhanced) increased damage vs. standard hand-to-hand.
Armor: 　None	Standard Earth Attunement resilience.

Josh explained to Sen his experience and then the details of his new skill and its impact of increasing durability and damage by 500 percent. Sen's eyes bugged out at that, and he immediately began working with his Essence. For the next sixty minutes, Josh guided Sen to *arc* his Essence. By the end, it was Sen's turn to be drenched in sweat with his hand white-knuckling his sword's pommel as he felt the Earth-Attuned Essence leave his meridians. His short sword took on the same golden-orange hue as Josh's. They smiled at each other dumbly.

"We need to test this out!" They said at the same time.

———————————★———————————

It was always challenging to find something functional but not needed just to destroy it. In fact, Josh knew an entire special division of the military corps of engineers spent most of its time building things just so they could be blown up.

Fortunately, this was not a problem Josh presently faced.

He walked over to the training dummy he had been striking moments before. Its transparent green energy shield covered a pristine, humanoid-shaped torso and head.

Josh cycled the Earth Essence from his sword back into his meridians and smiled. "My free Essence is back at 1200. No loss when I cycled the Essence back into my meridians from the sword."

Sen nodded sagely. "Essence is eternal. It is never lost or diminished. Just transferred."

Josh scowled. *~Like you knew before I checked... I can tell through the Bond you were just as uncertain as I was...~*

Nervous laugh. *~Well... someone... somewhere taught me... I just didn't remember until you pointed it out...~*

Rolling his eyes at Sen, Josh turned back to the business at hand, cycled his Essence to his hips and upper body and struck a standard midrange upswing. The shield crackled and hissed but held. Josh didn't feel bad at the lack of damage to the training dummy after watching the *Hegemon's* fire teams farther down range on this monorail gym get the same results with their heavy ordinance.

He then invested 200 Essence in his sword and restored its golden-orange hue. Repeating his swing, the glowing sword smashed through the shield like as much glass, evoking a brief static hiss from the apparatus powering it. The shattered pieces of its energy fell in broken shards and dissipated into floating motes before they hit the ground. Josh's sword continued on through the neck of the dummy, sending its head to fly off and slam against the wall thirty paces down range. Its trajectory of showering sparks took it over several of the still-shooting teams' line of fire. Smoke from the head's severed end died quickly as it wobbled face up before stopping.

The gym went silent, and all heads turned to stare at Josh.

With a deep smile, Josh looked around while sheathing his sword. "*Oops...*"

After that, they cleared out of the firing range in a hurry, the gym attendants throwing dirty looks in their direction as they sped away. Josh was glad no further Essence had been drained from his free Essence pool from the hit. He would have to keep an eye on it as he used it in the future.

Standing in the ten-foot cubical airlock of Epsilon 97, Josh and Sen looked through the heavily scarred, transparent doors as they slid to opposing corners and opened on diagonals.

The smell of pine and peat moss greeted their noses. The sound of birdcalls in the distance could be heard. They stepped through the doors onto ground covered in a thick mat of green grass. The temperature was a mild seventy-five degrees Fahrenheit. The airlock behind them began closing. The area was currently undergoing a daylight period. Overhead, light from an unseen source somehow shone down on them. Josh had no idea how long the day and night cycles were here or what triggered them.

Approximately ten steps in front of them, a line of trees marched off to the right and left. Near the airlock was a small kiosk with one of the recording devices that Naron had told them to look for to track the space marines.

Sen walked up to the device and entered the codes they had been given.

There was a split second of eight heavily armed and armored marines smiling in the light. Their body language and weapons at rest. It immediately cut to a nighttime closeup of a dark-haired woman who had obviously spent the last several days roughing it. Her hair was pulled back, but her headgear was gone. Leaves and pine needles poked out of it at odd angles as if she had just crawled through a day's worth of tall grass and forest-floor litter.

She began whispering in a rushed voice with an intense focus. "This is Lieutenant Nang, second in command of joint scout team delta six"—she glanced overhead briefly at a sudden noise—"with a likely . . . final daily log. I am the sole member of the team still at liberty. The other seven members have been captured, presumed killed. Pursuit is right behind me.

"The enemy organisms are sapient with colony-type intelligence. They function primarily in the form of large, physically powerful drones which attack from ambush. Thick, bony plates cover their surface, and they are resistant to all energy weapons. Only heavy, armor-piercing, mass-projectiles have been shown to be effective against them. They are primarily located in the anticipated location of the conduit breach we were sent to secure. They number between twenty and thirty individuals, including the ones cut down in the following video."

A set of coordinates blinked over the screen's lower portion, indicating where the joint team had encountered the parasites. Followed by what must have been body-camera footage. It was partially corrupted with static, and transmission artifacts abounded, without a doubt suffering from the EM disrupting forces from the exposed conduit. Despite this, the film adequately showed several seven-foot tall, mottled white and green, vaguely humanoid forms. Long limbs heavily supplemented with sharp-bony protuberances over all joints. Razor-sharp, blade-like shields lined their long, flat bones. A heavy triangular snout with narrow slits protected dark, black eyes. There was no apparent mouth . . . until it hinged open the top half of its head in a 180-degree movement, displaying rows of very sharp needlelike teeth. Josh absently thought of a moray eel.

The soldier whose camera was active was firing his weapon and yelling smack at the attacking monsters. A blatant attempt to taunt them to him. His large, mass-projector weapon tore the first and second beasts attacking him into large pieces. Rendering them into quivering masses with a white luminescent ichor spraying from the wounds and pooling around their shredded pieces. There was no acid hissing.

Thank heaven for small favors.

The soldier was finally taken out by a monster's hand reaching from behind that was briefly caught in the upper right corner of the screen. A mere instant later, the head-mounted camera was smashed against a nearby rock the shooter had been partially shielded behind.

"This footage is from CPO Tonda's bodycam. Moments ago, he sacrificed himself so I could get here to provide warning to those who would come after us.

"Honor his sacrifice. If you are not at company strength, do not, I repeat, *do not* come in here! *You will fucking die like we did!*"

She looked up again and to the side. "They've caught up. I'm going to lead them away from the airlock. Please tell my father I love him—"

The video ended.

The time stamp on the message was interpreted by his interface as being recorded one point five hours ago.

CHAPTER 22

Transfusion, Transfusion... I'm Never, Never, Never Gonna Speed Again!

ALYSA NANG was not having a good day. But to be sure, she was surprised she was still having any type of day at all. After leaving the message—hopefully, it would do someone some good—she had run from the airlock and positioned herself against a rock face. Then she opened up on the bastards with her armor-piercing rounds. For what they had done to her team, she wanted to blow them all to shreds. But...

Let's face it. It's dark and I'm firing an overpowered weapon from a standing position. She would have been amazed if she'd hit anything. *Maybe I got one.* The first few of them were pretty bunched up. But the gun show was just a feint anyway.

Her plan? To slow them down into as much of a group as possible. Then draw them in for a grand finale ... *I will not be an incubator for one of these nightmares!*

Dropping the gun, she pulled the spacer on her liquid-mix grenade. When she saw the red and clear elements diffuse into each other within the clear windows of the mechanized explosive she had expected that to be the last thing that she would ever see while she crouched there hoping she would be able to take two or three more of the aberrations with her ... things had gone pear-shaped from there.

The largest drone she had seen so far dropped from the rock above and landed directly at her twelve o'clock. Alysa had reflexively turned away from it, protecting the grenade from its reaching arms. No contest there! The giant monster had stripped the activated grenade from her hands with no effort. The monster then opened its giant mouth and shoved the grenade inside. Two other drones had dropped down and piled onto the first just as the grenade had gone off. All three were instantly killed with a muffled, meaty thud and a hail of sharp bone fragments spraying in all directions. She still had many of them stuck in her arms and face.

Not one to try and figure out stupid people ... or beasts in this case ... Alysa still had no idea why they would sacrifice so many of their number to add only herself to their colony. By definition, after all, internally gestating parasites were exclusively one host, one organism. The numbers didn't add up for the price they paid.

After the grenade, the remaining drones captured her and carried her back to the area near the conduit exposure. On their way in, she had been brought past the other seven members of her team. All were restrained in some type of organic resin and in varying stages of serving as gestational fodder. She had expected to be plugged in right next to them. As she passed the first of her crew, she could tell the multi-nodular root system functioning as the invasive element for this species hadn't used the mouth as the entry orifice to their alimentary canals. *This isn't going to be fun ...*

But the monsters hadn't stopped there. They continued to the back of the maintenance facility that housed the conduit junction they nested near, then kept going down several levels of stairs to the junction room. Upon arrival, Alysa confirmed what she had already guessed. The Stargen Conduit had been partially excavated and stripped of the lead-nickel alloy that shielded its massive power flow. Alysa's hair was blown back in an airless, static wind, and her teeth were practically wiggling in her gums, being this close to it.

They tied her hands and legs with simple but effective twine and set her down in a sitting position on a rock one of them had carried in. Then, in acts that spoke of pure supplication, they bowed their heads to the ground and backed out of the lower level, only turning around and regaining their feet once they were on the steps leading up. At that point, things had gone completely FUBAR.

"Yes, yes ... let's see what you are made of, my dear ..." The large, white boulder beside Alysa had opened its eyes and started talking in a coarse, rasping voice thick with age, speaking no less than flawless Intergalactic Common. The one language every member of every crew of the *Hegemons* spoke the iteration wide.

Stretching out its arms and legs, the rock stood. The new four-meter-tall menace began shuffling in a stooped fashion, apparently struggling with arthritic pain as it hobbled slowly to where Alysa sat.

There were prominent female organs. Six thin and depleted breasts lay flat against its chest, swaying slightly with its rocking gait. A pair of large, sagging labial lips dragged on the floor. Heavy black claws opened and closed on all four of its upper arms, with even thicker ones on its grasping feet.

Compared to the drones she had seen, it had a larger head with more defined humanoid features. When it stopped in front of her, the top of the creature's hinging head snapped open to taste the air. Leaving the turgid smell of the dying all about them from the expelled breath of its failing body. Hunching over Alysa, its slitted pupils wavered without

conscious control or focus, blind beneath opaque lenses that had calci-
fied with age.

Finishing its inspection of Alysa, the monstrosity straightened and
spoke, "Oh good! Oh, very good! I've waited so long for a viable candi-
date . . . I had only hoped for an appropriate female of age . . ."

Alysa's eyes widened in shock and disgust as its gigantic hand patted
her head gently. "But you will do nicely. An excellent specimen!"

Momentarily speechless, Alysa's slack-jawed befuddlement left her
gaping like a fish out of water.

Coming back to herself, Alysa elected to resist in the only way
she could. "Whatever you want from me, I won't give it to—" She
strained as she coughed up crimson-tinged sputum, followed by a
congealed glob of blood that dribbled down her chin as she caught
her breath to try again. "I won't . . . I won't give it to you!" Blood now
dripped down her lips to the front of her armored chest as her bleeding increased its pace.

Slowly chuckling in her thick and rasping way, the matriarch
responded to Alysa's feeble refusals with a mild tone and spread
hands as if explaining to a loved child. "Not that I would give you
a choice, young one . . . but you are already dying. Exposure to the
Stargen Conduit I've fed off all these years has already caused your
cell membranes to break down. You'll be dead in minutes if we don't
join. But do not be afraid! You are going to be my new vessel. Once
I've wrapped my mind around yours and seeded you with my genetic
code, we will leave here and find a new home. Just like when I came
here out of necessity within the body of a maintenance crew member
so many millions of years ago."

Four of the drones came down the stairs carrying a root system
with two large, blunted prongs connected with fleshy, mucous-covered
umbilicals. The white monstrosity standing next to her leaned back
onto the first prong and gave an initial sharp grasp of pain, then a deep
sigh of relief.

Alysa looked on with fear and mounting horror. She tried to tell the psychotic monster to screw right off, but a large blood clot came out instead and plopped onto her lap. She was starting to feel weak and dizzy.

"Hush, child. You don't understand the benefit of being my vessel. You will always be with me ... like they all are ... We will live to the end of this iteration and move on to find a new one ... and a new one after that. When we are united, I will show you what it means to have true power ... We will be together forever ... to Transcendence ..."

Some type of membrane must have been broken when the monster matron sat on the prong. A stream of vile ichor now flowed out from where the prong had entered. For a creature planning to live for billions of years, her time among the living must have been relatively short, as the matriarch was definitely rotting on the inside. But Alysa couldn't spare any more thoughts for the monster. It was clearly her turn as the lead drone grabbed the other probe and brought it forward. As it neared Alysa, the prong started wiggling in her direction as if it was going to insert itself on its own.

From that point, Alysa lost all sense of calm and collection. She immediately started to thrash and fight any way she could. But her strength ebbed, her motions grew more and more feeble every second. Alysa slipped from a seated position to a lying one, making it even more strenuous to move in her restraints as the tip of the prong started to worm between her clenched legs ...

And that was when two men jumped from the landing above and started cutting through the first rank of drones in the back of the room. Dressed in crew onesies, they were brandishing ... glowing swords?

She must have been dizzier than she thought. The one with the bald-topknotted head was moving through the monsters like a Tan Lao sword master. Leaving limbs and decapitated bodies behind him as he wove through their attacks like a dancer in the rain. The taller one was swinging his sword like a child's field baton, though to good effect. He chopped their bodies in half with powerful diagonal upswings, then went back to stab the heads if the bodies kept moving.

Once her drones had been destroyed, the monstrous matron tried to stand up and fight off the two men. But she was either too far gone or no match for them. The topknotted one sliced through three of her arms while the other slashed her back, opening a gaping wound. More of the horrible black ichor splashed around, flooding the area with the smell of rot and death. One last slash from the front, and her body and head fell in separate directions. Both tumbled into the trench onto the exposed conduit and were instantly vaporized.

Alysa tried to sit up and thank them. But she had lost control of her motor functions. The skin and muscles on her arms and hands started to slough off her bones. The cellular breakdown accelerated.

The one with hair turned to her and went to cut her bonds. "I'm Josh. This is Senyak. Your father sent us … are you all right? *Gods, Sen! She's falling apart!*"

"It's the electromagnetic field from the conduit. It would damage us, too, if not for the healing of our Essence. We need to get her out of here!"

Then Alysa was in someone's arms and moving. The last thing she knew was that she was moving much faster than she had thought was possible.

★

Josh held the dying woman in his arms as he sprinted with full cycling to his lower body.

He nodded. *~How far?~*

Sen thought for a moment. *~Twice as far as this.~*

Josh sped up.

Sixty seconds and two more miles later, he stopped and laid Alysa on the ground. Her breathing was shallow at 120 breaths per minute. Pulse was a rapid and thready 180 beats per minute. She was leaking clear fluid from all her pores, and her connective tissue was sagging off her boney structures. Even her bones were softening to his touch ... like she was breaking down at a molecular level.

He could never get her medical attention fast enough ... if it even existed?

Lifting his eyes to the heavens and pleading with anyone who would hear him ... *"This girl cannot die! I'm not sure how, but I do know that right now Karma is using her as some kind of stand in for Sophie ... like some kind of test to see if I'm worthy of having a shot to save my daughter ... For this moment, as far as Karma is concerned ... Alysa is Sophie ... and Sophie is her! What will happen to Sophie if I fail Alysa!? I can't lose either of them!"*

A voice in his head he couldn't identify, maybe just his own mind shattering as it broke under the strain ... *"You know all that you need to save her. She is a spiritual being like you."*

As if on instinct, he held his hand over her core and infused her with his Essence ... cycling all his free Essence into her. When that ran out, he broke down the concentrated Essence dedicated to his core and sent it to her. As his Essence flowed, she developed a fledgling core and the start of rapidly growing meridians cycling his Essence through her. He continued sending it, seeing it rushing to her heart, brain, lungs, limbs ... He pushed it faster. Faster! *Faster!!!*

She still needed healing. A quiet warning went off in Josh's head that he needed to stop. He was placing his spirit in jeopardy if he drained himself!

But Josh wasn't in the business of listening to a warning like that today! Alysa and Sofie's fates were entwined. If he needed to sacrifice himself ... so be it. Between him and them ... there was absolutely no contest. His last layer of dedicated Essence crumbled as he cycled it to her with no interruption—

"That's enough, brother, she's restored ... You've drained yourself ..." Sen gently lifted Josh's limp form and laid him beside Alysa.

Josh felt the truth of it … then it was his turn to fall into the bottom-less black again.

CHAPTER 23

———————————★———————————

A Reckless Prick Indeed...

JOSH'S EYES bulged slightly as he collected the Essence from the last of the twenty-eight drones he and Sen had ... *expunged* ... He would get used to that word at some point. It sounded like he was washing the shower out or something ...

Josh had drained his core to 4 percent while channeling Essence to Alysa. Sen had been right. Josh had almost been drained. Josh wasn't sure what would have happened if he had exhausted his Essence giving it to Alysa. But he didn't want to know. His intuition, which he decidedly trusted more lately, told him doing so was a way to walk the paths of the spiritual undead.

Right now, his core flashed. It was his third expansion in the last few minutes. The familiar red-blinking outline surrounded his green core icon in the top center of his interface. Two seconds later, it solidified. But instead of going green again, it changed to golden. Josh took this to mean his current core size was maxed out until he added another Attunement. Maybe the Lord Clone would come and disabuse him of this.

Till then I'm going with it! Josh engaged in the single thought micro-rebellion of his own mind ... perhaps only to have an ounce of control over all the insanity that had been raining down on him over the past few days.

Fifty-one percent flashed next to the half-filled golden circle.

It hadn't been comfortable. The drones were heavy with Essence compared to the wisps Josh had absorbed from the bat cannibals before. Two drones had been enough to fill his core from 4 percent to bursting. Of course, he had filled his meridians with Earth aura before using the drones' Essence. That had been a nonissue. He simply *Intended* to absorb the aura from the space around him, and his meridians had filled in less than sixty seconds as golden-orange aura streamed into him from all around. As he was attuned to it, no purification was necessary, like it was when they absorbed Essence from spirit beings. But Josh was getting good at that as well. Taking mere minutes to purify an entire core at this point.

Due to his Attunement, Josh's core and meridian capacities were significantly expanded compared to when he had absorbed the bats. The three full expansions he had just undergone had further increased their capacity. He sensed his core was approximately 400 percent bigger than it had been after the Attunement. This was reflected by his free Essence sitting at 3906. By his calculations, increasing the size of his core increased his free Essence by 25 percent per increase.

Physical Health Status:	5000/5000 Spherical Cultivation Units.
Free Essence:	3125/3906 Spherical Cultivation Units.

Not bad for a few overgrown bone bugs. *These organisms were more closely related to the phylum Mollusca of land-based shellfish than the phylum Arthropoda for insects . . .* Josh internally sighed at how easily his thoughts could be distracted down a science tangent.

Along with his core and free Essence capacity upgrades, Josh's meridians had also expanded. There was no question he could pack a significantly harder punch than before.

But what Josh was particularly proud of was the advancement of his sword skill during the battle with the parasites. Be they land-sea bugs or land-land bugs. He had gone from 20 percent at the junior basic to 17 percent at the basic level. Sen had confirmed that battle-driven, skill gains would always outstrip those on the training floor.

"At least it is that way in the Immortal realms. I suspect it is the same in the mortal realms as well..."

It sure seemed that way. Josh checked his status to bask in his increased digital awesomeness.

Body	Earth Attunement: 100% probability of increasing your health status by 500%. 100% probability of increasing the molecular density of your skin by 780%. Weapon Enhancement: Invest 200 units of Earth Attuned Essence into a weapon for 100% probability to increase the weapon's durability by 1000% and its damage rating by 500%. Duration dependent on use. Further increase your health status, connective tissue density and Earth attuned skills by increasing your level and cultivation.
Psyche	Mortal level.
Spirit	Spherical cultivation level 100% to stage 2/7.

Weapon:
  Titan Short Sword
Skill Level:
  Basic (17%)
Damage:
  Superior Mundane
  (Earth Enhanced)
	Quality: Mundane masterwork. Allows interface guidance for optimal usage. 100% probability of 1005% (x5 while Earth enhanced) increased damage vs. standard hand-to-hand.

Armor: None	Standard Earth Attunement resilience.

It didn't appear that the tiny step of maxing out his core at this intermediate step in his foundational stage would increase the Earth

Attunement bonuses. Josh would have to check again when he had a subsequent Attunement. Whatever came after completing the spherical core, Josh wasn't sure. But there was something beyond that. Josh had some suspicions about what it might be. But he would need more data points to make an accurate prediction and hypothesis . . . he was starting to get used to talking to himself in science mumbo-jumbo . . . *What is the world coming to?*

His mind flashed back to the battle with the gestational parasites. Even the basics that Sen had taught him had made a tremendous difference in how he approached them. More importantly, he had worked on his defense as well as not overextending himself with his attacks during the battle. In truth, if Josh had to make a comparison, he was approaching fighting with the sword a bit like he approached tennis matches. If he didn't make any mistakes to take himself out of the game, he was just waiting for his opponent to make a mistake and give him an opening.

He would mention this to Sen. But then again . . . maybe not. It would take Josh an hour to explain tennis to Sen . . . *yeah, definitely save it for later.*

Josh nodded to Sen. *~You ready to head back?~*

Sen nodded back. *~Ready, brother.~*

Josh picked Alysa up, and they headed for the airlock at a leisurely pace. The remaining ten or so miles back to the entry could accomplish in about thirty minutes with minimal Essence expenditure.

Sen had scouted the area yesterday after Josh had woken up from his emergency Essence transfusion. He had found no signs of any living drones within several miles of the conduit junction they had raided to get to Alysa. This would make sense from what Alysa had reported in her video. If they were clonal, they would tend to congregate en masse. Clearly, the matron they had cut down was attempting some kind of unique impregnation upon Alysa. They most likely would have all been there to protect her during this.

As they slowly walked back to the airlock carrying Alysa, Josh noticed that none of the other space marines who had been alive when they rescued Alysa were with them.

Josh tilted his head to Sen. ~*The other marines that were being... infused with the parasites... they didn't make it?*~

Downcast shake of the head. ~*I granted Lieutenant Nang's comrades the mercy of a warrior's death...*~

Wide eyed. ~*There was no way to... maybe... I dunno... surgically remove... the parasites?*~

With eyes squeezed shut, Sen just shook his head and continued on.

Josh wasn't certain but he thought he saw glistening in Sen's eyes before he turned away. He could definitely feel an intense remorse through their Bond for Sen's failure in getting there soon enough to save them.

Josh sensed Sen was certain there were no other viable options for the marines. No further questions were needed. In truth, it hadn't looked like there was much chance of saving them. But the level of medicine on the *Hegemon-4* wasn't something Josh was privy to. *Guess something like this is beyond even the advanced technology of a multi-billion-year-old, continent-sized spaceship.*

They arrived at the clearing with the recording device and the main airlock of Epsilon 97. Josh put Alysa down and again checked her vitals. Normal... no further sign of sloughing skin. Her pupils were responsive to light, and she responded appropriately to painful stimuli. She was just resting and recovering after being mostly dead. Josh could understand that.

Sen activated their communication device. "This is Senyak Marztanak, reporting out of Epsilon 97. We are ready for transport at the main airlock."

To no one's surprise, a heavily Chinese-accented and nasally voice came back over the transceiver. "How many for transport, Heir Marztanak?"

"Three. Myself, Joshua Elias Tanner, and Lieutenant Alysa Nang. She is well but still recovering from her injuries and is presently unconscious. Please send a stretcher team."

"The extraction team is on standby circling Epsilon 97. A strike team will be landing momentarily to facilitate exfiltration. EMS is standing by and ready to receive you at the forward section's main-medical hanger. Nang out."

Sen looked at Josh. "How will you tell him about the changes you brought to his daughter?"

"One problem at a time, Sen. I'm not even sure what I did do. And I have no idea how I will tell *her* yet. How much longer do you think she will need to sleep—"

A steady but fatigued voice cut Josh off. "She needs about two more weeks. But what she has gotten so far will have to do . . . Now, did you . . . *help* . . . the rest of my team in time? What is it you need to tell me? Why am I still among the living? And what is with the swords? In that order, please." Alysa raised herself to her elbows with an effort and looked at them.

Sen bowed at his waist. "Once we rescued you, your team's suffering was ended, Lieutenant."

"Thank you." Alysa said quietly, her eyes momentarily downcast—

The airlock cycled, and a fifteen-man platoon of space marines, equipped in what must have been half of Symbal's supply depot, ran through and secured the area. Were those surface-to-air guns being wheeled to the other side of the airlock? Subdued communications could be heard between the ground forces and those waiting on the landed shuttles outside the surface airlock as the special units efficiently secured the area.

The leader of the first fire team, a Beast Affin with robust tiger features, including a full snout, long fangs, and lanky but well-muscled limbs, ran up to them, leading a pair of medical corpsmen. Both were Jaralon and began unfolding a stretcher between them.

The Beast Affin spoke first, quickly nodding in greeting. "Sirs, ma'am. I'm Senior Chief Ishan." He turned to Alysa. "Ma'am, my orders are to immediately extricate you from this forward area to the main medical services hangar—"

"One minute, senior, I'm having a conversation with these gentlemen—"

"No, ma'am! Apologies, these orders come directly from your father. He made it *very clear* that if I was to disobey them, even at your orders, I would be eating nothing but cold rations on a very distant asteroid for the next two Ka nexus cycles . . . and I can't believe you would hate me that much . . . we've only just met. Now please lie down and let these two corpsman transfer you to their stretcher."

Gobsmacked, Alysa did just that. Her questions burned in her eyes as she tried to get Sen and Josh to follow. But the SCPO wasn't finished.

"Messrs. Marztanak and Tanner. Lieutenant Commander Shamla has asked for an immediate SITREP on the invasive species and the stripped Stargen Conduit. And after that, if someone could tell me what the fuck is going on, I would really appreciate it, sirs!"

Josh and Sen smiled at Alysa, quietly chuckling as they shrugged and turned from her inquisitive, ocular fury.

Josh called over his shoulder, "Don't worry, Alysa, we'll catch up with you as soon as we're finished here. In the meantime . . . try to feel your core . . . it's just under your navel."

The expression on Alysa's face could only be described as perplexed as she was carried away through the airlock, which immediately began to cycle closed.

Sen leaned over to the Beast Affin. "Of course, Senior Chief, let me quickly brief you and then report to the lieutenant commander."

———————————★———————————

The Clone floated in space far above the *Hegemon-4*. The continent-sized ship was only a speck of light below him. Still, nothing escaped his awareness.

His thoughts continued as he watched his two wards leave the research area designated Epsilon 97.

When Zenyak created a clone, it was never for a long-term assignment. If a task required the long-term involvement of a being at Zenyak's level of power and knowledge, he had always preferred that it was himself to do it. Even a perfect copy of himself would not do. Furthermore, the power ceded to a clone would become a permanent transfer unless restored before too long.

The Clone knew this ... as he knew everything about Zenyak. He also knew why, after billions of years, Zenyak was breaking this personal rule of his ... He and the other Immortals at his level were stretched thin containing the threat from outside iterational existence—

The quiet sound of space tearing and a brief flash of the deep-swirling blue of intact Reality indicating Zenyak's imminent arrival interrupted the Clone's ruminating.

"**Report?**" Zenyak asked.

Minuscule signs of fatigue only the Clone would recognize could be seen.

The Clone bowed his head, and Zenyak rested his hand on its crown.

Turning away from the Clone, Zenyak mumbled to himself. "**Using Earth aspect skills after only eighteen hours of Attunement was not probable. Less than one occurrence in 8,785,456 events. Externalizing his Essence to heal and create another cultivator was not even a predicted outcome in our probability predictions ...**" Turning back to the Clone, Zenyak asked. "**Did we orchestrate this?**"

"**No. Ka and Karma are wrapping themselves around Senyak and Joshua Elias Tanner in increasing amounts for Reality's own purposes. As is apparent, this ground is treacherous and fraught with peril. I merely facilitated Alysa Nang's soul birth by pointing out to Joshua what he already knew.**"

Zenyak's eyes narrowed at the Clone's statement knowing it to be an accurate appraisal of the situation. This was indeed perilous ground to tread. Karma and Reality were heavily invested here for purposes that Zenyak didn't fully understand.

Turning back to the Clone, Zenyak said, **"Analysis."**

"The synergistic association of Senyak and Joshua Elias Tanner is beyond all predicted expectations of mortal-level cultivation. To our knowledge, no mortals have ever advanced this rapidly. This is due primarily to their Karmic Bond and Ka and Karma shaping events around them, favoring advancement and growth for Reality's own purposes. Whatever they are. Furthermore, their motivation to fulfill the purpose of their Karmic Bond. Id est: Advance to sufficient cultivation to reestablish contact with Sophie Tanner is an event magnifier of unknown quantum ..." The Clone looked into Zenyak's grey eyes with his blazing-blue fractals to make his following statement unmistakable. **"For better or worse, Ka and Karma have brought Sophie Tanner's life force to be present in this iteration. I have felt it. She and Reality are laying a trail for Joshua Elias Tanner and Senyak. Shaping their actions and growth to bring the Karmic Bond of Senyak and Joshua Elias Tanner to fulfillment."**

Zenyak swallowed and looked at the Clone again. **"Unanticipated ... but perhaps useful. Recommendations."**

"Continued subsistence-level support with antagonistic motivation.

"No additional time should be spent on terrestrial organisms. They pose no challenge, and further growth will be minimal, even for Joshua's budding skill as a swordsman.

"Advancement to their next Attunement immediately following this meeting. If anything, we have been holding them back with our current exposures."

Zenyak eyed the Clone closely through his narrowed lids. **"Agreed with proviso ..."**

The Clone looked up to Zenyak, knowing what he would add. After all, the Clone was Zenyak, and the Clone had purposely left it off the list, hoping Zenyak's fatigue might have missed it. Not in this gigayear. Probability models were explicit that it was the one course of action that could further accelerate the pair's growth . . . but if it backfired . . . It was the one path forward that could unbalance Ka and Karma. Making all their planning detonate like a supernova . . . with uncertain probability outcomes that could end everything they were fighting for.

"Catalyze them with an exposure of the current iterational Sophie Tanner. She is the motivational fuel supplying this Karmic Bond. Let's see how far I can facilitate Senyak and Joshua's growth via Karmic intervention and their Bond. It is after all why I picked this cluster in the first place." A brief blue flash and Zenyak was gone.

I am a reckless prick. The Clone reflected. *A reckless prick indeed . . .*

CHAPTER 24

★

Two Times Around and Back Again...

"BÀBA, I'M fine. I need to get out of here and—"

"Nǚ'ér! You are the farthest thing from fine right now! The only thing you are going to do is rest in this place until both med bots and the attending spirit being clear you for duty. *That is an order, Lieutenant!*"

Josh and Sen rounded the corner in the med bay that Alysa Nang had been brought to, inadvertently stumbling upon the father-daughter confrontation mounting up to OK-Corral-Earps-vs-Clanton levels. Each resolutely stared steely eyed at the other.

Both he and Sen reflexively shifted a step back as the tension mounted. Josh wouldn't have wanted to go up against either one of them at the moment... but his money was on Symbal in this fight.

A full ten seconds later, Alysa relaxed back into a reclining position, mumbling under her breath. "It's the same order I've given to my own men..."

But Alysa was far from defeated. She remarshaled her forces to pick a fight she could win.

Focusing on him and Sen, a predatory look sprang into her eyes. "Well, gentlemen. No more senior chiefs to save you from me. I'll have my explanations about who you are and what you did to me now!"

Symbal's brows narrowed at her words, and he shifted the gravitas of his stare to them as well.

Confronted with what felt like two tigers about to pounce, Josh's brain accelerated into defensive mode, a million-watt smile sprang upon his face. "Ahh ... yeah ... about that ..."

None of the scans run by the med bots showed the presence of her core or meridians. Alysa had immediately accepted what they said about being cultivators and needing to awaken her own cultivation to save her from the Stargen Conduit's radiation as true. But the circumstances were in favor of this.

For one thing, Alysa remembered what condition she had been in. For another, she could feel her core and the Essence set in motion by Josh. Her meridians were brimming with it as it spun through her. Only now, hours later, after Josh's Intention had been realized and all Alysa's injuries had been healed, was the Essence starting to slow down.

Symbal's acceptance, however, had been a different matter. He had shot some very calculating glances at Josh and Sen as they explained what cultivation was and how Josh had given her his Essence to keep her alive.

Both he and Sen were patient, feeling that they needed his acceptance as well. They repeated themselves several times, and even gave visual demonstrations. It was obvious that Alysa felt her father was being overly protective again, but Symbal's hesitance was understandable. After all, how quickly *was* a father supposed to accept that a strange man has infused part of his soul into his unconscious daughter when she was on the brink of death? Gratefully, Alysa had diffused the situation immediately.

Taking hold of Symbal's hand with both of hers, she had looked into his eyes. "Bàba. It was the only way. Without it, I would not have survived even one more minute . . . of that, I'm sure."

After searching her eyes, Symbal spun around and bowed deeply at the waist to Sen and Josh. "I am forever in your debt. Whatever is in my power is yours, anytime, anywhere." He stayed that way for several long moments and then stood with tears running silently down his cheeks to his smiling lips. "Thank you!" he harshly whispered as he turned back to focus on his daughter.

Briefly mentioning they would be back in a few hours to continue explaining things as best they could, Josh and Sen had slipped quietly away to let them have their time of reunion.

Three hours later, they returned. Josh and Sen told Alysa what they knew of cultivation. How to recharge her free Essence. The difference between her core Essence and free Essence. How she could absorb from other spiritual organisms. Not to try and absorb any undead Essence. They evaluated her by sensing the Essence in her core. Both agreed that she was essentially as they had been back in the alley with the Clone.

They explained the possibility of expanding her core and not trying to do it without medical support.

They also explained Attunement and what they had learned about it so far.

Symbal had sat next to her, taking quick notes. Alysa had sat in her bed and taken it all to heart silently.

Collecting Essence from food animals had been Symbal's idea. And it had worked. He had a chicken brought in and killed right there behind the curtains of the medical bay. Josh couldn't help but think it paid to be the lieutenant commander in charge of supply.

———————————— ✶ ————————————

Josh looked at the chicken's carcass and saw a wisp of essence in a tiny core near its center of mass, "It's got Earth Essence." He smiled to Alysa and handed her the small fowl. "Use your Intent to feel its Essence like you can your own. Then move it to your hand meridians and absorb it. Then move it to your core. It will feel ... ungainly to be sure. But don't give up. You'll get it."

Alysa accepted the small dead bird Josh handed her with a serious intensity that, if he was honest, scared him. He and Sen both academically knew that cultivation and its actions were much easier for them compared to others because of the benefit of Josh's mastery of physical laws and their Karmic Bond to share it. But here they got to see it firsthand with Alysa's struggles. She chased the hint of Earth Essence around the dead bird's meridians like a toddler chasing food around a plate the first time they used cutlery.

Wink. ~*Do you think she is struggling too much?*~

Sen's knowing smile. ~*Alysa is a very competent soldier and, I am certain, an excellent student. But cultivation is a learning process for all that don't have our ... particular benefits. We are seeing the difference between us and even a very motivated person ... but watch out ... she has all the markings of someone who doesn't give up. I am sure she will ultimately run down her prey through sheer tenacity.*~

Admiring glance. ~*I agree with that! One thousand percent!*~

The next day had been spent explaining how to cycle Essence and use it for healing. Enhanced hearing and sight as well as improved physical performance.

Again, what had taken them moments to learn had been the work of several hours of guided teaching. But both felt Karma demanded they care for the life they had caused to be reborn. There was no other road to walk here.

Alysa could now enhance her eyes and ears. She was still working on enhancing her meridians for actions. But she would have the rest of her life to dedicate to it.

Over these days, Josh and Sen continued their sword training. Josh had some slowdown in his training gains but continued as Sen told him how small his personal training gains were. Josh getting 8 percent on his basic sword level per ninety-minute lesson was huge compared to Sen, now only getting 1 percent after he had broken through 90 percent in his advanced level. Josh's level sat at 43 percent of basic.

Weapon: Titan Short Sword Skill Level: Basic (17% → 43%) Damage: Superior (Earth Enhanced)	Quality: Mundane masterwork. Allows interface guidance for optimal usage. 100% probability of 1005% (x5 while Earth enhanced) increased damage vs. standard hand-to-hand.

———————————✳———————————

Josh dodged to the right, fully enhancing his upper and lower body. Alysa's spear slash hit the mat where he had been standing less than one tenth of a second before. Alysa wielded one of the Titan dory's heads mounted on one of the ship's practice shafts. It had been Sen's idea, and Josh had agreed a budding cultivator needed the best mundane weapon they could provide. She would still need an Earth Attunement to enhance her weapon as they did ... but for now, it seemed to be a good fit for her.

"Missed me by a mile!" Josh laughed, standing behind Alysa.

She gritted her teeth and spun around with a diagonal slash from a partially crouching position.

"Whoa!" Josh raised his sword and blocked an attack that had come faster than expected due to Alysa successfully cycling her Essence. "Aha! Now that was much better at cycling your Essence. You are getting the hang of it!"

Her follow-up spinning-leg sweep was less effective as she was nearly out of free Essence. Josh's interface showed the recommended action to avoid her attack and an appropriate counterattack. He jumped over her sweeping leg and pushed her back onto her backside with a light kick to her shoulder.

Defeated, Alysa flattened out on her back and lay panting on the ground. Cycling Essence was new to her, and there had been no chance for her to increase her baseline core yet. She also didn't benefit from a probability interface like Josh and Sen did. But based on Josh's backward calculations . . . if she had the same size core he and Sen had started out with, her free Essence was likely only forty cultivational units.

"You've had some hand-to-hand training, haven't you?" Alysa asked, pulling herself up, a fine sheen of perspiration on her brow.

"Well, a little as a kid. Some formalized grappling and boxing as a teenager. Some fights in the streets. But the sword is new. Just like for you." He grinned. "I'm also cheating. My cultivation units are significantly higher than yours, and I can keep myself fully enhanced during our whole fight . . . not really fair to you."

"Nothing fair about fighting. You win, or you lose. I'll figure it out. You better watch your back. I'm coming for you and Senyak!" A wicked grin spread over her lips and reached her eyes.

And Josh believed it! "Warning noted!" Josh laughed. "Are you sure you're not from Chicago?" Josh offered her his hand to get up off the floor and channeled Essence into her meridians, refilling her tank, as it was.

She perked up immediately. "Thanks. That saves me a trip to the ship's forward-section animal pens. Half a waking period's travel time to go back and forth. My father is having a satellite slaughter pen opened up nearer here in supply, but it is still two days until it's fully set up . . . I really don't like being empty, you know?"

Josh nodded and toweled off his head. "Yeah, I know exactly what you mean."

Josh looked down, sheathing his sword, when Alysa put her hand on his cheek.

"Thank you *soooo sooooo* much, Daddy!" Sophie's voice and the intonation of a four-year-old came from Alysa's mouth!

Josh's head flashed up, and he stared wide-eyed at Alysa. She blinked several times. Then her eyes rolled up into her head as she fell forward into his arms.

———————————✳———————————

Josh, Sen, and Symbal were standing in the medical bay over an angry Alysa's bed. And she was having none of the paternal actions of any of them. Pulling off the vitals meter from her hand, Alysa stood and donned her duty jacket while pushing through them to the passageway beyond.

There she turned around and faced them, starting with Josh. "I know what I said. Have you forgotten? I was there!" Next came Symbal. "No, I don't fully understand it. Yes ... I am ... *linked* ... to Josh's daughter. If she hadn't reached out to me ... I'm sure I wouldn't have survived ... she *lent me strength* when I needed it ... and I owe her a debt I am going to try and repay." She finished with Sen. "I would appreciate it if you could discuss with me the ... bond you and Josh share. It's not exactly what Sophie and I have ... but I think it might be close."

Sen's overriding politeness caused him to nod in the affirmative, which instantly drew glares from both Josh and Symbal. He held his hands up in surrender as they chased Alysa down the hall.

At the door to the lift, she turned back to Josh. "Look ... she's been with me since I woke up in Epsilon 97. I can't really explain it. Usually, it's just a feeling or fleeting vision. A girl running through her backyard. Picking flowers to give to her blonde mommy ... chasing the cat that keeps sneaking in and staring at her hamster ..."

"Mr. Snipps!"

"Yes ... *him.* I'm not sure how Sophie came through as strongly as she did. She was suddenly much closer for an instant and couldn't help herself... I can feel that she is very, very sorry. She didn't mean to scare you..."

Josh closed his wide-open mouth then spoke with a dry throat. "Can you tell her... tell her I love her to the mo—"

"To the moon around two times and back again." Smiling, she grabbed his hands with both of hers. "She knows, Josh. I swear she knows!"

A smile split his wooden face. Silent tears ran down his cheeks.

Alysa next turned to Symbal, whose mouth was hanging open as well. "Bàba... and I am sorry for scaring you..." She grabbed her father in a hug, then looked into his eyes. "This is just part of my new... *normal*. I'm trying to get used to it... just like you are. Please give me the time and understanding I need?" Pulling back from their hug, she finished by looking at him with a raised left eyebrow.

Looking her dead in the eye, his nasal voice spoke clearly, "Ancestors give me strength! Now you are channeling your mother's power looks at me! How many of you are in there!" Symbal smiled, warmly shaking her shoulders and hugging her tighter. "Of course, I—" He looked to Josh and Sen, who were nodding vigorously as well. "We... will be here to support you, nǚ'ér"

"**It is time to depart.**" The unmistakable voice cut through their conversation.

And Josh and Sen were gone from the passageway.

———————————————✶———————————————

"**We have arrived at the long-abandoned Sanctuary of the Mind Breaker, orbiting Baroo-7 on the atmospheric moon of Mwezi. There are Items of Power located within this outpost that will attune your Mind Aspect. Acquire them.**"

Josh raised his clenched fist with an index finger, pointing at the Clone with a firm frown on his face. He opened his mouth on the verge of shouting angry words.

But Sen was faster. It didn't matter how angry you were, or how unreasonable Zenyak was. Nobody approached him in rage . . . and expected to get away unscathed.

Sen body-checked Josh; wrestled him to the ground and put him in a rear-naked choke. "Th-thank you, Lord Clone . . ." Sen managed to get out as he struggled, only able to subdue Josh after fully cycling his Essence to his upper body.

Sen could tell through their Bond Josh didn't have the heart to fight with him . . . he just wanted to scream at the Clone. "We are ready to depart when necessary!"

"I see . . .

"This is for free, gentlemen. Just because this sanctuary is abandoned doesn't mean it is desolate. You have progressed much too far not to have competition. Be ready for it."

And they were gone again . . . appearing in a small courtyard of a crumbling ruin. Knee-high green and yellow weeds grew through cracks in the few flat grey stones not covered over by large blocks coming from the tumbledown stone building that had once stood here. A large, amber sun rose behind the pink and orange striated gas-giant planet covering most of the horizon.

A feral scream exploded from Josh's throat. No different from an animal gnawing its own leg off to escape a deathtrap. Blood in his eyes, he closed them tightly for thirty seconds . . . then sanity reigned . . . again.

Josh nodded to Sen. ~*Thank you, brother . . .*~

Sen nodded back and narrowed his eyes. ~*When the time comes . . . I will need you to do the same for me.*~

EPILOGUE

———————✷———————

THE PARAMOUNTS, the three most powerful Immortals in all Reality stared from the fifty-fifth aspect doorway into the face of absolute nothingness... *Oblivion.* Awestruck, knowing that despite their countless ages of absolute Authority, they were now confronted by something so much greater than themselves there was no path to safety. The only thing they truly knew was that if they didn't do something... anything... in relative short order, all probability calculations confirmed that Oblivion's continued advance was the terminal end of... well, everything...

Oblivion was not darkness, not light, not the crushing gravity of a singularity that mortals made such great noises about.

It's just a rotting, Ka-less grey mire that devours any underlying aggregate without discrimination and leaves the absence of all.

Zenyak Marztanak, the Penultimate Combatant's nostrils flared at their powerlessness to deal with it. Everything that made contact with Oblivion faced absolute and complete annihilation. Regardless of whether it was physical, spiritual, Karmic, mortal Essence, or Immortal Ka... All substrates were impotent against Oblivion's procession.

No strength could withstand penetration through it. No perception had been able to quantify its properties. The only real information they had learned was the rate normal iterations were obliterated by it.

All Immortals who touched it had succumbed instantly. No residual remainder of their Ka was detectable by any of them.

Zenyak's shared his thoughts in frustration. **"We've only been able to slow it down. And the cost to accomplish that was on the edge of insanity!"**

Neither Chiteki, the Prime Motivator nor the entity known only as the Principal Master responded to the truth of his statement of the obvious.

It had taken the total implosion of a wide swath of complete iterational cuboids to curb Oblivion's pace. The resetting of twenty-seven complete realities per cuboid from the fifty-eighth aspect doorway to the fifty-fifth where they now stood.

"If I hadn't seen it with my own perception, I would never have believed it."

Very few Immortals knew or even cared to know that the Reality frequented by spirit beings, mortal or Immortal was only in the iterational cuboids of the first thirty-five aspect doorways branching from Zenyak's own Polar Neutral Iteration. This was because the iterations beyond the thirty-fifth were abstract substrates with too few dimensional vectors to support mortal life. As such, they had apparently never given rise to Immortal existences and had very little to attract anyone for permanent residence.

Imploding these iterations down to their primordial singularities had created a metaphysical fire line of sorts.

Trench digging ... that's what we are reduced to ...

A barrier Zenyak had originally hoped would slow Oblivion down, allowing their subordinates to find a way to gather some information for a better next step.

And it had hindered Oblivion. The original spread between iterational cuboids was assessed at one per 2,500 Ka nexus rotations ... And one aspect doorway per 10,000 Ka nexus rotations. After their implosion tactic, this had stretched to 4,000 and 17,000 respectively.

But, in all this time, no information had been able to be gathered. Zenyak and his companions had used the intervening time to regather the Cultivated Ka they had sacrificed for the implosion strategy so they could do it again ... if necessary ... If nothing new presented itself after this line in the sand was crossed ... Zenyak and his colleagues could only think of one last sacrifice to slow things down. For his friends' sake, Zenyak hoped it wouldn't come to that eventuality ... But all three were united and willing if necessary ...

The Prime Motivator, having stared into nothingness for long enough, turned to Zenyak, **"Regretting not ascending into the Great Unknown before this was found? I know I am!"**

Zenyak turned the strong and wizened visage he emulated as his avatar to the lithe fourteen-year-old avatar preferred by the Paramount Immortal who had become his friend over the last hundred million Ka nexus rotations. Chiteki currently floated in a lotus position upside down and rotating so fast all that could be seen of him was a blurring inverted tetrahedron of Ka and his face-up palms.

"Grow up, Chiteki!" Zenyak chided with a half chuckle.

The Principal Master, stoic as always, ignored both of their antics and proceeded to the matter at hand extending his Intention to begin the desiccation of entire cuboidal clusters of iterations. **"Are we ready to restart the implosion protocol. Buy more time ... I** *hope* **we use more wisely—"**

A scaled lash shot from the center of Oblivion's grey mass and swept across the ranks of Immortals arrayed before it. None were spared. Not the Masters in service to the Principal Master. Not the Seraph who served Chiteki, the Prime Motivator. Nor did the combat-focused followers of Zenyak, serving him as the Penultimate Combatant, do any better. All were instantly annihilated as the lash crashed through them heading toward the three leaders,

Zenyak, always the fastest in combat, erected his Ka core shield and stood before the other two as they opened a Reality portal back toward safety, several aspect doorways away.

The grey lash struck Zenyak's shield, and his knees instantly buckled. It had partially penetrated his bulwark—a barrier that had for time immemorial been unscathed to *all* forces. Zenyak's Ka meridians began draining like a leaking sieve as his shield flared trying to match the force exerted on it. He had no choice but to open his Immortal Ka core and sacrifice converted essence to keep the shield between his friends and the ultimate stillness that terminal proximity with the tentacle promised. He had to keep the shield up for all of them until they could pass through the deep blue hues of Reality. Or there was no further hope for them, Reality . . . the multiverse as a whole.

As if Oblivion could tell they were escaping, the force of the lash's attack intensified. Zenyak was driven to his knees and his vision narrowed.

From a distance, he heard the alarmed voice of the Principal Master yelling. **"Chiteki! Grab him! His core meridians are rupturing from the strain!"**

Then all was the swirling blue of the Way.

THE END
Josh & Sen Save the Multiverse
Book One: The Path of One

Come adventure with Josh & Sen again in:

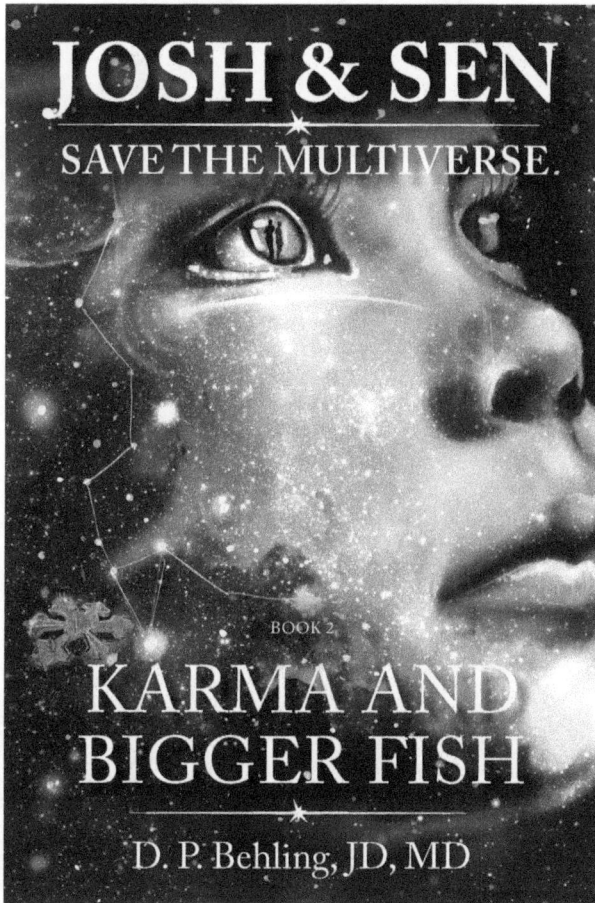

Keep reading for an excerpt!

Are you Special?

"I'M GOING to rise through human cultivation. Transcend and continue through Immortal cultivation. And then... I'm going to send that blue-glowing-Lite-Brite muther home with a rupture!" Josh, the forty-four-year-old divorced Chicago lawyer turned multiversal galavanter, thrashed his hands around violently as he shouted to the sky and the surrounding fields.

For their Mind Attunement item of power, the Clone had sent them to the terrestrial moon Mwezi that orbited the massive pink and orange gas giant Baroo-7. The giant's wispy pastel stripes dominated the sky and cast everything with a gentle orange-pink tint.

When they had first arrived Sen, the Immortal combat specialist, reduced to mere humanity as part of his grandfather's design, had looked around to find that...

They were on a small hill...

In the tumbledown ruin of an ancient stone building...

Smack dab in the middle of exactly...

Nowhere...

Rolling fields of wild grains and thistles covered the countryside around them. Far off in the distance, on the rising slopes of the valley wall, they could see a large ... castle?

Even with his enhanced sight, Sen wasn't exactly sure from this distance. It was large and white, surrounded by large white walls with several grand, white towers.

With no other signs of civilization, and Josh far too distracted cursing the Clone's existence to actively participate, Sen decided to cross through the grass toward it.

They could have run using their cultivation. But Josh's tirade against the Clone's existence was slacking, so he must be finding the slower pace with time to reflect, *therapeutic* ...

Sen had learned a bit about his brother over the last week. Josh's passion for life and to win were a significant part of their growth thus far. He was honest and would tell a person what he thought about them, good or bad ...

But to be overly passionate about the snares others caught him in would keep Josh from identifying his adversary's agenda. In fact, the snare was most likely laid to keep them from seeing the plot in the first place. A lesson Sen had learned the hard way from the genocidal harvester, Brundox. But now his eyes were open to many things he had ignored. Sen had been taught this very point by his political tutors as a child.

"In the midst of chaos, there is also opportunity ... Victorious warriors win first and then go to war, while defeated warriors go to war first and then seek to win."

Josh's mind was quick, and he could focus it to a photon's edge when necessary. Sen nudged Josh's intellect to see the Clone's acts for what they were. Control.

"Yes ... yes, brother ... without question ... we will send that incestuous fornicator back to the Polar Neutral Iteration with a crushed scrotum ... But you must have noticed that the timing was amazingly convenient ... even for a being as callused as the Clone ... What could his motivation possibly be?"

Josh's head snapped up. Already on edge at the continued existence of, well, just about everything, Josh's eyes thinned. "What!?" The words out, Josh's head dropped in immediate self-reproach.

Sen felt everything through their Bond.

Josh spoke again. "Sorry, brother ... you don't deserve my angst." Josh's cheeks puffed up as he forced a calming breath. "Yes, his timing was inconvenient in the extreme! Much too perfect to be a coincidence ..." Josh looked up to the sky, thinking seriously about Sen's point for a second before answering. "Well, he made it plain that he doesn't give a rat's booty about Sophie. Or me seeing her ... His constant and stated objectives are for us to rise through mortal cultivation and to transcend to the Immortal realms of cultivation ... So, he must have pulled us out of there—at the very instant I had a real chance to communicate with Sophie—to force me to work harder to get back ... From his perspective ... to accelerate our growth!" Josh's teeth clenched to the point of grinding. "He's separating me from my daughter as a motivational aid! That mother-frakker. *Arrghhhh* . . . I'm going to send him home with a *rupture!*" Josh stamped his feet impotently on the ground and pointed his index finger at the sky as he cursed the Clone for the next thirty seconds of their walk.

Sen smiled quietly as Josh went on with his tirade. Sorry to have started Josh up again ... but it was necessary he understood the political machinations of Sen's family. Better now than later.

———————✦———————

"It's been three hours, Sen. I know we're getting closer because that castle looks more like a *palace. But how much farther do you think it is?*"

Chuckle. ~Still farther, brother, still farther.~

Josh rolled his eyes and laughed quietly at himself. *What should I expect. I basically asked how much longer our car ride was going to be.*

But the ... palace was significantly closer. Its massive walls and tow-ers dominated the side of the valley they were walking in. *It reminds me of the Maharaja's stronghold described in* The Arabian Nights ... *Or maybe some fantastically elaborate north African Kasbah.*

Tall, white spires, surrounded by minarets with pointed conical tops, reached over 300 meters into the sky. The larger ones were capped with broad, rounded domes tapering to needlepoint peaks. All were colored in faded hues of red, orange, and yellow, well placed under the sun's warm amber glow and the pink and orange of Baroo-7 above. Flocks of white and yellow birds, barely pinpricks at this distance, rode the thermal updrafts between and around the pinnacles. Such freedom made any onlooker wish to be there soaring with them.

After an hour, they came across a well-packed dirt road winding in the direction of the palace. Thirty minutes later, they could make out smaller buildings forming a town around the palace's 100-meter-tall alabaster walls. Small trails of smoke from cooking or other working fires rose around the outbuildings. And grey plumes floated up from distant roads, dust from vehicles that moved along them.

Neatly fenced and cultivated fields of well-organized crops started to line the roads. Josh noticed a species like corn, along with wheat, soybeans, tomatoes, and several orchards of citrus-bearing trees. The field's produce looked to be three to four weeks from harvest. The plants' fruiting bodies were well-laden, but no discernible, vegetative head was visible in the center of the—

"Get a grip. The science is only going to distract you, Josh" he mut-tered to himself.

Josh took a sip from the canteen Sen had been drinking from and put it back in his bag. Or aspect facet as Symbal had called it. The can-teen slid back in. Somehow. To someplace inside there. And came out again when he called it. He would have to spend time with the facet to learn more about how it worked. While the facet was a *nice luxury* to

Sen, its workings were of no interest to him. He had seen many things like it in the past. But it was pretty cool to Josh.

It's not just the bag. I need answers for a lot of things. I know how to use Essence. But what is it really? Does it come from matter? From energetic-solar ejections as particles or rays? There is undoubtedly a spiritual requirement. Is life required? Consciousness? Could Intelligence on the Hegemon-4 *see it or use it?*

He had no answers for any of these questions. Yet learning these things was vital to maximize his use of Essence, increase his cultivation, and get back to Sophie ...

There were a ton of questions about Sophie.

What is the link between Alysa and Sophie? How did I drag my daughter into this insanity? Is she in any danger!? Alysa and Sophie's Karma are obviously tied together ... but across so many iterations? How has it happened? How strong is it? Do I need to bring them together? Keep them apart?

These questions were going to keep him awake until he was able to find some form of resolution.

The Clone also knew Sophie and Alysa shared a bond in some way similar to the one Josh and Sen did and could likely answer all of Josh's questions. He tended to reward them with some information when they successfully achieved his objectives. Maybe Josh could get some answers after they got this mind fruit and completed their next Attunement.

Questions aside, Josh was grateful to Sen for getting his brain reengaged to do more than rage hating on the old blue bastard.

Nod. *~You are welcome, brother. I wonder how Sophie and Alysa's bond formed as well.~*

Nod. *~I thought saving Alysa would meet Karma's price of balance.~*

Blink. *~As did I. The Clone can answer these questions just as any Immortal Fate Glancer could trace the ties of Reality and Balance between them. But let me bring it up. You are too close to act in Sophie's best interest.~*

Blink. *~You are right ... but it's hard ...~*

Sen smiled reassuringly. Then, because he could keep no secrets from his Karma Bonded brother, particularly about Sophie .,, the source of their Bond ... Sen added, ~*It could be a test of you. Somehow instigated or fostered by Zenyak. Never speak of your doubts or concerns about it out loud ... just in our Bond. I suspect that even the Clone cannot completely read our shared Karmic communications.*~

Josh nodded in affirmation and continued walking toward the town, trying to take his mind off things that were beyond his ability to change. It would only slow him down from gathering the strength to get back to Sophie.

———————————★———————————

They walked for another hour, and Josh noticed Sen began to have trouble concentrating. In fact, he had started dancing a little jig on one leg, then the other while he held his legs together like a little kid who had to pee.

"Senyak. Do you need to ... urinate?"

"Um ... yes ... but there are no proper facilities in the area. So ... I was waiting for one. The last time I urinated outside of the proper facilities ... it didn't go so well ..."

Josh held back a chuckle, remembering their first face-to-face meeting in the alley. What seemed like a lifetime ago ... but counting quickly ... it was really less than seven days. "Okay ... that was a unique set of circumstances. And yes ... it is better for mortals to always use the facilities when available. But right now, we are out in the open, the great outdoors. It's okay to go off to the side, out of the way, and pee if we need to ... I kinda have to go myself." Josh pointed out the fence between the growing crops and the road. "I go here. You go maybe five feet away. Facing apart from each other ..."

Sen lined up at the fence, facing away from Josh, and they both relieved themselves.

"See. Perfectly ok—" Josh was cut off by a voice to their left,

"What in the Ascending Hells are you guys doing to my maize?" The figure stood off to the side, on the top slat of the fence they were peeing through.

Startled by the fact they hadn't heard his approach, even with their hearing enhanced, they both turned . . . their pants down and still holding their business . . .

"Oh, gods! Please put 'em away, fellas!" And then, with a voice reserved for a young child or a mentally handicapped adult. "Friends, are you both . . . *special?*"

Sen and Josh quickly pulled up their pants.

Eye glare. ~*I knew I should have waited!*~

Head hung. ~. . .~

ABOUT THE AUTHOR

DAVE BEHLING is a Chicago born sci-fi, fantasy, and video game admirer. When he was younger and stronger, he was able to fight off his infatuation long enough to work as a Honolulu-based plaintiff's malpractice lawyer for five years before attending med school and residency. Now he treats his patients on Oahu, where his office has been for the last fifteen years.

He has trained in several fields of martial arts over the years, including Tae Kwon Do and Brazilian Jiu-Jitsu. Older now, he would rather be surfing, snowboarding, and skating when he is brave enough!

Most importantly, he is the proud father of four amazing children: Indigo, Tristan, Kireina, and Nina. They even text him sometimes. He is also the lucky owner of the world's cutest chihuahua, Rosie.

Contact information:

Instagram: https://www.instagram.com/davidbehlingauthor/

Facebook: https://www.facebook.com/David.Behling.Author/

Website: joshandsen.com

Special Thanks to GameLit Society
https://www.facebook.com/groups/LitRPGsociety

LITRPG!

To learn more about LitRPG, talk to other authors including myself,
and to just have an awesome time, please join the LitRPG Group

www.facebook.com/groups/LitRPGGroup

FACEBOOK

There's also a few really active Facebook groups I'd recommend you join, as you'll get to hear about great new books, new releases and interact with all your (new) favorite authors! (I may also be there, skulking at the back and enjoying the memes...)

www.facebook.com/groups/LitRPGsociety/
www.facebook.com/groups/LitRPG.books/
www.facebook.com/groups/LitRPGforum/
www.facebook.com/groups/gamelitsociety/

Printed in the USA
CPSIA information can be obtained
at www.ICGtesting.com
LVHW050847240524
781042LV00002B/187

9 798988 653509